THE AMBER WAVES OF AUTUMN

Edited by David M. Olsen

Kelp Books, LLC

1491 Cypress Drive #475
Pebble Beach, Ca 93953

TABLE OF CONTENTS

TABLE OF CONTENTS

THE SEVEN SEALS

by Francesca Lia Block

For P.L. (1954-2024)

When all six of my black-haired, green-eyed, seal-sleek brothers disappeared, I drove up the coast to look for them.

I got up at dawn, sensing something was wrong—a certain weight to the fog, a melancholy in the song of the blue glass wind chimes—and they were not in their beds in the sage-green Santa Monica craftsman house with the glassed-in sun porch draped in morning glories; their cell phones were gone, the yellow VW van gone. They had left a note:

Jude, we will be back. Go to school. Don't try to look for us. The fridge is stocked. WE LOVE YOU. Matthew, Mark, John, James, Andrew & Thomas

I usually did whatever my brothers said, but after I texted them and received no response, I packed some water, got into the blue VW Bug with my brother Thomas's extra surfboard attached to the top, and went looking.

First, I stopped in Venice Beach, where my brothers played drums on the boardwalk every weekend. Sonny nodded as I approached, his dreads swinging. Even on that overcast morning, warmth radiated off him in waves.

"Jude, girl. Aren't you supposed to be in school?"

"Hi, Sonny. How've you been?"

"Doing okay. Good as can be in this besieged world. How are you, my little one?"

"Have you seen them?" I asked him. I didn't have to say their names. My brothers were the only people I spent time with, unless you counted their ever-changing cycle of girlfriends. The pouting ballerina and performance artist. The golden-tressed actress named after a muse. The activist who wore embroidered cotton peasant dresses and plaited her hair in Frida Kahlo braids. The freckled, cherubic drummer. The shy poet who ran off crying to the bathroom almost every time she visited the house. And Luna. Those were only *Matthew's* girlfriends!

"Not since last weekend at the circle. Why?"

"I woke up this morning and they were gone. I texted and called, and no one answered."

"That's odd," Sonny said, scratching his scalp with his long-fingered, drum-calloused hand. A beam of light, which had somehow managed to break through the clouds, hit and sparked the silver ring he wore.

"Please text me if you see them," I said, staring at the ring.

"Of course. And maybe try Luna," Sonny said, glancing up at the pale blue apartment building across the boardwalk. "She talking to Matthew these days?"

"Off and on, from what I can tell."

"Sounds like those two. You take care, Jude."

I went over to knock on Luna's door. She answered, wearing one of the dresses she made and sold on the boardwalk—a pale pink velvet slip with silver rose flocking. I smelled weed and sandalwood incense. Inside her apartment, the blue walls and ceiling glamoured with glow-in-the-dark stars.

Maybe Luna and Matthew were *off*, because she didn't smile at me. "Matt's not here if you're looking for him."

"He said he was going away," I told her. "With all of them. But they didn't say where."

Luna frowned and played with her blond braid, rubbing the tail back and forth over her upper lip like a mustache. "Well I wouldn't know. Your brother is a piece of work."

"Sorry," I said. I didn't know what else to say. My brothers had collectively left a chain of broken hearts—not unlike the jagged-edged halves on the silver charm bracelet Luna wore—dangling all up and down the California coastline. "Let me know if you hear from him."

Luna glared at me with those moon-mad eyes, as Matthew called them. "I won't hear from him. If *you* do, tell him I'm going to eat him alive," she said.

"I think something might be wrong," I said to the pale blue door.

I remember my mother's be-ringed hands playing a lute, her black, jasmine-scented hair hanging down over her face. Her green eyes that glittered like leaves in the wind. Matthew, Mark, John, James, Andrew, and Thomas all look exactly like her. I have her eyes and hair color, but my hair is wiry, and my skin is a darker shade. My mother died when I was three. By then our father had already left, so it was Matthew who kind of raised me with the help of the others, and sometimes with Sonny's guidance. It wasn't easy for Matthew to try to work all those jobs, go to school, and take care of so many kids, but he did it. He'd even nursed me through all those illnesses I'd had. No wonder it was hard for him to settle down with a girlfriend. I would have told Luna this if she hadn't slammed the door in my face, but it would never have worked anyway; each girlfriend thought she would be the one to change him. To take care of him the way he'd had to take care of us. Matthew had done well. We were always sheltered, fed, and clothed, but also there was always music; there was always surfing. My brothers took me with them everywhere though I was small and sickly. We got in the van and drove up the coast, and I watched them surf or listened to them play in their band, Six Seals. That was why it scared me that they had left like that with no warning and no explanation.

I drove all the way up the coast to Ventura, to the mini-mall vegan fast-food place with all the flyers of 1980s punk bands like Black Flag and Fear and the Adolescents on the walls. Matthew had scrupulously educated me on the origins and influences of punk rock, as well as world music, funk, soul, and techno. He even knew about polka and klezmer.

The owner of the vegan place wasn't there, but the guy working the counter texted him and made me a vegan Reuben sandwich on rye with a sauerkraut side and a natural cream soda, and said it was on the house. People loved my brothers. Well, unless those people were girlfriends whose hearts they had broken like the charms on Luna's bracelet. Although those girlfriends probably still loved my brothers, too.

After I'd finished my sandwich, the owner still hadn't texted back, so I thanked the guy, gave him my cell phone number, and left. I drove to the beach and sat on the dirty sand, stared at the waves, drank some water, and thought about what to do. I could go back, or I could keep driving, stopping at places where I thought my brothers might be. I didn't even know why I was looking for them at all. I should have stayed home. That's what they'd told me in the note. Go to school, eat the food in the fridge, we'll be back. They would be back, I told myself. Of course they would. Unlike our father, they had never abandoned me.

That was the problem. This was unprecedented. But also, when your father is a leaver, you become one, too. If you are abandoned, you abandon. It just made sense. The girlfriends would all tell me that very thing if I had asked them.

I saw some graffiti on a low wall that separated the boardwalk from the sand. It said, *Marry me*. I thought how that would make my brothers uncomfortable. They would hate that graffiti, I thought.

My phone dinged. My youngest brother, Thomas.

Come here, it said. The address was in Morro Bay.

I texted back, but Thomas didn't respond. So I got in the Bug and continued on up the coast.

I drove inland for a while. Near the oil rigs, I saw something on fire in the distance, a swarm of black clouds. Every song on Spotify made me want to cry because it reminded me of how much I loved my brothers before those black clouds of smoke took them away. The heat had made me morose. *It's making you morose, Jude*, Matt would have said.

Once, my brothers and I went to Morro Bay. We walked down to the water and ate veggie burgers at a wooden picnic table on the rotting pier, and Matthew bought me a pink hoodie with a hibiscus flower on it, and then we saw a charming otter lying on its back devouring a crustacean of some sort.

"Otters are the only animals other than humans who use tools," Matthew had told me when I was in fourth grade and did a report on them. "They lie on their backs and crack shells with rocks." This otter was so merry, chewing away in the swirls of blue bay water while we watched him perform for us. My brothers and I saw a pelican land on the surface of the water, then dive and spear and devour a fish—the whole thing visibly sliding down its throat. "Every creature just feeding violently and yet with no malice," Matthew had said. We went to get some Mediterranean food at a hole-in-the-wall where the owners made everything fresh—the best fattoush salad I'd ever had, "With real sumac," Matthew said, and homemade pita bread and hummus. We sat at a metal table on the sidewalk on the dark street and chatted with the owner, who was proud of his cuisine and brought us fresh slices of watermelon for dessert. With our hands still sticky from watermelon, we walked back to the water, where the sea lions called out in the near distance, where they lounged on buoys in the darkness near the tiny lights from boats. "How did the people who lived in the boats sleep, even people who lived in the surrounding homes?" I asked Matthew. "It was a lullaby," he said. "Zip up your hoodie, Jude. You're shivering." The sea animals in the bay serenaded all night. I heard them from my motel room overlooking the water. My brothers shared the two rooms on either side.

In the morning, we ate breakfast and drank matcha tea lattes with almond milk—because Matthew said it was better for us than cow milk, soy, or oat—in a café garden and drove to San Simeon and watched the sea elephants draped on the sand. Some of the bulls were molting, dotted with pink splotches. The sea lions looked dead except when one raised and waved a fin, or a couple snuggled together head to tail and then shifted positions, and one lone pup wriggled down the sand to the sea and threw himself in; I never saw him return, but Matthew reassured me that he would.

On the way back we stopped in Cambria with its Victorian houses and antique stores and found another hidden garden restaurant and drank green smoothies and ate blue corn waffles that left a blue corn sugar scent in my nostrils even after we left.

Later, at sunset, pink and orange clouds blazed overhead, gilded at the edges. Matthew showed me how to hold my phone out the window as we drove into Los Angeles. In the video I took, palm tree silhouettes fly by against that electric sky, and I can hear my brothers' voices marveling.

In Morro Bay, a sea breeze cooled the charred air. I parked and went up to the door of the yellow clapboard house, the address Thomas had sent me, and I knocked. A tan, blond woman answered. I thought of my dead mother with her black hair and green eyes and the rings on her lute-playing fingers.

"Hi," I said. "Sorry to bother you. I'm looking for my brothers. Are they here?"

The woman seemed like she was trying to frown at me, but her tan, polished face hardly moved. "They all left," she said. "They were here and then they left. He's gone, too."

"Who?" I asked.

"Your father," she said. "Or should I say *their* father. He's dead. They scared him to death. Good riddance." She slammed the door in my face just as Luna had done.

Matthew is the best at everything, the lead guitar player, the singer, the songwriter, the surrogate father to all of us. He wears, on a chain around his neck, our mother's silver ring. A ring coveted by all the girls whose hearts he breaks. Mark is the smartest in his poindexter glasses, a computer whiz, and he plays keyboards. John tosses black curls, juggles, stands on his hands, plays drums, and makes the girls laugh. James is surly and models himself exactly after Matthew, even down to the way he dresses, in sharkskin suits and finely patterned shirts, and that he, too, plays a Fender Stratocaster—red instead of blue like Matt's. Andrew is a quiet hipster, wears a goatee and a porkpie hat, and plays bass; I never quite know what he is thinking. Thomas the drummer who feels the beat in his chest writes short stories and the lyrics to Matthew's songs. They all wear Ray-Ban Wayfarers. They walk in sync like slow-motion movie boys in a high school hallway; they surf and play music in sync. They finish each other's sentences.

They also have the same fear.

Once, before I was born, our father, a veteran, took my brothers to the desert and detonated improvised explosive devices. My brothers huddled together and cried, begged him to stop. He said it was to get them inured to loud sounds, but they all became terrified of noise and had to play their music at high volume in order to hide this fear from the chain of brokenhearted girlfriends. And then Thomas went deaf.

After that, my brothers said, our father tried to drown Thomas, but Matthew had taught Thomas to surf, to hold his breath for a long time underwater, so he fought back and survived. This is what killed my mother, my brothers said, the drowning incident. I was too young to remember any of it, but I always believed my brothers were telling the truth. Now I knew for sure.

When I got to Ventura again, the sun hovered low above the sea. After I found a bathroom where I could pee, I got Thomas's wetsuit from the trunk and took his extra board and walked down to the sand, where I sat shivering in my pink Morro Bay hoodie and watched the last flare of light disappear behind the horizon and tried to calm myself and think clearly about what had happened, but I could not calm down or think clearly, and then I fell asleep.

I must have fallen asleep.

A man sat on the sand, wearing a black cloak. He turned his face to me. I saw the cleft in his chin and his pale cheekbones, his face as pointy as a star. He beckoned me over, so I went to him without thinking. In front of the man sat a chessboard covered with small bones and other animal parts. The man held out what resembled a bat's foot. Five tiny sharp claws like a miniature, mummified hand.

"It will open the castle," said the man. "Take it into the water."

Six seal silhouettes pranced on the horizon in some kind of danse macabre.

Matthew had taught me that term, too.

I had never surfed before, because my brothers worried I'd hurt myself or get sick, but I had watched them surf since I was a baby. So I carried Thomas's board down to the water. I lay on the board and paddled out. My rib cage pressed into the polyurethane. The waves towered cold and sleek like a castle made of glass. I held the bat's foot in my hand. It was the key.

In the glass castle, I stood shakily. I saw, as if on a watery screen, my six brothers entering a yellow house. I saw them surrounding a pale dwarf while a tan, blond woman slept with her back turned away. I saw Matthew reach out and touch the man, shake him awake.

"You fucked us all up," Matthew said. Then he nodded at Thomas, who held up a boom box over his head, like that actor in that late 80s movie Matthew once showed me, and blasted one of my brothers' songs as loud as it could go.

The man reached for the gun by his bed but then stopped and grabbed his own chest.

I wasn't sure I wanted to leave the castle made of glass. My skin no longer felt cold. Everything sparkled—prisms. I thought I heard the serenade of the sea mammals calling me away.

But then I thought of my six brothers, sleek and black in neoprene.

"Go home, Jude," said a voice. I turned and saw a woman translucent as water in the sun. She held the hand of a man with dreads.

They both wore matching silver rings.

When I emerged from the water, my hands were empty, and the hooded man was gone.

I arrived the next day and saw the van parked at the curb. Music wafted from inside the house, and I smelled weed when I opened the door. Mark, John, and James sat at the big, scarred, wooden table, chopping up onions, garlic, tomatoes, and basil and grating Parmesan cheese. Andrew and Thomas signed to each other and laughed and tossed strands of spaghetti onto the kitchen wall already covered with dried noodles, seeing if the pasta would stick. Sonny was there, too. He smiled at me, and for the first time, I recognized the tilt of my own cheekbones and the curve of my lips. "*Their dad*," the blond woman had said. Something clicked perfectly in my chest, like the last puzzle piece.

Matthew stood apart; his nearsighted green eyes huddled a bit close together, he had a hooknose and a perpetual scowl on his face, but it all only made him look more handsome. The tallest, most beautiful, and most talented of my brothers. The one who had raised me, raised all of us, really.

Matthew wore a shirt of Tiffany blue velvet with gray, silk fleur-de-lis flocking. He held a woman in his arms, burying his long, high-cheekboned face in her pale hair. She turned and looked at me, showed me her carnivorous teeth, and held up her left hand. My mother's ring—the one Matthew always wore on a chain around his neck, the one, I realized, for the first time, matched Sonny's silver ring—circled Luna's finger.

A TAWNY BROWN LIVEABOARD

by Bev Vincent

Living on a houseboat in a marina wasn't as idyllic as Travis McGee made it seem in Benjamin Kane's favorite amateur-detective novels. Not that he was actually living on this small boat, the *El Halcón*, moored in San Diego's Shelter Cove Marina. No—that was down to his younger brother, Nate, who'd failed to mention that the first *b* in the Airbnb he'd booked Kane into meant *boat* and the second was purely theoretical. Since arriving, he'd had to fend for himself at the food trucks parked near the main entrance to the marina.

McGee's boat had been rigged with a pressure sensor that silently alerted him whenever anyone tried to board the *Busted Flush*. Kane's floating accommodations had nothing similar, but the boat was small enough that an unusual rocking motion jolted him out of an uneasy sleep. Waterbeds had once been all the rage, but Kane never saw the attraction. He liked to feel terra firma beneath his body. The world was unsteady enough as it was.

He rolled onto his back, waiting for the swaying to subside. Angry voices and the distinctive sounds of a struggle came from the dock outside the cabin window. He squinted at the bedside clock: nearly three in the morning. Drunks having a besotted argument, he decided.

The voices grew louder, more insistent. Kane debated getting up to tell them to take their disagreement elsewhere. There didn't seem much point in calling the cops. The two drunkards would, no doubt, be long gone before the authorities arrived. He made a mental note to pack earplugs the next time he traveled. Being jarred awake in the middle of the night wasn't going to leave him in a good mood come morning, when he had to deliver a speech at the California Private Detectives Association's annual conference.

A gunshot startled him upright. He instinctively reached for his own pistol on the nightstand. Of course, it wasn't there. He was traveling light—carry-on luggage only—so his trusty sidearm was in a lockbox in his house back in Houston. He grabbed his cell phone instead and dialed 911. While explaining the situation to the person on the other end of the line, he scanned his accommodations for something to use as a weapon. The best he could come up with was a rack of ornamental belaying pins, one of which looked substantial enough to serve as a cosh.

Kane eased open the door to the sleeping quarters and crept up the steep, short staircase to the main deck. Strategically placed lampposts in the marina provided a little illumination, but the closest one was at least thirty yards away, so his immediate surroundings were nearly dark. He slipped his phone into his pocket and clenched the belaying pin as he emerged onto the deck.

Heavy footsteps reverberated in the distance. He looked in that direction in time to see a figure disappearing into the next pool of darkness. He couldn't make out if it was a man or a woman. The person was heading toward the parking lot, as near as Kane could tell.

Wielding his makeshift weapon, Kane gingerly descended the gangway. A man was lying face up on the wooden dock. Kane pulled his phone back out and activated its flashlight. The bright light revealed a pool of blood oozing from beneath the man's body. It dripped between the planks and into the water below. Kane had a mental flash of a shark being attracted by the blood.

With the police presumably on the way, Kane approached the injured man. He was Hispanic, maybe forty or forty-five. It was hard to tell in the dim light. Besides that, impending death aged a person. What little life remained in him was rapidly draining away. Kane knelt beside him to examine the wound. He'd seen more than a few similar injuries during his years with HPD. They were almost always fatal unless a fully equipped paramedic happened to be standing by. He pulled off his T-shirt and used it to try to stanch the flow of blood coming from the man's chest. The exit wound in his back was probably worse, but Kane did what he could.

Despite his grave injuries, despite bubbles of blood forming in his mouth, the man struggled to say something.

Kane leaned closer.

"My ring," the man said between wheezing breaths.

Kane looked at the man's hands. On his right index finger, he wore an ornate ring that gleamed in the beam of Kane's flashlight.

"Get it to Jacobi," the man said. He repeated the name, then fell silent. His eyes were watery, but his gaze was insistent.

Kane could hear a siren approaching as he slipped the ring from the man's finger and pushed it into the pocket of his shorts without a second thought. He ran the risk of being charged with obstructing justice if caught, but it seemed important to fulfill the dying man's request.

The man's body relaxed then. Kane pressed his fingers against the side of the man's throat but couldn't detect a pulse. The shooting victim was gone.

Kane stepped away from the body. When two police officers appeared in the distance, he slipped the belaying pin into the waistband at the back of his shorts so trigger-happy cops wouldn't decide he posed a threat.

The officers quickly secured the scene. While they waited for reinforcements, they took Kane's preliminary statement. Paramedics arrived a few minutes later but soon ascertained there was nothing they could do.

Fortunately, the crime scene tape didn't hinder his access to the boat, so Kane was able to go aboard while awaiting the next phase of the investigation, a process with which he was intimately familiar. He tossed the belaying pin on a bench and surreptitiously pushed the ring into a crack between two waterproof pillows on a deck chair. He doubted the police would search him, but he didn't want to take that chance.

A pair of detectives arrived in due course. Kane invited them aboard the *El Halcón*. The lead, a woman named Detective Nguyen, sat in the chair with the hidden ring. Kane didn't catch the other detective's name.

Nguyen posed the same questions the patrol officers had already asked, throwing in a few others for good measure. The silent detective took notes. Kane repeated the timeline of events to the best of his ability, which could be confirmed by his 911 call, he said. No, he didn't know who the dead man was, and he had no idea why the man had decided to get himself murdered outside his rental boat. Yes, he'd seen someone leaving the marina who might have been the perpetrator, but he couldn't provide a useful description. Kane neglected to tell the detectives he was a private investigator and former cop. When Nguyen gave him her business card and said she'd like him to stay in town for a few days, Kane nodded as if he was agreeing with her request.

After the detectives were finished with him, Kane took a shower and shaved in preparation for the conference. By the time he left the boat, the man's body had been removed, but the bloodstains on the wooden dock remained. Crime scene investigators were still combing the marina for clues. One of them gave Kane a pair of booties to put over his shoes until he cleared the area.

He grabbed a breakfast burrito from a food truck near the parking lot and ate it while navigating the unfamiliar streets of San Diego. As he drove, he called Nate to fill him in on the situation, asking him to find out what he could about the man who'd been murdered. "I know it's a long shot," Kane said, "but he told me to give something to a man named Jacobi."

"Give him what?"

"A ring," Kane said.

"Which you failed to mention to the cops," Nate said.

"Well."

"OK. I'll get back to you."

The conference was being held at the Marriott Marquis near the Gaslamp historic district. Kane entrusted his rental car to a valet who might have been old enough to shave, and made his way inside. He found the registration desk outside the Grand Ballroom and signed in. After draping his lanyard around his neck, he grabbed a much-needed cup of coffee and found a quiet corner. He wasn't scheduled to talk for another twenty minutes.

While he waited, he examined the dead man's ring, mentally reconsidering his spur-of-the-moment decision to not mention it to the detectives. He didn't have much time to track down this Jacobi person. Come tomorrow, he would be headed back to Houston, and the murder would be in the capable hands of the SDPD.

There was nothing written inside the band, not even initials. The ring itself, though, looked like some kind of puzzle box. He poked and prodded and twisted it without getting anywhere.

"That looks intriguing." A thin man with a tiny mustache was standing beside him. The man's voice was high-pitched. "I rather enjoy a good puzzle. Would you mind if I looked at it?"

He also had a conference lanyard draped around his neck. Kane tried to catch the man's name, but his badge was turned to face his chest. Kane realized his own was the same way and flipped it around. "Sure, but I only have a few minutes."

"I know, Mr. Kane. I'm here for your talk."

The man sat across from Kane, who handed him the ring. The man peered at it for a moment, then gave the top a few quick twists. It popped off to reveal a small, black object nestled inside. The man handed it to Kane. "Your presentation, I presume."

Kane accepted the micro SD card. "That's a relief. I was sure I was going to have to wing it." He offered a twisted grin. "My brother didn't trust me to not lose it." He glanced at his watch and got up. "You saved the day. I'll see you inside, Mr..."

"Hamilton," the other man said after a pause. "Happy to be of service." He also stood, gave Kane a stiff bow, and headed toward the conference room.

Kane didn't have time to examine the memory chip. If he'd been back in Houston, he would have given it to Hector, the agency's tech expert. Kane knew enough not to stick a drive of unknown origin into a networked computer. It could offload a virus or install ransomware. Hector would have set up an isolated virtual machine to examine its contents, but Kane had no idea how to do that. He returned the micro SD card to its hiding place, reassembled the ring, and stuck it in his shirt pocket. Then he finished his coffee and made his way to the conference room.

It should have been Nate giving the presentation, but his brother had been called to testify at a trial related to one of their cases. He was by far the more gregarious of the two brothers. Still, Kane thought the audience was entertained by his anecdotes about working with the various reality TV shows with which their firm had contracts to provide security and investigative services. Even though this was San Diego and not Los Angeles, it was close enough to Tinseltown for people to be intimately familiar with showbiz. Kane described how they had leveraged a single gig into a regular revenue stream and the ways they had lured other production companies into enlisting their services. Some of their exploits on reality programs had garnered national headlines, which was why Kane Investigations had been invited to the convention. During his talk, he noticed Mr. Hamilton in the audience, occasionally stroking his mustache.

After the Q&A session, most of the audience headed out to the lobby for free coffee and donuts. Hamilton, though, drifted toward the front of the room as Kane retrieved his USB drive from the A/V tech. Kane was pretty sure Hamilton had clocked the fact that it wasn't the minidisk he'd extracted from the puzzle ring.

Kane saw someone else familiar enter the conference room—Detective Nguyen. When Hamilton spotted the detective, he made an abrupt U-turn and headed out to the lobby as well. Kane wondered if Hamilton knew the woman was police.

"Detective," Kane called out when Nguyen was a dozen yards away. "I didn't expect to see you here. Don't tell me you're thinking about joining the dark side."

Nguyen shrugged. "You didn't tell me you already had."

"And yet you managed to track me down."

"Once I found out you were a private detective, it seemed like a reasonable place to look."

Kane gathered his papers and stepped down from the dais. "And why might you be looking for me? I told you everything I know."

"Did you, though?"

"What makes you think otherwise?"

"I'm naturally suspicious. Occupational hazard. When I find out a private investigator was staying a few yards from where a man was gunned down, it seems like more than a coincidence."

Kane nodded. "In your position, I'd probably think the same thing."

"That's all you have to say?"

He sighed. "You haven't asked me any questions. I'm just agreeing with you." He looked toward the conference room entrance. "We're going to have to vacate the premises soon. There's another presentation here in five or ten minutes."

"Would you mind coming to HQ to answer some more questions? It's not that far from here."

"Gee, I wish I could," Kane said, "but I promised someone I'd attend their talk at ten thirty." He glanced at his watch. "Best I can do is give you a few minutes out in the lobby."

Nguyen nodded as if she'd been expecting his response. Kane led her to the remote corner of the lobby where he'd been sitting earlier. As they walked, he looked around for Hamilton, but the mystery man was nowhere to be found.

Once seated, Nguyen got straight to the point. "Are you sure you didn't recognize the man who was killed outside your boat this morning?"

"Not my boat," Kane reminded her. "Just my room for a couple of nights. And, no, as I said, I have no clue who he was. Never saw him before. Have you identified him?"

"I'll ask the questions."

"Sure, go ahead."

"You didn't tell us you were a PI."

"It didn't seem germane. I could be a plumber, and it wouldn't change what I saw."

"Still, it seems like something you might have mentioned."

"I told you I was in town for a conference."

"Not here on a case, then. Following a suspect?"

"Nope. We have enough of those back in Texas without importing them from California."

Clearly frustrated, she made him go through the morning's events one more time. Kane didn't have to worry about getting caught in a lie, since he was telling the truth—omitting only one small detail. Nguyen wanted him to describe the person he saw leaving the scene, but he didn't have anything to add to what he'd already said.

Eventually she closed her notebook. "Why do I think you aren't telling me everything?"

"Occupational hazard?" Kane said with a raised eyebrow.

Detective Nguyen frowned. "Dealing with people in your occupation is always a hazard, in my experience."

"Some might say the same is true of yours," Kane said as he got to his feet. His cell phone buzzed in his pocket. He took it out and looked at the notification on the lock screen. "I have to get this. Will you be sticking around for the next session? Maybe you'd gain some insight into how the other side works."

"No thanks. I have a pretty good idea already. Enjoy the convention, Mr. Kane. I'll be in touch, I'm sure."

Kane waited until she was at the hotel entrance before checking his phone again. The message was from Hector. *The man who owns the boat where you're staying is named Jacobi. He'll be at the Fathom Bistro at eleven. Click the link for directions.* Hector, for all his tech savvy, always texted in complete, properly punctuated sentences.

Fathom Bistro, which billed itself as San Diego's only taphouse on the water, wasn't far from where the *El Halcón* was moored. Kane dropped his car off at the parking lot near the marina and walked to the rustic restaurant. It doubled as a bait and tackle shop for those who wanted to fish from the pier, which seemed to be a popular pastime.

Several people occupied the outdoor tables—the only kind of seating Fathom offered—but one man was sitting by himself. "Mr. Jacobi?" Kane said as he approached the man, who had the same grizzled look as Robert Shaw in *Jaws*. There was a pint of amber beer on the table in front of him, along with a half-consumed pulled pork sandwich. As Kane got closer, he detected an unpleasant odor coming from the table.

Jacobi looked up, noticed Kane's reaction, and grinned. "Kimchi. Want some?"

"No thanks," Kane said. "Can't say I've ever acquired the taste." He looked at the chalkboard's lengthy list of available draft beers. "I will have a drink, though. It's been a morning." A roving waiter took his order.

When Kane's drink arrived, Jacobi dumped the remains of his lunch in a nearby trash can, much to Kane's relief. "What can I do for you, Mr. Kane? The other Mr. Kane—the one on the phone—said you were staying aboard my boat. I hope the accommodations are to your liking."

"They're fine. Had a little excitement earlier this morning, though."

"Oh?"

"A man was murdered on the dock next to the boat."

"*Quatsch*!" Jacobi said.

Kane had no idea what the word meant, but Jacobi seemed upset by this news. "Yes. I'm not sure if the police have identified him yet. Maybe you know him?" He described the deceased.

"Hmm," Jacobi said. "I'm not sure."

"He mentioned your name."

"What?"

"I was there when he died. He said the name Jacobi. That's why my brother tracked you down."

Jacobi's eyes narrowed. After looking over his shoulder, he leaned in closer. "What exactly did he say?"

"He was in pretty bad shape by the time I got to him. He died less than a minute later."

"What did he *say*?"

Kane took a sip of his English porter. "Just your name. I wondered if he was trying to identify who killed him."

"That's preposterous," Jacobi said, sitting up straight. "Esteban was a friend. Well, more of a colleague, but anyway. I was home in bed with my wife when this happened."

"So, you do know him?"

"Yes, all right. You're sure he didn't say more? He didn't, perchance, give you something?"

"Like what?"

"Oh, I don't know. It would have been something small." He muttered to himself. "Dammit. The police probably have it by now." He looked up again. "You didn't see a ring?" His voice sounded hopeful.

Kane shook his head, hoping the ring wasn't making a conspicuous bulge in his shirt pocket. "No. Sorry. Was it valuable?"

"Not really. A family heirloom, that's all."

"You were related to—what did you call him? Esteban? I don't see the resemblance."

Jacobi barked a nervous laugh. "Not his family, of course. Mine. My family. Esteban recovered it for me. It has been missing for the better part of a generation."

Kane didn't believe a word of the story. "I'm not sure the police have identified Esteban yet. It might be helpful if you called the lead detective to let her know the man's name. They might have the ring."

Jacobi looked aghast. "Oh, no. I couldn't do that. I avoid getting involved in police matters."

I'll bet you do, Kane thought. "If you gave me his full name, I could pass it on to them."

"Only if you promise to leave me out of it."

"Absolutely."

Jacobi stared at Kane for several seconds before speaking. "His name is…was…Esteban Navarro." He stood. "Now, if you will excuse me, I have business to attend to. I bid you a good day."

Kane took another sip of his beer and decided to stay for lunch. It was a nice day, the view of San Diego Bay and the Pacific beyond was spectacular and, kimchi aside, the food smelled terrific. He ordered a Greek hamburger and a second beer. He didn't have to be anywhere, so sitting dockside for a while seemed like a good way to pass the time.

On his way back to the *El Halcón*, behind an art installation called *Endless Wave*, Kane saw a rare object: a pay phone. He plunged his hand in his pocket and came up with enough coins for a local phone call. There were probably CCTV cameras in the area, but he couldn't see any in the vicinity of the phone itself. Instead of dialing the number on Nguyen's business card, he called the SDPD non-emergency number and conveyed the murder victim's name to the person who answered. For all he knew, Nguyen already had that information. Then he continued into the lobby of the nearby Island Palms Hotel and emerged through a side exit several minutes later.

There were worse places to spend a lazy afternoon than on the deck of a boat in San Diego, Kane decided. He made a brief detour across the causeway joining the island to the mainland to pick up a case of beer, which he carried back to Shelter Cove Marina. When he reached the *El Halcón*, though, he discovered he had an unexpected visitor. The enigmatic Mr. Hamilton was making himself at home on the boat's covered deck.

"Permission to come aboard?" Kane called out, his voice dripping with sarcasm.

"Humble apologies, Mr. Kane. I did not know how to reach you otherwise, so I decided to wait here for you."

Kane climbed the gangplank. "I don't believe I told you where I was staying." He brushed past the man and put the beer in the galley fridge. He removed a can for himself but did not offer his visitor a drink.

Hamilton stroked his mustache and shrugged. "I have come to make a bargain with you."

"Do tell," Kane said.

"That ring you had earlier, and its intriguing contents. I wish to purchase them from you."

Kane sat on a bench on the starboard side of the boat, as far from Hamilton as possible. "Sorry to be the bearer of bad news, but it's not for sale. Not by me, at least."

"Whatever do you mean?"

Kane popped open his beer and took a long sip. "Only that I don't have the ring anymore."

Hamilton frowned. "I don't believe you. I saw you with it a few hours ago."

"Time passes. Circumstances change."

When Hamilton suddenly reached inside his jacket, Kane dropped his beer, leaned over, grabbed the belaying pin from where he'd tossed it that morning, and hurled it at the man. His aim was decent—the wooden pin struck Hamilton on the right temple, knocking him off-balance. Before the man had a chance to recover, Kane was on him. He extracted the pistol from Hamilton's jacket pocket after a solid punch left the man slumped over in his seat. He backed out of Hamilton's reach in case he recovered, verified the gun was loaded, pulled out his phone, and dialed Nguyen's number.

The police responded rapidly to the scene, taking Hamilton into custody. The gun went into an evidence bag. Nguyen indicated the belaying pin lying on the deck. Traces of blood dotted one end.

"It came in handy as an impromptu weapon," Kane said.

"Who is he? And what did he want?"

"He called himself Hamilton. He was looking for this." Kane retrieved the ornate ring from his shirt pocket. Nguyen had him drop it into an evidence bag. "You might find some touch DNA. His, the guy who got shot...and mine."

"And how exactly did you come into possession of it?"

"The dead man gave it to me. Well, he was still alive, but you know what I mean. He wanted me to give it to someone named Jacobi, but I have no idea who that is."

Nguyen frowned. "Why am I just hearing about it now?"

"It was a dying man's request. How could I refuse him? Turns out there's a memory chip inside. I didn't know about it until Hamilton—if that's really his name—opened it. I thought it was just a ring, you know, a family heirloom. I didn't realize there was something hidden in it. I have no idea what's on the disk, but Hamilton was sure eager to get his hands on it."

"You should have told me about this sooner."

"I know. Poor judgement. Did you ever identify the murder victim?" Kane nodded in the direction of the dock, where the bloodstains were still clearly visible despite someone's valiant efforts to remove them.

"We did. Got an anonymous tip, would you believe?"

"Sure. It happens. It'll be interesting to hear if that gun you just bagged is a match for the bullet in—what did you say his name was?"

"I didn't. But this boat is owned by a man named Abraham Jacobi. We're trying to track him down."

"Jacobi, eh? Makes sense—I'm pretty sure the dead man was trying to come on board when he was shot. I remember the boat rocking."

"I'm glad you don't live around here. I think you'd turn into a major pain in my ass." Nguyen nodded at Kane's spilled can. "Shame about the beer."

"Collateral damage. There's plenty more where that came from. Can I offer you one?"

"Tempting," the detective said. She sighed. "I'm still on the clock, though."

"Come back later, if you like," Kane said. "Join Benjamin Kane's perpetual floating house party."

"John D. MacDonald. I approve."

Kane smiled. "Have a nice afternoon, Detective."

"Drop by HQ in the morning to formalize your statement."

"Aye, aye," he said.

After Nguyen and her colleagues were gone, Kane called his brother. "The situation has been resolved to everyone's satisfaction," he told Nate. "Well, not the guy who tried to kill me a while ago. Or the dead man. Me, basically. My satisfaction. And Detective Nguyen, more or less."

"Are we going to get in trouble because of this?"

"No more than usual," Kane said, stifling a yawn. "Gotta run. My beer's getting warm."

"That was supposed to be me, sitting on a boat deck, getting a tan."

"Luck of the draw," Kane said. "Sucks to be you."

After he hung up, he cleaned up the spilled beer and got another can from the fridge. A few minutes later, a tall redhead emerged onto the deck of the boat in the adjoining slip. She was wearing a flimsy swimsuit and huge sunglasses. "What was that all about?" she called out to him.

Kane smiled. "I guess you missed last night's excitement. Want a beer? Come on over, and I'll tell you all about it."

THE END

HAMPTON BAYS TOMMY ON THE BACKSTAIRS

by Mike Newirth

In the Hamptons it's the way people talk about the Hamptons that tells you everything about them. Not the yearning--all our voices share that-- when you grow up and live and wake up next to the happy masters of the higher rungs of the ladder, it happens. Nor the blowsy, bitchy, petty *Don't you know who I am?* of the Summer Sharers. Anybody who calls it "The Hamptons" is not from the Hamptons. This is still Long Island, where township is everything, and the only locals who count are the ones you grew up around. When I say I'm fifth generation Wainscott it means nothing to most people, but around here it means my roots return to the days when planting potatoes here would seem a heretic's idea. You won't meet anybody more East Hampton than me on your overpriced summer excursion, which makes my chosen path (second generation, there) seem much more surprising. I'm more East Hampton than any Jewish Oscar-winning family filmmaker or brittle, closeted Euro billionaire is what I'm saying, no matter where I lay my head at night or what time at night my workday ends.

Funny, I should have been at home that night in the first place, enjoying a few beers in my tiny yard as the sun crept down. But I was at my desk in the muster room, patiently staring at a backlog of paperwork forms I was too tired to actually complete, when the call came in. It took me a moment to connect the voice on the other end -- "Ah, Vasquez, badge number three-ought-five, calling in code E-nine, Eskimo-nine"-- with the fresh-faced, caramel-skinned young new hire I'd seen around town, monitoring a traffic post in a Challenger, still on it like an egg rested beneath that official gas pedal. *Man or woman down, perpetrator gone on arrival.* I could hear an excited nausea in his young voice. Not an everyday call for any of us on the job in the East Hampton PD to be making.

I myself kept my excitement in check and my speed to sixty as I pushed the Dodge over pitch-black roads, past some unfinished mansions and the back nine of the Wainscott country club. It was only two weeks past Labor Day but already the annual hinge had swung; the swollen crowds of summer people and trendies and party monsters (potential backroad traffic fatalities all) were mostly gone. I passed a winery that used to be a potato field, slowed down as the roads narrowed, nearing Georgica Beach. My destination had a private drive and thick privacy hedges.

They called these properties "summer cottages." As I pulled up, the depth of the mansion was concealed by the slight rise it was built on, and I heard the low mutter of the ocean, the beach frontage behind the pool and guest cabana. Behind the hedge and the drive and the tumescent cottage's double lot was the grail they all sought-- frontage on Georgica Beach, which was properly restricted from the mobs who clogged Main Beach all summer long. Here it was as though only millions guaranteed a place on the sand to spread out designer toys and togs, and gently burn away by the respectfully murmuring Atlantic, even the jellyfish knew to keep their distance. It was said that Martha Stewart nearly took a pernicious daughter to court over their spread at nearby Georgica Pond. Although it's also said that she's become nicer in the years since doing time.

I remember when I first would see the owner of this cottage. I'd spent teenage summers, then some prior to the academy, first bussing then bartending in local restaurants, Rowdy Hall and Citron. One summer in the early 1990s he had just appeared, bossing his way through the circuit. It was after he got the whole Gotti crew acquitted a second time, and everyone in New York had seen his shiny head and heard his arrogant rasp day after day on channel 5 at six, and everyone in those crowded, expensive summer restaurants wanted to be his friend. He was curt to the help, and he tipped well. In those days he sweated arrogance and money. But that was some years ago.

Now three or four scattered rooms were lit, and many dark windows. Vasquez's unit and a South Shore ambulance were in the graveled lot by the dark carriage house, lights off and silent, respectful of sleeping millionaires in proximity.

I met Officer Vasquez in the kitchen. It's a close call, but you could cater a hundred thousand dollar wedding in that kitchen. Lonely acres of stainless steel and rich-blue Italian tile. I could sense Vasquez vibrating from across the room. He explained what he'd seen in a breathless voice.

"Did you get sick up there, buddy?" I said. "In one of the twenty bathrooms?"

"No sir," breathless.

"It's all right if you did, you know. It's all part of coming upon a thing like this."

"Did you, ever?"

I chuckled. "Nah."

I glided through the set-open double doors of the vast first floor, all white walls hung with occasional investment art, large pieces, angry and abstract color slashes. Up the ultramodern cantilevered-wedge central staircase, Vasquez a trembling presence just behind me. There was a large picture window set at the stair bend, and out in the darkness the silver surf line of the Atlantic undulated; a red buoy winked indistinctly.

The master bedroom suite had been recently redone. The current flavor was *Town & Country* with a central arcade-like room with a properly tufted and canopied bed, probably Ralph Lauren or something bespoke, and his and her vanity and toilet chambers. He was in his dressing room, arms akimbo on the floor.

Recently, he had been among the top five criminal defense attorneys in New York City, but now his money and power had spilled all over the terrazzo and he appeared no different than any unfortunate seventeen-year-old prom king we found off the deceptively clear straightaways of Route 27, poured through his windshield. He was in a nice bathrobe, and like men of a certain age must, he'd applied advanced cosmetics to the cause of maintaining his wispy remaining strands of hair to appear more coherent, but now those efforts were for nothing, as the remaining strands were crushed into a roughly punctured crater in the rear quarter of the old attorney's cranium. He'd buckled when he fell, skinny calves at unnatural doll's angles, and he'd voided himself, and the blood spray was more fevered than the curated art downstairs. Long strands of red told the story, across the terrazzo and reaching up the immaculate white cabinetry of ties and hosiery, never to be seen in court again. I noticed the large glass ashtray rolled up against one wall, though it looked spotless, though that was up to the labbies.

Hazard pay when the Realtor contracts this cleanup, I couldn't stop myself from thinking.

"The, uh, new widow," Vasquez whispered, hesitant to speak above the scent of blood and waste and death between us, coppery-sharp enough to nearly hear. "She asked the paras keep her company down the hall."

"We just say widow," I told him, kindness in my voice. "Put her down as 'wife of the decedent.'"

They were in the clubby study at the far end of the hall, past several closed doors. It was bright inside, light reflecting off the immaculate mahogany paneling and cigar-colored leather furniture, tufted and overstuffed couch and chairs. The two paramedics who had, pro forma, coded the old man had obviously been resting their bones on the couch but leapt up when they heard us coming, and now stood comically at half-attention, their faces caught between boredom and wonderment at the grim situation. I didn't recognize them; they were youngsters, a Black girl and a pimple-faced white guy. I did recognize Coraline Stegner, anyone would. That fine, cruelly reserved (but always polite) face, framed by lush blond hair descending, was not easily forgotten. Even though she was getting older, as is true for all of us (except her husband now), and looked puffy and shocked and slack now. It was obvious they had given her something.

Coraline Stegner was only a model briefly but, in her twenties, had that fragile and imperious beauty which made an ad campaign not forgotten, because her slim poise captured anyone's imagination. Less remembered were her wild years, unless you were out here late at night in the most exclusive night spots. I was not, but I heard the stories of her debauches, the powder on the bar from her tiny Chanel bag, the evenings capped off by her unsteady perching to piss in the bar triple sinks. And I saw her sometimes, around town, with her blond posse, speaking with gravity across untouched seafood towers. And then the marriage to David Benowitz, a careful and appropriate life plan--the pitbull lawyer turned genteel *of-counsel* man of leisure, cared for by a loving woman who understood Hamptons society, visibly happy in repose in their mansion astride the exclusive beachside paths--which now lay tragically shattered and bleeding in the dressing room down the hall.

I introduced myself. "I know you've already met Patrol Officer Vasquez." He stepped forward, and nodded, awkward like he was remembering stage directions in a school play. "Mrs. Benowitz, I am so shocked and sorry to see this. Is there anyone we can call for you right now?"

"I don't want to bother anyone," she said in a broken whisper.

I nodded like I understood that.

"I caught a late jitney out from the city," she whispered. I felt badly for her, could see she was in shock and only upright from the miracles of Xanax or whatever stronger dram had been called for. "I met friends at the Palm bar for a late supper. I knew David would not want to be awakened. That's what I *thought*." She cried a little.

We all exchanged uneasy glances. Everyone so determined to do their jobs, that they all forgot their manners. There was a bathroom off the study, so I strode in and plucked a few tissues for Mrs. Benowitz.

"Thank you," she breathed.

The old attorney's wide desk was mostly pristine, with some separate piles of clipped papers and manilla folders, emeritus work, I supposed, which now would land back on the desk of some lowly associate.) There was a heavy desk set of green onyx, and no photos. Under a gold-trimmed onyx blotter weight was an untidy assemblage of paper carbons and bulldog clips. Habits of lawyers and those who spent time among them. This collage clearly represented months if not years of dicey negotiations over home renovations - to the extent we'd call a full-bore triple-lot estate which went empty four months of the year a "home." I looked down at a list on a yellow pad, several groupings of names. I recognized a few. Tommy Guardiello, who I knew still lived in Hampton Bays, where he'd grown up. Hampton Bays was the community that supplied the bartenders and tradesmen and the white gardeners (when white gardeners were still permissible). It was some coincidence that this run-down, dismal Hamptons community never made it into the society pages or the Styles section, but if you've driven through and smelled the sour air and spied the tight-packed unrenovated houses, you'd know why. He wasn't the only one on the list who had a reputation as a backstairs boy. A skilled South Fork tradesman who wasn't above ticking the extra boxes on a contract for the sole benefit of the lady of the house.

She looked toward the rear of the property, toward the solarium, I presumed, which we'd seen was still covered with the sad pageantry of flapping blue tarpaulins. Her abrupt laugh whistled through them. "The work here was never done. David always said, one more renovation, one more set of contractors left to sue."

I pondered that. Cause and effect? "Do you know these men?" I named the three contractors that I'd recognized.

"I remember the one. Thomas Guardiello and Sons." Her voice was listless. Tommy was one of the sons. "He asked a lot of questions."

I bet he did, I thought, then looked at the faces of the other people in the room. They were all in various poses of pretending not to listen to us, although Vasquez still appeared genuinely shocked. I wondered if a night like this could propel an earnest young officer to reconsider the vocation, but of course, he wasn't second generation with the job like I was. And he didn't go back any further than that like I did. But then, neither did Coraline Stegner, even though Backstairs Tommy did.

We all felt the tick of lights splashing up the private drive. That would be whichever overnight-catching county investigator had just chanced into the supreme misfortune of being first responding on such a death scene, his job obviously to take enough notes to prepare his bosses to establish chain of command among a flood tide of media attention from The City, due west. I saw Coraline wince at the very thought of it. I raised my hands to them, placating vaguely, and went downstairs.

Sure enough, the lone sixty-something white-haired man climbing out of the unmarked Explorer looked supremely pissed off to be awake and here. He'd have trucked over from Manorville barracks, only half-awake. He was unshaven and exuded his hangover (*why not have a taste, what could happen on an overnight?*) and I think myself and Vasquez both could have fit into his pants. Out on the courtyard's crunching gravel, I extended my hand, which he ignored. I could tell he had a special sneer for the modified Sam Browne style uniform we'd always worn, even though we'd long since traded Colts for Glocks, to the op-ed distaste of the summer Spielbergs (bad optics, I suppose). "The fuck are you?"

I explained that I was a sergeant in the East Hampton PD and that I had been alone in the building when the patrol officer called in, so came by to assist.

"So, you really don't even need to be here."

"I live in this town." I tried to control the petulance. "Look, Vasquez? He's got plenty of potential but this has got to be his first major scene. I was just playing catch-up anyway."

"That's the initiative we expect from you vacation rangers, but why don't you let the proper investigative authorities take it from here."

I gave him my best smile. The thing about dealing with Suffolk cops is you're never sure if they were of the inner circle of the recent chief who got caught tuning up the local Oxy fiend who'd thieved the chief's beloved dildo collection from the chief's county Escalade. "Couldn't agree more, Detective," I said.

I told Vasquez so long. I was remembering the stories of him as an Eagle Scout in Hampton Bays, how his parents worked two jobs each and his *abuela* kept on cleaning houses in the Hamptons, her knees giving out while he stacked merit badges. I thought he had his responsibilities well in hand. I looked in on Mrs. Benowitz, where the paramedics were watching her like teenagers gauging a video game played by someone else. Lovely blond Coraline--the epitome of the good summer class, she should have been suntanned in a pale bikini in a chaise a thousand yards away, on Georgica beach, watching as a robin's-egg blue summer sky split the ocean's horizon-- was staring at the wall like a housecat, medicated somewhere between shock and grief.

"Ma'am, let me say again that you have all of our--the East Hampton Police Department's--deepest sympathies. Officer Vasquez is downstairs and will see to all your immediate needs." She looked at me with drowning eyes.

Before I left I instructed Vasquez on the protocol for signing off as First On Scene for the county investigators and state police and evidence techs, who even now were rushing through the night, toward the rich old lawyer's beach house, smelling the salt of their own ambition. I insinuated they should be told the recently widowed Mrs. Benowitz was trembling in prescription sleep, even though I figured that wouldn't slow them down much. "You're doing fine. Remember: these are rich people, powerful people. Part of our job now is to see that gets respected. No press, you see what I'm saying? Don't spread any rumors. I can follow up with all who need to know how this looks in the morning."

Aren't you going to stay?" Vasquez gulped.

I chucked him hard on the shoulder and forced a smile. "Chain of command, champ. You and I, we wear the same badge. You just report to that catching D who's chugging an airport Scope right now out there, and they gonna send you home, just like me." I paused like it was just occurring to me. Mentorship is important. "You just make sure you tell them everything you saw. You'll do fine."

The back route to Sag Harbor led from Georgica through a few sharp turns and lights turned yellow blinkers now, then under an old stone railroad bridge, but then it opened up like the horizon. It was one of my favorite places to unwind a car like the Dodge, the sinuous curves only occasionally punctuated by private drives and the forest preserve access road, begging you to punch it to eighty, ever since I was a teenager, and the cops who pulled me over would have to give me only a finger-wagging warning when they found out who my dad was. Not long before I was the one pulling over the summer speeders in their Porsche 911s. And sometimes when they told me who their daddy was, it did work, while other times their evening took a different turn which wound up with their names listed (shame, shame) in the *East Hampton Star*.

Then you slowed down when passing the old Jewish and Black cemeteries. The water sounded different here as you approached the small town center. It was late enough that the neon was off at the old movie theater. The main street looked prosperous as it had forever, but then I turned by the Whaling Museum, that prim, white cube still salty with the unfortunate ghosts of eighteenth century predator technology, and it dipped sharply into a scrubby, sadder street, small saltbox houses set back and dark and sullen behind cluttered yards. At the end of the block was a rambling clapboard building that was almost like one of those sad houses, but the dirt parking lot suggested crowdedness of lives and transactions, here at Pudgy's.

There was a square-jawed, large-framed man behind the bar, in a dingy apron, and a slight woman at the far end doing her end-of-night tasks, a small pile of tip money next to a pad. A few drinkers remained at the bar; the tables were empty. At this hour they'd just look down at the scent of the uniform.

I nodded at the bartender, whom the summer people who wandered in inevitably believed to be Pudgy, the jolly owner of a neighborhood tavern, although none of that was accurate. If a weekend visitor stopped in, he'd certainly be permitted to overpay for a plate of totally adequate fried clams, and would leave feeling only slightly creeped out.

After ten p.m. it was a rough and surly place, locals only. Rich boy would find his Porsche keyed outside at the very least, after ten. But it's not like the hollow-eyed man who was not Pudgy poured many Cosmopolitans. He nodded at me and brought me a beer. At one end of the bar sat three older fellows, and at the far end, a curvy woman with long, dark hair pulled back was finishing her shift work.

It felt good to rest for a moment on the torn vinyl of the crooked barstool. I sipped my beer and looked the three over, but all were well into their personal oblivion, barely recognizable though clearly old locals. The waitress, Jolie, had seen me come in of course, and kept her eyes focused on the tools of her trade: silverware and threadbare napkins and a spike of orders and a pile of cash.

When she had completed her sidework and marshaled an evening's tips into neat piles of silver and singles, she looked up at me, then eased off her stool and tossed her crumpled apron on it, then wandered toward the dim door that led to the stairway and upstairs apartment. I finished my beer slowly, tossed down a few singles, and followed her.

She was sitting back on the sprung, burnt-orange nubbly couch. There were a kitchenette and a small bedroom--that was it. The apartment was dusty and partly a maze of stacked liquor boxes, some crumbling with forgotten orders and spillage, so a faint sour wine aroma pervaded. But things happened here and had for years. Jolie's hands were on her knees. She wore jeans and a lacy, black top. From a night of running drinks and food her clothes would creak with sweat and her scent and Long Island iced tea splasheroo. She was a pretty woman, exhausted, with eyes older than she was.

"We need to talk again about Tommy," I said.

"I'll *bet* we do," she said.

"How is he doing?"

"Fine, I'm sure."

"He in here tonight?"

"No." She answered so quickly, I was totally convinced. "Not last night neither."

"He been making money lately, running schemes?"

"*Schemes*? I ain't his mother."

I had no reason to believe Jolie and Tommy were locked in any sort of significant relationship, any more than those broken-down whalers down there still cluttering up the bar (instead of going back to beachfront houses full of warmth and kindness which for them had never existed) had reason to believe she and I had any sort of relationship. But they had known each other since high school, in Hampton Bays, and I knew they saw each other and partied together sometimes. Everyone who grew up out here and stayed has those connections, whether or not they hooked their way into the summer glamour and never looked back.

"I need you to think back." As I spoke I laid the blue pills out one by one, five of them, rolling off my fingertips, a neat sleight of hand you wouldn't expect of them. "To the conversation you and Tommy had, which you and I talked about."

Her eyes counting five, she spoke dully. "Tommy and me were partying. We was sitting in his car in the parking lot outside here. He kept complaining about his latest job. Said the old lawyer had drawers full of watches, big-time jewels. Said he never bothers setting the burglar alarm. Said the old lawyer sleeps like he's a hundred, not eighty."

"What kind of watches?"

"Rolexes and shit. French types."

"Swiss," I said, feeling a slight pulse at the temple. "The watches are Swiss. 'Running like a Swiss watch.' That's what those kinds of people all say."

"Right. Okay."

I looked at Jolie while her eyes took their time flickering between me and the pills. When she finally focused back on the here and now, I gripped her forearm, hard. "They will come around, next day or two. They'll be asking general questions about him and probably some other people. All you got to do is say what he said, and you just say you heard it at the bar. If it comes up later, anyone says, 'But you knew him,' you say 'I just remembered it wrong.'"

There didn't seem much to say while she went to work with a razor blade and the heel of a tiny shopworn Altoids tin and ground down one of the blue marvels. I watched as she did her bumps and then I glared at her when she offered me the straw. *But why not.* Life is short, as David Benowitz, Esq. would remind any client.

After she collected the remainder and stashed them in her tin, she drifted over to the sprung couch in the room's shadows, and I could see her muscles relax without moving. She threw her head back like she could cough out an evening's exhaustion, but I knew she was just feeling the kneading effect of the synthetic opiate. She cast sleepy eyes in my direction. Sometimes I had her do things in moments like this on that very same couch, it was true. Sometimes I went there with her, in the small hours when the entire town was so quiet and even the ancient waterfront streets could forget centuries worth of grudges, like there was no such thing as class and there never had been and we could all be summertime friends.

Jolie was a cute South Shore gal, a princess neverwas, and she looked all right, but even in the haunted apartment's dim light her flesh was grainy and slack. You could see the stone-cold junkie she would one day be swimming beneath its surface, clawing its way up. I had been in bed with Coraline

Stegner, together in the cozy pool cabana when I gave her Tommy's name and asked her how much she thought a backstairs boy like Tommy would need to see, to be strayed. She estimated a hundred thousand. I laughed. "Depending on how you approach it, guy like him, he'd do it for ten."

Jolie looked toward the back bedroom. I knew the last thing she needed now.

I wanted to give it to her. I touched her arm with great tenderness. I felt badly about what was bound to happen to her.

"It looks like somebody had better wake up the chief," I said.

END

Mike Newirth grew up on Long Island and now lives in Chicago. His fiction received a Henfield-*Transatlantic Review* award and a Pushcart Prize, and his stories, essays, and reviews appear in many publications and anthologies, including *The Baffler*, *The Louisville Review*, *Another Chicago Magazine (ACM)*, *VOLT*, and *They're at It Again: Stories from Twenty Years of Open City*. He's a faculty member of the Department of English at the University of Illinois--Chicago.

KELLER'S THERAPY

by Lawrence Block

I had this dream," Keller said. "Matter of fact I wrote it down, as you suggested."

"Good."

Before getting on the couch Keller had removed his jacket and hung it on the back of a chair. He moved from the couch to retrieve his notebook from the jacket's inside breast pocket, then sat on the couch and found the page with the dream on it. He read through his notes rapidly, closed the book, and sat there, uncertain how to proceed.

"As you prefer," said Breen. "Sitting up or lying down, whichever is more comfortable."

"It doesn't matter?"

"Not to me."

And which was more comfortable? A seated posture seemed more natural for conversation, while lying down on the couch had the weight of tradition on its side. Keller, who felt driven to give this his best shot, decided to go with tradition. He stretched out, put his feet up.

He said, "I'm living in a house, except it's almost like a castle. Endless passageways and dozens of rooms."

"Is it your house?"

"No, I just live here. In fact I'm a kind of servant for the family that owns the house. They're almost like royalty."

"And you are a servant."

"Except I have very little to do, and I'm treated like an equal. I play tennis with members of the family. There's this tennis court in back of the house."

"And this is your job? To play tennis with them?"

"No, that's an example of how they treat me as an equal. And I eat at the same table with them, instead of eating downstairs with the servants. My job is the mice."

"The mice?"

"The house is infested with mice. I'm having dinner with the family, I've got a plate piled high with good food, and a waiter in black tie comes in and presents a covered dish. I lift the cover and there's a note on it, and it says, 'Mice.'"

"Just the single word?"

"That's all. I get up from the table and I follow the servant down a long hallway, and I wind up in an unfinished room in the attic. There are tiny mice all over the room, there must be twenty or thirty of them, and I have to kill them."

"How?"

"By crushing them underfoot. That's the quickest and most humane way, but it bothers me and I don't want to do it. But the sooner I finish, the sooner I can get back to my dinner, and I'm very hungry."

"So you kill the mice?"

"Yes," Keller said. "One almost gets away but I stomp on it just as it's getting out the door. And then I'm back at the dinner table and everybody's eating and drinking and laughing, and my plate's been cleared away. Then there's a big fuss, and finally they bring my plate back from the kitchen, but it's not the same food as before. It's . . ."

"Yes?"

"Mice," Keller said. "They're skinned and cooked, but it's a plateful of mice."

"And you eat them?"

"That's when I woke up," Keller said. "And not a moment too soon, I'd have to say."

"Ah," Breen said. He was a tall man, long-limbed and gawky, wearing chinos and a dark green shirt and a brown corduroy jacket. He looked to Keller like someone who had been a nerd in high school, and who now managed to look distinguished, in an eccentric sort of way. He said "Ah" again, and folded his hands, and asked Keller what he thought the dream meant.

"You're the doctor," Keller said.

"You think it means that I am the doctor?"

"No, I think you're the one who can say what it means. Maybe it just means I shouldn't eat Rocky Road ice cream right before I go to bed."

"Tell me what you think the dream might mean."

"Maybe I see myself as a cat."

"Or as an exterminator?"

Keller didn't say anything.

"Let us work with this dream on a very superficial level," Breen said. "You're employed as a corporate troubleshooter, except that you used another word for it."

"They tend to call us expediters," Keller said, "but troubleshooter is what it amounts to."

"Most of the time there is nothing for you to do. You have considerable opportunity for recreation, for living the good life. For tennis, as it were, and for nourishing yourself at the table of the rich and powerful. Then mice are discovered, and it is at once clear that you are a servant with a job to do."

"I get it," Keller said.

"Go on, then. Explain it to me."

"Well, it's obvious, isn't it? There's a problem and I'm called in and I have to drop what I'm doing and go and deal with it. I have to take abrupt arbitrary action, and that can involve firing people and closing out whole departments. I have to do it, but it's like stepping on mice. And when I'm back at the table and I want my food—I suppose that's my salary?"

"Your compensation, yes."

"And I get a plate of mice." He made a face. "In other words, what? My compensation comes from the destruction of the people I have to cut adrift. My sustenance comes at their expense. So it's a guilt dream?"

"What do you think?"

"I think it's guilt. My profit derives from the misfortunes of others, from the grief I bring to others. That's it, isn't it?"

"On the surface, yes. When we go deeper, perhaps we will begin to discover other connections. With your having chosen this job in the first place, perhaps, and with some aspects of your childhood." He interlaced his fingers and sat back in his chair. "Everything is of a piece, you know. Nothing exists alone and nothing is accidental. Even your name."

"My name?"

"Peter Stone. Think about it, why don't you, between now and our next session."

"Think about my name?"

"About your name and how it suits you. And" —a reflexive glance at his wristwatch— "I'm afraid our hour is up."

Jerrold Breen's office was on Central Park West at Ninety-fourth Street. Keller walked to Columbus Avenue, rode a bus five blocks, crossed the street, and hailed a taxi. He had the driver go through Central Park, and by the time he got out of the cab at Fiftieth Street he was reasonably certain he hadn't been followed. He bought coffee in a deli and stood on the sidewalk, keeping an eye open while he drank it. Then he walked to the building where he lived, on First Avenue between Forty-eighth and Forty-ninth. It was a prewar high-rise, with an Art Deco lobby and an attended elevator. "Ah, Mr. Keller," the attendant said. "A beautiful day, yes?"

"Beautiful," Keller agreed.

Keller had a one-bedroom apartment on the nineteenth floor. He could look out his window and see the UN building, the East River, the borough of Queens. On the first Sunday in November he could watch the runners streaming across the Queensboro Bridge, just a couple of miles past the midpoint of the New York marathon.

It was a spectacle Keller tried not to miss. He would sit at his window for hours while thousands of them passed through his field of vision, first the world-class runners, then the middle-of-the-pack plodders, and finally the slowest of the slow, some walking, some hobbling. They started in Staten

Island and finished in Central Park, and all he saw was a few hundred yards of their ordeal as they made their way over the bridge into Manhattan. Sooner or later the sight always moved him to tears, although could not have said why.

Maybe it was something to talk about with Breen.

It was a woman who had led him to the therapist's couch, an aerobics instructor named Donna. Keller had met her at the gym. They'd had a couple of dates, and had been to bed a couple of times, enough to establish their sexual incompatibility. Keller still went to the same gym two or three times a week to raise and lower heavy metal objects, and when he ran into her they were friendly.

One time, just back from a trip somewhere, he must have rattled on about what a nice town it was. "Keller," she said, "if there was ever a born New Yorker, you're it. You know that, don't you?"

"I suppose so."

"But you've got this fantasy, living the good life in Elephant, Montana. Every place you go, you dream up a whole life to go with it."

"Is that bad?"

"Who's saying it's bad? But I bet you could have fun with it in therapy."

"You think I need to be in therapy?"

"I think you'd get a lot out of therapy," she said. "Look, you come here, right? You climb the Stair Monster, you use the Nautilus."

"Mostly free weights."

"Whatever. You don't do this because you're a physical wreck."

"I do it to stay in shape."

"And because it makes you feel good."

"So?"

"So I see you as all closed in and trying to reach out," she said. "Going all over the country and getting real estate agents to show you houses you're not going to buy."

"That was a couple of times. And what's so bad about it, anyway? It passes the time."

"You do these things and don't know why," she said. "You know what therapy is? It's an adventure, it's a voyage of discovery. And it's like going to the gym. It's . . . look, forget it. The whole thing's pointless anyway unless you're interested."

"Maybe I'm interested," he said.

Donna, not surprisingly, was in therapy herself. But her therapist was a woman, and they agreed he'd be more comfortable working with a man. Her ex-husband had been very fond of his therapist, a West Side psychologist named Breen. Donna had never met the man herself, and she wasn't on the best of terms with her ex, but—

"That's all right," he said. "I'll call him myself."

He'd called Breen, using Donna's ex-husband's name as a reference. "But I doubt that he even knows me by name," he said. "We got to talking a while back at a party and I haven't seen him since. But something he said struck a chord with me, and, well, I thought I ought to explore it."

"Intuition is a powerful teacher," Breen said.

Keller made an appointment, giving his name as Peter Stone. In his first session he talked some about his work for a large and unnamed conglomerate. "They're a little old-fashioned when it comes to psychotherapy," he told Breen. "So I'm not going to give you an address or telephone number, and pay for each session in cash."

"Your life is filled with secrets," Breen said.

"I'm afraid it is. My work demands it."

"This is a place where you can be honest and open. The idea is to uncover those secrets you've been keeping from yourself. Here you are protected by the sanctity of the confessional, but it's not my task to grant you absolution. Ultimately, you absolve yourself."

"Well," Keller said.

"Meanwhile, you have secrets to keep. I can respect that. I won't need your address or telephone number unless I'm forced to cancel an appointment. I suggest you call in to confirm your sessions an hour or two ahead of time, or you can take the chance of an occasional wasted trip. If *you* have to cancel an appointment, be sure to give me twenty-four hours' notice. Or I'll have to charge for the missed session."

"That's fair," Keller said.

He went twice a week, Mondays and Thursdays, at two in the afternoon. It was hard to tell what they were accomplishing. Sometimes Keller relaxed completely on the sofa, talking freely and honestly about his childhood. Other times he experienced the fifty-minute session as a balancing act; he was tugged in two directions at once, yearning to tell everything, compelled to keep it all a secret.

No one knew he was doing this. Once when he ran into Donna she asked if he'd ever given the shrink a call, and he'd shrugged sheepishly and said he hadn't. "I thought about it," he said, "but then somebody told me about this masseuse, she does a combination of Swedish and shiatsu, and I've got to tell you, I think it does me more good than somebody poking and probing at the inside of my head."

"Oh, Keller," she'd said, not without affection. "Don't ever change."

It was on a Monday that he recounted the dream about the mice. Wednesday morning his phone rang, and it was Dot. "He wants to see you," she said.

"Be right out," he said.

He put on a tie and jacket and caught a cab to Grand Central and a train to White Plains. There he caught another cab and told the driver to head out Washington Boulevard and let him off at the corner of Norwalk. After the cab drove off he walked up Norwalk to Place and turned left. The second house on the right was a big old Victorian with a wraparound porch. He rang the bell and Dot let him in.

"The upstairs den," she said. "He's expecting you."

He went upstairs, and forty minutes later he came down again. A young man named Louis drove him back to the station, and on the way they chatted about a recent boxing match they'd both seen on ESPN. "What I wish," Louis said, "I wish they had like a mute button on the remote, except what it would do is it would mute the announcers but you'd still hear the crowd noise and the punches landing. What you wouldn't have is the constant yammer-yammer-yammer in your ear." Keller wondered if they could do that. "I don't see why not," Louis said. "They can do everything else. If you can put a man on the moon, you ought to be able to shut up Al Bernstein."

Keller took the train back to New York and walked to his apartment. He made a couple of phone calls and packed a bag. At 3:30 he went downstairs, walked half a block, and hailed a cab to JFK, where he picked up his boarding pass for American's 6:10 flight to Tucson.

In the departure lounge he remembered his appointment with Breen. He called and canceled the Thursday session. Since it was less than twenty-four hours away, Breen said, he'd have to charge him for the missed session, unless he was able to book someone else into the slot.

"Don't worry about it," Keller told him. "I hope I'll be back in time for my Monday appointment, but it's always hard to know how long these things are going to take. If I can't make it I should at least be able to give you the twenty-four hours' notice."

He changed planes in Dallas and got to Tucson shortly before midnight. He had no luggage aside from the piece he was carrying, but he went to the baggage claim area anyway. A rail-thin man with a broad-brimmed straw hat stood there holding a hand-lettered sign that read NOSCAASI. Keller watched the man for a few minutes, and observed that no one else was watching him. He went up to him and said, "You know, I was figuring it out the whole way to Dallas. What I came up with, it's *Isaacson* spelled backwards."

"That's it," the man said. "That's exactly it." He seemed impressed, as if Keller had cracked the Japanese naval code. He said, "You didn't check a bag, did you? I didn't think so. Car's this way."

In the car the man showed him three photographs, all of the same man, heavy-set, dark, with black hair and a greedy pig face. Bushy mustache, bushy eye-brows. Enlarged pores on his nose.

"That's Rollie Vasquez," the man said. "Son of a bitch wouldn't exactly win a beauty contest, would he?"

"I guess not."

"Let's go," the man said. "Show you where he lives, where he eats, where he gets his ashes hauled. Rollie Vasquez, this is your life."

Two hours later the man dropped him at a Ramada Inn and gave him a room key and a car. "You're all checked in," he said. "Car's parked at the foot of the staircase closest to your room. She's a Mitsubishi Eclipse, pretty decent transportation. Color's supposed to be silver-blue, but she says gray on the papers. Registration's in the glove box."

"There was supposed to be something else."

"That's in the glove box, too. Locked, of course, but the one key fits the ignition and the glove box. And the doors and the trunk, too. And if you turn the upside down it'll still fit, 'cause there's no up and down to it. You really got to hand it to those Japs."

"What'll they think of next?"

"Well, it may not seem like much," the man said, "but all the time you waste making sure you got the right key, then making sure you got it right side up."

"It adds up."

"It does," the man said. "Now, you got a full tank of gas. It takes regular, but what's in there's enough to take you upwards of four hundred miles."

"How're the tires? Never mind. Just a joke."

"And a good one," the man said. "'How're the tires?' I like that."

The car was where it was supposed to be, and the glove box held the car's registration and a semiautomatic pistol, a Horstmann Sun Dog, loaded, with a spare clip lying alongside it. Keller slipped the gun and the spare clip into his carry-on, locked the car, and went to his room without passing the desk.

After a shower, he sat down and put his feet up on the coffee table. It was all arranged, and that made it simpler, but sometimes he liked it better the other way, when all he had was a name and address and no one on hand to smooth the way for him. This was simple, all right, but who knew what traces were being left? Who knew what kind of history the gun had, or what the string bean with the NOSCAASI sign would say if the police picked him up and shook him?

All the more reason to do it quickly. He watched enough of an old movie on cable to ready him for sleep, then slept until he woke up. When he went out to the car he had his bag with him. He expected to return to the room, but if he didn't he'd be leaving nothing behind, not even a fingerprint.

He stopped at Denny's for breakfast. Around one he had lunch at a Mexican place on Figueroa. In the late afternoon he drove up into the hills north of the city, and he was still there when the sun went down. Then he drove back to the Ramada.

That was Thursday. Friday morning the phone rang while he was shaving. He let it ring. It rang again just as he was ready to leave. He didn't answer it this time, either, but went around wiping surfaces a second time with a hand towel. Then he went out to the car.

At two that afternoon he followed Rolando Vasquez into the men's room of the Saguaro Lanes bowling alley and shot him three times in the head. The little gun didn't make much noise, not even in the confines of the tiled lavatory. Earlier he had fashioned an improvised suppressor by wrapping the barrel of the gun with a space-age insulating material that muffled most of the gun's report without adding much in the way of weight or bulk. If you could do that, he thought, you ought to be able to shut up Al Bernstein.

He left Vasquez propped in a stall, left the gun in a storm drain half a mile away, left the car in the long-term lot at the airport.

Flying home, he wondered why they had needed him in the first place. They'd supplied the car and the gun and the finger man. Why not do it all themselves? Did they really need to bring him all the way from New York to step on the mouse?

"You said to think about my name," he told Breen. "The significance of it. But I don't see how it could have any significance. It's not as if I chose it myself."

"Let me suggest something," Breen said. "There is a metaphysical principle which holds that we choose everything about our lives, that in fact we select the very parents we are born to, that everything which happens in our lives is a manifestation of our will. Thus there are no accidents, no coincidences."

"I don't know if I believe that."

"You don't have to. We'll just take it for the moment as a postulate. So, assuming that chose the name Peter Stone, what does your choice tell us?"

Keller, stretched full length upon the couch, was not enjoying this. "Well, a peter's a penis," he said reluctantly. "A stone peter would be an erection, wouldn't it?"

"Would it?"

"So I suppose a who decides to call himself Peter Stone would have something to prove. Anxiety about his virility. Is that what you want me to say?"

"I want you to say whatever wish," Breen said. "Are you anxious about your virility?"

"I never thought I was," Keller said. "Of course it's hard to say how much anxiety I might have had back before I was born, around the time I was picking my parents and deciding what name they should choose for me. At that age I probably had a certain amount of difficulty maintaining an erection, so I guess I had a lot to be anxious about."

"And now?"

"I don't have a performance problem, if that's the question. I'm not the way I was in my teens, ready to go three or four times a night, but then who in his right mind would want to? I can generally get the job done."

"You get the job done."

"Right."

"You perform."

"Is there something wrong with that?"

"What do you think?"

"Don't do that," Keller said. "Don't answer a question with a question. If I ask a question and you don't want to respond, just leave it alone. But don't turn it back on me. It's irritating."

Breen said, "You perform, you get the job done. But what do you feel, Mr. Peter Stone?"

"Feel?"

"It is true that peter is a colloquialism for the penis, but it has an earlier meaning. Do you recall Christ's words to the first Peter? 'Thou art Peter, and upon this rock I shall build my church.' Because Peter *means* rock. Our Lord was making a pun. So your first name means rock and your last name is Stone. What does that give us? Rock and stone. Hard, unyielding, obdurate. Insensitive. Unfeeling."

"Stop," Keller said.

"In the dream, when you kill the mice, what do you feel?"

"Nothing. I just want to get the job done."

"Do you feel their pain? Do you feel pride in your accomplishment, satisfaction in a job well done? Do you feel a thrill, a sexual pleasure, in their death?"

"Nothing," Keller said. "I feel nothing. Could we stop for a moment?"

"What do you feel right now?"

"Just a little sick to my stomach, that's all."

"Do you want to use the bathroom? Shall I get you a glass of water?"

"No, I'm all right. It's better when I sit up. It'll pass. It's passing already."

Sitting at his window, watching not marathoners but cars streaming over the Queensboro Bridge, Keller thought about names. What was particularly annoy-ing, he thought, was that he didn't need to be under the care of a board-certified metaphysician to acknowledge the implications of the name Peter Stone. He had very obviously chosen it, and not in the manner of a soul deciding what parents to be born to and planting names in their heads. He had picked the name himself when he called to make his initial appointment with Jerrold Breen. *Name?* Breen had demanded. *Stone,* he had replied. *Peter Stone.*

Thing is, he wasn't stupid. Cold, unyielding, insensitive, but not stupid. If you wanted to play the name game, you didn't have to limit yourself to the alias he had selected. You could have plenty of fun with the name he'd borne all his life.

His full name was John Paul Keller, but no one called him anything but Keller, and few people even knew his first or middle names. His apartment lease and most of the cards in his wallet showed his names as J. P. Keller. Just Plain Keller was what people called him, men and women alike. ("The upstairs den, Keller. He's expecting you." "Oh, Keller, don't ever change." "I don't know how to say this, Keller, but I'm just not getting my needs met in this relationship.")

Keller. In German it meant *cellar,* or *tavern.* But the hell with that, you didn't need to know what it meant in a foreign language. Just change a vowel. Keller = Killer.

Clear enough, wasn't it?

On the couch, eyes closed, Keller said, "I guess the therapy's working."

"Why do you say that?"

"I met a girl last night, bought her a couple of drinks, went home with her. We went to bed and I couldn't do anything."

"You couldn't do anything."

"Well, if you want to be technical, there were things I could have done. I could have typed a letter, sent out for a pizza. I could have sung 'Melancholy Baby.' But I couldn't do what we'd both been I would do, which was have sex with her."

"You were impotent."

"You know, you're very sharp. You never miss a trick."

"You blame me for your impotence," Breen said.

"Do I? I don't know about that. I'm not sure I even blame myself. To tell you the truth, I was more amused than devastated by the experience. And she wasn't upset, perhaps out of relief that I upset. But just so nothing like this ever happens again, decided I'm changing my name to Dick

"What was your father's name?"

"My father," Keller said. "Jesus, what a question. Where did that come from?"

Breen didn't say anything.

Neither, for several minutes, did Keller. Then, eyes closed, he said, "I never knew my father. He was a soldier. He was killed in action before I was born. Or he was shipped overseas before I was born and killed when I was a few months old. Or possibly he was home when I was born, or came home on leave when I was very small, and he held me on his knee and told me he was proud of me."

"You have such a memory?"

"I have no memory," Keller said. "The memory I have is of my mother telling me about him, and that's the source of the confusion, because she told me different things at different times. Either he was killed before I was born or shortly after, and either he died without seeing me or he saw me one time and sat me on his knee. She was a good woman but she was vague about a lot of things. The one thing she was completely clear on, he was a soldier. And he got killed over there."

"And his name—"

Was Keller, he thought. "Same as mine," he said. "But forget the name, this is more important than the name. Listen to this. She had a picture of him, a head-and-shoulders shot, this good-looking young soldier in a uniform and wearing a cap, the kind that folds flat when you take it off. The picture was in a gold frame on her dresser when I was a little kid, and she would tell me how that was my father.

"And then one day the picture wasn't there anymore. 'It's gone,' she said. And that was all she would say on the subject. I was older then, I must have been seven or eight years old.

"Couple of years later I got a dog. I named him Soldier, I called him that after my father. Years after that two things occurred to me. One, Soldier's a funny thing to call a dog. Two, whoever heard of naming a dog after your father? But at the time it didn't seem the least bit unusual to me."

"What happened to the dog?"

"He became impotent. Shut up, will you? What I'm getting to's a lot more important than the dog. When I was fourteen, fifteen years old, I used to work afternoons after school helping out this guy who did odd jobs in the neighborhood. Cleaning out basements and attics, hauling trash, that sort of thing. One time this notions store went out of business, the owner must have died, and we were cleaning out the basement for the new tenant. Boxes of junk all over the place, and we had to go through everything, because part of how this guy made his money was selling off the stuff he got paid to haul. But you couldn't go through all this crap too thoroughly or you were wasting time.

"I was checking out this one box, and what do I pull out but a framed picture of my father. The very same picture that sat on my mother's dresser, him in his uniform and his military cap, the picture that disappeared, it's even in the same frame, and what's it doing here?"

Not a word from Breen.

"I can still remember how I felt. Like stunned, like *Twilight Zone* time. Then I reach back in the box and pull out the first thing I touch, and it's the same picture in the same frame.

"The whole box is framed pictures. About half of them are the soldier and the others are a fresh-faced blonde with her hair in a page boy and a big smile on her face. What it was, it was a box of frames. They used to package inexpensive frames that way, with a photo in it for display. For all I know they still do. So what my mother must have done, she must have bought a frame in a five-and-dime and told me it was my father. Then when I got a little older she got rid of it.

"I took one of the framed photos home with me. I didn't say anything to her, I didn't show it to her, but I kept it around for a while. I found out the photo dated from World War Two. In other words, it couldn't have been a picture of father, because he would have been wearing a different uniform.

"By this time I think I already knew that the story she told me about my father was, well, a story. I don't believe she knew who my father was. I think she got drunk and went with somebody, or maybe there were several different men. What difference does it make? She moved to another town, she told people she was married, that her husband was in the service or that he was dead, whatever she told them."

"How do you feel about it?"

"How do I feel about it?" Keller shook his head. "If I slammed my hand in a cab door, you'd ask me how I felt about it."

"And you'd be stuck for an answer," Breen said. "Here's a question for you. Who was your father?"

"I just told you—"

"But someone fathered you. Whether or not you knew him, whether or not your mother knew who he was, there was a particular man who planted the seed that grew into you. Unless you believe yourself to be the second coming of Christ."

"No," Keller said. "That's one delusion I've been spared."

"So tell me who he was, this man who spawned you. Not on the basis of what you were told or what you've managed to figure out. I'm not asking this question of the part of you that thinks and reasons. I'm asking that part of you that simply knows. Who was your father? What was your father?"

"He was a soldier," Keller said.

Keller, walking uptown on Second Avenue, found himself standing in front of a pet shop, watching a couple of puppies cavorting in the window.

He went inside. One whole wall was given over to stacked cages of puppies and kittens. Keller felt his spirits sinking as he looked into the cages. Waves of sadness rocked him.

He turned away and looked at the other pets. Birds in cages, gerbils and snakes in dry aquariums, tanks of tropical fish. He was all right them. It was the puppies that he couldn't bear to look at.

He left the store. The next day he went to an animal shelter and walked past cages of dogs waiting to be adopted. This time the sadness was overwhelming, and he felt it physically as pressure against his chest. Something must have shown on his face, because the young woman in charge asked him if he was all right.

"Just a dizzy spell," he said.

In the office she told him that they could probably accommodate him if he was especially interested in a particular breed. They could keep his name on file, and when a specimen of that breed became available—

"I don't think I can have a pet," he said. "I travel too much. I can't handle the responsibility." The woman didn't respond, and Keller's words echoed in her silence. "But I want to make a donation," he said. "I want to support the work you do."

He got out his wallet, pulled bills from it, handed them to her counting them. "An anonymous donation," he said. "I don't want a receipt. I'm sorry for taking your time. I'm sorry I can't adopt a dog. Thank you. Thank you very much."

She was saying something, but he didn't listen. He hurried out of there.

"'I want support the you do.' That's what I told her, and then I rushed out of there because I didn't her thanking me. Or asking me questions."

"What would she ask?"

"I don't know," Keller said. He rolled over on the couch, facing away from Breen, facing the wall. 'I want to support your work.' But I don't even know their work is. They find homes for some animals, and what do they do with the others? Put them to sleep?"

"Perhaps."

"What do I want to support? The placement or the killing?"

"You tell me."

"I tell you too much as it is," Keller said.

"Or not enough."

Keller didn't say anything.

"Why did it sadden you to see the dogs in their cages?"

"I felt their sadness."

"One feels only one's own sadness. Why is it sad to you, a dog in a cage? Are you in a cage?"

"No."

"Your dog, Soldier. Tell me about him."

"All right," Keller said. "I guess I could do that."

A session or two later, Breen said, "You have never been married."

"No."

"I was married."

"Oh?"

"For eight years. She was my receptionist, she booked my appointments, showed clients to the waiting room until I was ready for them. Now I have no receptionist. A machine answers the phone. I check the machine between appointments, and take and return calls at that time. If I had had a machine in the first place I'd have been spared a lot of agony."

"It wasn't a good marriage?"

Breen didn't seem to have heard the question. "I wanted children. She had three abortions in eight years and never told me. Never said a word. Then one day she threw it in my face. I'd been to a doctor, I'd had tests, and all indications were that I was fertile, with a high sperm count and extremely motile sperm. So I wanted her to see a doctor. 'You fool, I've killed three of your babies already, why don't you leave me alone?' I told her I wanted a divorce. She said it would me."

"And?"

"We were married eight years. We've been divorced for nine. Every month I write an alimony check and put it in the mail. If it was up to me I'd rather burn the money."

Breen fell silent. After a moment Keller said, "Why are you telling me all this?"

"No reason."

"Is it supposed to relate to something in my psyche? Am I supposed to make a connection, clap my hand to my forehead, say, 'Of course, of course! I've been so blind!'"

"You confide in me," Breen said. "It seems fitting that I confide in you."

A couple of days later Dot called. Keller took a train to White Plains, where Louis met him at the station and drove him to the house on Taunton Place. Later Louis drove him back to the train station and he returned to the city. He timed his call to Breen so that he got the man's machine. "This is Peter Stone," he said. "I'm flying to San Diego on business. I'll have to miss my next appointment, and possibly the one after that. I'll try to let you know."

Was there anything else to tell Breen? He couldn't think of anything. He hung up, packed a bag, and rode Amtrak to Philadelphia.

No one met his train. The man in White Plains had shown him a photograph and given him a slip of paper with a name and address on it. The man in question managed an adult bookstore a few blocks from Independence Hall. There was a tavern across the street, a perfect vantage point, but one look inside made it clear to Keller that he couldn't spend time there without calling attention to himself, not unless he first got rid of his tie and jacket and spent twenty minutes rolling around in the gutter.

Down the street Keller found a diner, and if he sat at the far end he could keep an eye on the bookstore's mirrored front windows. He had a cup of coffee, then walked across the street to the bookstore, where there were two men on duty. One was a dark and sad-eyed youth from India or Pakistan, the other the slightly exophthalmic fellow in the photo Keller had seen in White Plains.

Keller walked past a whole wall of videocassettes and leafed through a display of magazines. He had been there for about fifteen minutes when the kid said he was going for his dinner. The older man said, "Oh, it's that time already, huh? Okay, but make sure you're back by seven for a change, will you?"

Keller looked at his watch. It was six o'clock. The only other customers were closeted in video booths in the back. Still, the kid had had a look at him, and what was the big hurry, anyway?

He grabbed a couple of magazines at random and paid for them. The man bagged them and sealed the bag with a strip of tape. Keller stowed his purchase in his carry-on and went to find himself a hotel room.

The next he went to a museum and a movie, arriving at the bookstore at ten minutes after six. The young clerk was gone, presumably having a plate of curry somewhere. The jowly man was behind the counter, and there were three customers in the store, two checking the video selections, one looking at magazines.

Keller browsed, hoping they would decide to clear out. At one point he was standing in front of a whole wall of videocassettes and it turned into a wall of caged puppies. It was momentary, and he couldn't tell if it was a genuine hallucination or just some sort of mental flashback. Whatever it was, he didn't like it.

One customer left, but the other two lingered, and then someone new came in off the street. And in half an hour the Indian kid was due back, and who knew if he would take his full hour, anyway?

He approached the counter, trying to look a little more nervous than he felt. Shifty eyes, furtive glances. Pitching his voice low, he said, "Talk to you in private?"

"About what?"

Eyes down, shoulders drawn in, he said, "Something special."

"If it's got to do with little kids," the man said, "no disrespect intended, but I don't know nothing about it, I don't want to know nothing about it, and I wouldn't even know where to steer you."

"Nothing like that," Keller said.

They went into a room in back. The jowly man closed the door, and as he was turning around Keller hit him with the edge of his hand at the juncture of neck and shoulder. The man's knees buckled, and in an instant Keller had a loop of wire around his neck. In another minute he was out the door, and within the hour he was on the northbound Metroliner.

When he got home he realized he still had the magazines in his bag. That was sloppy, he should have discarded them the previous night, but he'd simply forgotten them altogether and never even unsealed the package.

Nor could he find a reason to unseal it now. He carried it down the hall, dropped it unopened into the incinerator. Back in his apartment, he fixed himself a weak scotch and water and watched a documentary on the Discovery Channel. The vanishing rain forest, one more goddam thing to worry about.

"Oedipus," Jerrold Breen said, holding his hands in front of his chest, his fingertips pressed together. "I presume you know the story. Unwittingly, he killed his father and married his mother."

"Two pitfalls I've thus far managed to avoid."

"Indeed," Breen said. "But have you? When you fly off in your official capacity as corporate expediter, when you shoot trouble, as it were, what exactly are you doing? You fire people, you cashier entire divisions, you close plants, you rearrange human lives. Is that a fair description?"

"I suppose so."

"There's an implied violence. Firing a man, terminating his career, is the symbolic equivalent of killing him. And he's a stranger, and I shouldn't doubt that the more important of these men are more often than not older than you, isn't that so?"

"What's the point?"

"When you do what you do, it's as if you are seeking and killing your unknown father."

"I don't know," Keller said. "Isn't that a little far-fetched?"

"And your relationships with women," Breen went on, "have a strong Oedipal component. Your mother was a vague and unfocused woman, incompletely present in her own life, incapable of connection with others. Your relationships with women are likewise blurred and out of focus. Your problems with impotence—"

"Once!"

"—are a natural consequence of this confusion. Your mother herself is dead now, isn't that so?"

"Yes."

"And your father is not to be found, and almost certainly deceased. What's called for, Peter, is an act specifically designed to reverse this entire pattern on a symbolic level."

"I don't follow you."

"It's a subtle point," Breen admitted. He crossed his legs, propped an elbow on a knee, extended his thumb, and rested his chin on it. Keller thought, not for the first time, that Breen must have been a stork in a prior life. "If there were a male figure in your life," Breen went on, "preferably at least a few years your senior, someone playing a faintly paternal role vis-à-vis yourself, someone to you turn for advice and direction."

Keller thought of the man in White Plains.

"Instead of killing this man," Breen said, "symbolically, I need hardly say—I am speaking symbolically throughout—but instead of killing him as you have done with father figures in the past, it seems to me that might do to nourish this man."

Cook a meal for the man in White Plains? Buy him a hamburger? Toss him a salad?

"Perhaps you could think of a way to use your particular talents to this man's benefit instead of his detriment," Breen went on. He drew a handkerchief from his breast pocket and mopped his forehead. "Perhaps there is a woman in his life—your mother, symbolically—and perhaps she is a source of great pain to your father. So, instead of making love to her and slaying him, like Oedipus, you might reverse the usual course of things by, uh, showing love to him and, uh, slaying her."

"Oh," Keller said.

"Symbolically, that is to say."

"Symbolically," Keller said.

A week later Breen handed him a photograph. "This is called the Thematic Apperception Test," Breen said. "You look at the photograph and make up a story about it."

"What kind of story?"

"Any kind at all," Breen said. "This is an exercise in imagination. You look at the subject of the photograph and imagine what sort of woman she is and what she is doing."

The photo was in color, and showed a rather elegant brunette dressed in tailored clothing. She had a dog on a leash. The dog was medium size, with a chunky body and an alert expression in its eyes. It was that color which dog people call blue, and which everyone else calls gray.

"It's a woman and a dog," Keller said.

"Very good."

Keller took a breath. "The dog can talk," he said, "but he won't do it in front of other people. The woman made a fool of herself once when she tried to show him off. Now she knows better. When they're alone he talks a blue streak, and the son of a bitch has an opinion on everything. He tells her everything from the real cause of the Thirty Years' War to the best recipe for lasagna."

"He's quite a dog," Breen said.

"Yes, and now the woman doesn't want other people to know he can talk, because she's afraid they might take him away from her. In this picture they're in the park. It looks like Central Park."

"Or perhaps Washington Square."

"It could be Washington Square," Keller agreed. "The woman is crazy about the dog. The dog's not so sure about the woman."

"And what do you think about the woman?"

"She's attractive," Keller said.

"On the surface," Breen said. "Underneath it's another story, believe me. Where do you suppose she lives?"

Keller gave it some thought. "Cleveland," he said.

"Cleveland? Why Cleveland, for God's sake?"

"Everybody's got to be someplace."

"If I were taking this test," Breen said, "I'd probably imagine the woman living at the foot of Fifth Avenue, at Washington Square. I'd have her living at number one Fifth Avenue, perhaps because I'm familiar with that particular building. You see, I once lived there."

"Oh?"

"In a spacious apartment on a high floor. And once a month," he continued, "I write out an enormous check and mail it to that address, which used to be mine. So it's only natural that I would have this particular building in mind, especially when I look at this particular photograph." His eyes met Keller's. "You have a question, don't you? Go ahead and ask it."

"What breed is the dog?"

"The dog?"

"I just wondered," Keller said.

"As it happens," Breen said, "it's an Australian cattle dog. Looks like a mongrel, doesn't it? Believe me, it doesn't talk. But why don't you hang on to that photograph?"

"All right."

'You're making really fine progress in therapy," Breen said. "I want to acknowledge you for the work you're doing. And I just know you'll do the right thing."

A few days later Keller was sitting on a park bench in Washington Square. He folded his newspaper and walked over to a dark-haired woman wearing a blazer and a beret. "Excuse me," he said, "but isn't that an Australian cattle dog?"

"That's right," she said.

"It's a handsome animal," he said. "You don't see many of them."

"Most people think he's a mutt. It's such an esoteric breed. Do you own one yourself?"

"I did. My ex-wife got custody."

"How sad for you."

"Sadder still for the dog. His name was Soldier. Is Soldier, unless she's gone and changed it."

"This fellow's name is Nelson. That's his call name. Of course the name on his papers is a real mouthful."

"Do you show him?"

"He's seen it all," she said. "You can't show him a thing."

"I went down to the Village last week," Keller said, "and the damnedest thing happened. I met a woman in the park."

"Is that the damnedest thing?"

"Well, it's unusual for me. I meet women at bars and parties, or someone introduces us. But we met and talked, and then I happened to run into her the following morning. I bought her a cappuccino."

"You just happened to run into her on two successive days."

"Yes."

"In the Village."

"It's where I live."

Breen frowned. "You shouldn't be seen with her, should you?"

"Why not?"

"Don't you think it's dangerous?"

"All it's cost me so far," Keller said, "is the price of a cappuccino."

"I thought we had an understanding."

"An understanding?"

"You don't live in the Village," Breen said. "I know where you live. Don't look so surprised. The first time you left here I watched you from the window. You behaved as though you were trying to avoid being followed. So I bided my time, and when you stopped taking precautions, that's when I followed you. It wasn't that difficult."

"Why follow me?"

"To find out who you were. Your name is Keller, you live at 865 First Avenue. I already knew what you were. Anybody might have known just from listening to your dreams. And paying in cash, and all of these sudden business trips. I still don't know who employs you, the crime bosses or the government, but then what difference does it make? Have you been to bed with my wife?"

"Your ex-wife."

"Answer the question."

"Yes, I have."

"Christ. And were you able to perform?"

"Yes."

"Why the smile?"

"I was just thinking," Keller said, "that it was quite a performance."

Breen was silent for a long moment, his eyes fixed on a spot above and to the right of Keller's shoulder. Then he said, "This is disappointing. I had hoped you would find the strength to transcend the Oedipal myth, not merely reenact it. You've had fun, haven't you? What a naughty little boy you've been! What a triumph you've scored over your symbolic father! You've taken his woman to bed. No doubt you have visions of getting her pregnant, so that she can give you what she so cruelly denied him. Eh?"

"Never occurred to me."

"It would, sooner or later." Breen leaned forward, concern showing on his face. "I hate to see you sabotaging your own therapeutic process this way," he said. "You were doing so *well*."

From the bedroom window you could look down at Washington Square Park. There were plenty of dogs there now, but none of them were Australian cattle dogs.

"Some view," Keller said. "Some apartment."

"Believe me," she said, "I earned it. You're getting dressed. Going somewhere?"

"Just feeling a little restless. Okay if I take Nelson for a walk?"

"You're spoiling him," she said. 'You're spoiling both of us."

On a Wednesday morning, Keller took a cab to La Guardia and a plane to St. Louis. He had a cup of coffee with an associate of the man in White Plains and caught an evening flight back to New York. He caught another cab and went directly to the apartment building at the foot of Fifth Avenue.

"I'm Peter Stone," he told the doorman. "I believe Mrs. Breen is expecting me."

The doorman stared.

"Mrs. Breen," Keller said. "In Seventeen-J."

"I guess you haven't heard," the doorman said. "I wish it wasn't me that had to tell you."

"You killed her," he said

"That's ridiculous," Breen told him. "She killed herself. She threw herself out the window. If you want my professional opinion, she was suffering from depression."

"If you want *my* professional opinion," Keller said, "she had help."

"I wouldn't advance that argument if I were you," Breen said. "If the police were to look for a murderer, they might look long and hard at Mr. Stone-hyphen-Keller, the stone killer. And I might have to tell them how the usual process of transference went awry, how you became obsessed with me and my personal life, how I couldn't seem to dissuade you from some inane plan to reverse the Oedipal complex. And then they might ask you why you employ aliases, and how you make your living, and . . . do you see why it might be best to let sleeping dogs lie?"

As if on cue, the dog stepped out from behind the desk. He caught sight of Keller and his tail began to wag.

"Sit," Breen said. "You see? He's well trained. You might take a seat yourself."

"I'll stand. You killed her, and then you walked off with the dog, and—"

Breen sighed. "The police found the dog in the apartment, whimpering in front of the open window. After I went down and identified the body and told them about her previous suicide attempts, I volunteered to take the dog home with me. There was no one else to look after it."

"I would have taken him," Keller said.

"But that won't be necessary, will it? You won't be called upon to walk my dog or make love to my wife or bed down in my apartment. Your services are no longer required." Breen seemed to recoil at the harshness of his own words. His face softened. "You'll be able to get back to the far more important business of therapy. In fact" —he indicated the couch—"why not stretch out right now?"

"That's not a bad idea. First, though, could you put the dog in the other room?"

"Not afraid he'll interrupt, are you? Just a little joke. He can wait for us in the outer office. There you go, Nelson. Good dog. . . Oh, no. How dare you bring a gun to this office? Put that down immediately."

"I don't think so."

"For God's sake, why kill me? I'm not your father. I'm your therapist. It makes no sense for you to kill me. You've got nothing to gain and everything to lose. It's completely irrational. It's worse than that, it's neurotically self-destructive."

"I guess I'm not cured yet."

"What's that, gallows humor? it happens to be true. You're a long way from cured, my friend. As a matter of fact, I would say you're approaching a psychotherapeutic crisis. How will you get through it if you shoot me?"

Keller went to the window, flung it wide open. "I'm not going to shoot," he said.

"I've never been the least bit suicidal," Breen said, pressing his back against a wall of bookshelves. "Never."

"You've grown despondent over the death of your ex–wife."

"That's sickening, just sickening. And who would believe it?"

"We'll see," Keller told him. "As far as the therapeutic crisis is concerned, well, we'll see about that, too. I'll think of something."

The woman at the animal shelter said, "Talk about coincidence. One day you come in and put your name down for an Australian cattle dog. You know, that's a very uncommon breed in this country."

"You don't see many of them."

"And what came in this morning? A perfectly lovely Australian cattle dog. You could have knocked me over with a sledgehammer. Isn't he a beauty?"

"He certainly is."

"He's been whimpering ever since he got here. It's very sad, his owner died and there was nobody to keep him. My goodness, look how he went right to you! I think he likes you."

"I'd say we were made for each other."

"I can almost believe it. His name is Nelson, but of course you can change it."

"Nelson," he said. The dog's ears perked up. Keller reached to give him a scratch. "No, I don't think I'll have to change it. Who was Nelson, anyway? Some kind of English hero, wasn't he? A famous general or something?"

"I think an admiral. Commander of the British fleet, if I remember correctly. Remember? The Battle of Trafalgar Square?"

"It rings a muted bell," he said. "Not a soldier but a sailor. Well, that's close enough, wouldn't you say? Now I suppose there's an adoption fee to pay, and some papers to fill out."

When they'd handled that part she said, "I still can't get over it. The coincidence and all."

"I knew a man once," Keller said, "who insisted there was no such thing as a coincidence or an accident."

"I wonder how he'd explain this."

"I'd like to hear him try," Keller said. "Let's go, Nelson. Good boy."

LAST NIGHT IN OCEAN BEACH

by Curtis Ippolito

Carrie kissed and snapped, beckoning her dachshund-terrier mix, Dash, to keep pace as they darted across West Point Loma Boulevard on their way to Dog Beach for the last time.

Dash yanked his leash, pulling Carrie to a favored clump of bird-of-paradise. Full bladder or not, he habitually lifted his leg on the tropical plant, as if he refused to piss on the beach. Too much on his agenda, then, with dozens of dog asses to sniff, snacks to beg for from other dog owners, and washed-up, dead crustaceans to investigate.

Today, though, she didn't care. He could do whatever. She wanted them to soak up every moment possible on her one-hour lunch break.

Normally, they'd take a second shorter beach break in the afternoon—a nice luxury thanks to her working from home full-time as a graphic designer—but today she was slammed with tasks, and this would be their only trip while the sun shone.

While Dash emptied his bladder, Carrie gazed at the Ocean Villa Inn. A two-story, white, blue-trimmed dump of a motel. Its only redeeming feature was the two or three dozen mature Mexican Palm trees encompassing the property. She didn't know what was worse—that tourists actually booked a vacation in San Diego only to stay at this supremely sketch place, or that she'd miss watching the all-night food deliveries, random fistfights, and prostitute busts from her tiny studio across the street.

Dash tore up blades of sandy grass with his back paws.

"C'mon," said Carrie.

He whipped his dopey head up to her, panting with his long tongue, and darted back to the sidewalk. They continued toward the beach. A blue, cloudless sky above, the sounds of gently crashing waves surrounding them. The aroma of weed wafted on the breeze, overpowering the smells of salt and beach. Goddamnit, she would miss it all. She wasn't leaving San Diego and made a promise to herself they'd go to the beach every day after work, even if it had to be a different beach. Best intentions aside, a nagging voice told her she was fooling herself. Moving five miles inland might as well be fifty. She'd be lucky if they hit the beach both days of the weekend from here on out.

They reached the parking lot with access to the beach just past the concrete barricades. Seagulls squawked and hopped all around them. Dash loved to chase them when given the opportunity. He hadn't caught one yet. Carrie grimaced, hoping to hell he never did.

"Suh, Carrie!" Ryan. A one-time hookup of hers calling out from his Dodge Coachmen. He was parked at the barricades separating the parking lot from the volleyball courts.

Offering a weak smile, she waved. "Hey."

"Come here a sec."

Dash was locked onto the beach. She, too, wanted to get down there, sink her toes into the sand one last time. But she figured saying good-bye to Ryan fit the theme of this last trip, this last day in Ocean Beach. Besides, he never hurt the eyes.

"C'mon, Dash." After some hesitation, he submitted, and they traipsed over to Ryan.

Sliding door open, tan legs dangling off the side, Ryan sat there, his chest glistening in the sun. He wore only faded-blue boardshorts. The only pair she'd ever seen him in.

"Hey, Ryan. How are you?"

He popped up, his bare feet smacking the blacktop. Pulled her into a hug. "Suh, girl. You look fine as always. How you been?" He smelled like way too much body spray and not enough soap and water. Why did that do it for her?

"Oh, you know… It's our last day as locals. So that blows."

Ryan sucked his teeth. "Damn. I was hoping you'd find a place, but I guess no-go? Offer still stands. You and Dash can totally crash in the Coachmen. Plenty of room."

Carrie laughed. A little too hard. "Sorry. That's sweet of you, but I'm not the vanlifer type. My work desk is bigger than the inside of your…home."

"It's all good. So, where you headed, then?"

How much information to divulge? In many ways, she had enjoyed their fling. It had been fun. Totally spontaneous, a trait she was always challenging herself to flex. Being a military brat, her childhood had been incredibly regimented and controlled by her Navy father. Even at thirty, she still had to push herself to break out of her routine and live. For that reason alone, she didn't regret fucking Ryan. She hadn't even hesitated bringing him back to her place, because doing it in his van was a nonstarter. To his credit, he never stalked her or parked outside her apartment or anything. So why worry now about giving him too much info?

"Clairemont. Balboa and Genesee area."

Ryan grimaced.

"What?"

"Nothing, sorry," he said. "Clairemont? You sure? It's so…domestic."

"Yeah, I'm renting a house with a couple of co-workers. I'll have double the room at half what I'm paying now, and it's only five miles from PB and Mission Bay."

Ryan raised his hands. "Fuck. I live on wheels, and that still sounds too far. You and Dash gonna get down this way much?"

"For sure. On the weekends."

He grimaced again. Ran a hand through his thick, jet-black hair. "Sounds bleak."

Carrie shrugged. "Hand I was dealt."

"Want me to beat some sense into your landlord? Force him to keep your rent the same?"

"Ha! I wish." Carrie playfully shoved Ryan's shoulder. "I mean… No, just kidding. Already signed the new lease."

"Okay, then my parting gift: a fist to that fool's face it is."

"You're crazy."

Ryan smiled. The sun made his big brown eyes gleam.

"Remind me why we didn't go out again," he said.

Maybe it was all the mixed emotions of moving out of OB, Ryan looking so damn hot, or simply because that small voice told her to be spontaneous, but Carrie felt a wave of emotion.

She lunged at Ryan, kissed him on the lips.

* * *

Her work desk was the last thing needing packed. The issue wasn't her computer monitors and laptop. It was all the paperwork: brochure samples, notebooks of stock samples, remit envelopes—clutter, clutter, clutter. She'd recycle it all if up to her, but for some reason the nonprofit she worked for still sent out print appeals and brochures in this digital age, so she needed to keep samples on hand. She sighed, packing away a crystal trophy for "Best Spread."

Carrie moved to the couch to take a break. Pulled up a food delivery app on her phone and ordered a plant-based California burrito from her favorite vegetarian fast-food joint. She didn't know how they did it, but their "carne asada" tasted superior to real meat. Once she completed the order, she scanned her small apartment.

Dash was curled up in his doggy bed to her right. Snoring. Hard to believe they wouldn't call this home after tonight. Eight years. Her first and only apartment postcollege. The movers would arrive at ten the next morning, and that would be that.

Two months ago, her landlord, Gary, sent a notice he was raising her rent by two hundred and twenty bucks once she renewed. And after it had gone up one hundred and eighty the year before. Hilarious for a derelict complex with zero amenities.

She did her due diligence looking for a cheaper place in the neighborhood. Stalked listings, schmoozed landlords and Realtors alike. But try as she might, it felt as if she couldn't submit an application fast enough.

The only places she could afford—and that was straining the definition of the word—got snatched up the same day as being listed.

Sure, she'd miss living so close to the beach. And the Ocean Beach Pier, Dog Beach, sunsets at the tide pools. Not to mention all the bars and restaurants on Newport, and OB's funkiness as a whole. Like the drum circle on Wednesday nights. It took all the nerve she had to make herself take part that first time. She would miss it all desperately because there was no way she could afford three grand a month in rent.

Recounting all this made Carrie wish she had given Ryan the green light to beat Gary's ass. Wouldn't change a thing, but maybe she'd feel a little sense of justice on her way out.

* * *

Hours later, a buzzing sound woke her. Dash barked twice but stayed anchored to her side. Groggy, she rolled to the nightstand. Found her cell phone lit up.

A string of short texts from Ryan.

Then, a soft knock on the front door.

Dash jolted, growled.

"Carrie, let me in," said a hushed voice.

Dash barked a defensive, timid bark, jumped off the bed, and ran to the front door.

Carrie got out of bed. Checking the time, she muttered, "Two thirty?"

At the door, Dash sniffed through the doorjamb, tail wagging furiously.

"Go away. Don't you know what time it is?" Carrie looked through the peephole and saw nothing more than a shadowed figure in the darkness.

"It's Ryan. Can you let me in?" he whispered.

"Why are you here?"

"Did you get my texts?"

"Yeah, but I haven't…wait a…" She hadn't read them yet, but this was going nowhere fast, so she unlocked the door, and Ryan wedged his way in, turned, and locked the door.

"Sorry to show up like this, but I need your help. I fucked up."

Carrie rubbed her eyes. His words didn't connect. "What?"

"I fucked up. I need your help."

Dash sniffed Ryan's feet, his tail continuing to wag and now knocking against the wall.

"Go lie down, Dash." Carrie pushed him toward his doggy bed. Dash went there and got in, panting and wagging his tail. She turned to Ryan. "So, what's going on?"

His face was a blotchy, sweaty mess. Hair matted to his forehead, and he was shaking.

"I went to your landlord's to, you know…give him my going-away present for you…and… Oh god, Carrie. He's dead!"

"What? Are you serious?" She hugged herself, feeling incredibly confused and suddenly vulnerable. "What happened? What did you do?" He had to be pranking her, right?

"I don't know. I mean, I do. I just can't believe it." Ryan brushed past her and began to pace. After taking several shallow breaths, he continued. "I went over an hour ago, and he was up. He opened the door, and I pushed my way in. He grabbed me by the shoulders, and we struggled. I tried to push him off me so I could punch him and get out of there, but he held tight. Finally, his grip loosened, and I gave him one hard shove. He tripped over the entryway where the living room ends and the kitchen begins…flew backwards and nailed the back of his head on the corner of the counter. He dropped like a rock."

Ryan stopped. Looked up at Carrie. His eyes wet, panicked. "There's so much blood."

"Holy fuck." She held out her arms for him, and he nestled himself into her, like a hurt ten-year-old seeking his mother's comfort.

After a couple minutes, he gained some composure and looked at her.

"I'll call the police," Carrie said.

"No!" Ryan pushed away. "You can't."

"It was an accident. We have to."

"I basically broke into the dude's house. They'll arrest me. I came here to ask you to help me get rid of his body—"

"Ryan. No!"

"Don't give me that look. He was a piece of shit. No reason either of us has to get into trouble for his death."

"Either of us?"

"C'mon, Carrie. I went there to beat his ass for you."

"Are you fucking serious?"

Ryan arched his eyebrows, gave her a sad puppy-dog face. "No one will ever know. I have a bulletproof plan. I just need another set of arms, and we have to do this *now*."

Shit.

"At least see what I'm dealing with. Then, I'll tell you my plan."

"I really hate this. Never thought you'd really beat the guy up… Fine. Let me put on a T-shirt first."

* * *

Carrie leashed Dash, and the three of them went to Gary's office apartment, around the other side of the complex. On the way, Dash stopped to pee, making Ryan antsy.

The night sky was moonless but full of stars. The complex around them desolate. They were in that rare three-hour window of time when all of OB either slept or was passed out drunk. By four thirty, the beach would begin humming again, beginning with surfers.

Once they reached Gary's door, Ryan put a finger to his lips. He pushed open the door, and Carrie followed him in. Only the light over the oven was on, but still bright enough to illuminate the tiny efficiency apartment. Carrie's eyes watered immediately from the pungent smell of wintergreen chewing tobacco hanging thick. Gary was a dipper, and apparently a hoarder, too, because the glass-topped coffee table in the middle of his living room was dominated by In-N-Out cups filled to the brims with tobacco spit.

Carrie wrinkled her nose. Ryan nodded sideways for her to follow. They cut in front of the couch, pushing through empty takeout cups, fast-food bags, and pizza boxes. Dash sniffed it all with great intrigue.

When they made it to the kitchen, Carrie gasped, seeing a pool of black blood on the floor. It coated the ceramic tile and lapped along the cabinet baseboards. She lost a grip on Dash's leash for a second—long enough for him to yank free and dart to the blood. He stopped right at the edge and began lapping feverishly.

"Gross!" said Ryan, covering his mouth.

Carrie's stomach lurched. She lunged for Dash. Scooped him up by his belly, turned, and ran out the front door. After plopping him in the grass and squeezing his leash tight, she pitched to the side and puked on the trunk of a palm tree.

Ryan showed at her side. "Are you okay?"

She wiped her lips. "Yeah. Let me put Dash back in my apartment."

Ryan mouthed, "Okay."

After returning Dash home, Carrie came back down and took several deep breaths before reentering the apartment. Once inside, she noticed Gary this time, or what had been Gary. Rolled up in cheap Persian carpet behind the couch. She'd rushed right past him on the way to throw up.

Ryan was standing in the kitchen, staring at the blood.

"So what's your plan?" she asked.

He turned, face white as a lifeguard tower. "I'll come back and clean this up after we get rid of the body."

"Excuse me?"

He walked over to her. Touched her shoulder. She didn't pull away.

"Here's the plan: We load Gary into my van. Drive to Sunset Cliffs. Park at a pullout. We roll him out of the rug and over the cliff. When they find his body, everyone will think he just fell off the cliff—happens all the time, and his injury will match. I'll drive us back. You go home and take a shower. I'll take care of everything else, including hosing down your vomit."

"You've thought of everything." She said it with more snark than she intended.

"What do you say?"

"You're really serious. I still think we should call the cops."

Ryan grabbed her elbow. "No, you can't." A pause. "When they ask why I was here...I don't know what I would say. I did it for you."

His tone wasn't threatening, but the subtext that he'd drag her into this made a vein in her neck start throbbing.

"I really don't want to go to prison, Carrie."

"I don't want that, either. Just let me think a sec."

"Hurry. We only have a couple hours until surfers show up. Not to mention, parking along the cliffs opens then too. This is the only time we can do this."

Maybe it was her uncaffeinated, groggy brain, but the plan made sense. Seemed riskier to call the police, honestly. She couldn't trust Ryan not to implicate her, even non-maliciously. And, he was right. People did fall off the cliffs all the time, and no one would think otherwise about Gary.

Her palms went clammy and her heart drummed in her ears.

Was she really talking herself into doing this?

* * *

The Coachmen didn't sputter as long as Ryan kept it under twenty-five miles per hour. They wound their way along Sunset Cliffs Boulevard, the vast Pacific unseen to their right. It was too dark to see anything in that direction, except when the road cut sharply and the van's headlights illuminated sandstone cliffs, boulders, and black ocean for the briefest of moments.

"What about there?" Carrie pointed to a large parking lot on the right.

"No good."

He kept driving. Carrie snuck a peek over her shoulder at the carpet roll. Gary's body hadn't weighed as much as she expected when they loaded him into the van, although Ryan had taken the heavier upper-body end.

"Here," Ryan said.

He pulled into a smaller pullout containing a half dozen parking spots. A low metal barricade separated them from the cliff. Ryan pulled the passenger side of the van parallel to the barricade, turned off the headlights, and put the van in park. Kept it running.

"What about porch cameras at the mansions across the street?" Carrie asked.

"We'll climb in the back, go out through the sliding door. Even if they get the van on camera, who's going to connect it with finding him washed-up way down the beach in a few hours? We're cool. Let's just get this done."

She followed Ryan into the back. Made a mental note to remind him to burn his sheets, bedding—everything Gary had touched. Ryan quietly opened the sliding door, offered a hand, and helped Carrie down. Feet planted, she righted herself and brushed her T-shirt smooth.

"I've never seen you wear a shirt before," she said to Ryan.

"We can flirt later. Here, help me." He grabbed the carpet by one end and tugged. One side swung to him. Then he pulled the other side. "We'll have to lift him over the barricade to roll him over."

They each took one end of the carpet, Ryan hugging his and Carrie grasping hers with her hands. Together, they lifted the body out of the van and heaved it onto the barricade. Ryan leaned over the side to look. "There's more land here than I expected," he whispered. "We're gonna have to get on the other side so we can walk it closer to roll him off the cliff."

"Okay." Carrie breathed deeply. Tucked her chin. She stepped one leg over the barricade while keeping hold of the carpet. Then the other. Her sneakers crunched on the crusty soil.

Ryan did the same. Once they were on the other side, he gestured for them to carry the carpet closer to the cliff. Slowly, they stutter-stepped several paces until Ryan said, "Good."

They set the carpet down. Carrie wiped her hands on her pajama shorts.

"Okay, move back," Ryan said. "I'll roll him out and over."

Carrie backpedaled to the barricade. Rested her butt against it. She watched Ryan come around to the long end of the carpet. He bent down, grabbed the edge, and tugged. The carpet unfurled quickly, and Gary's body popped out like some kind of sick magic trick.

But it didn't go over.

The body stopped short, resting on the lip of the cliff.

"Fuck," Ryan whisper shouted.

They both walked over to investigate.

"Careful," Ryan said. "The ground's slippery."

Reinforcing his message, a sign to their left read, *Unstable cliffs. Watch your step.*

Gary was face down, thank god. But it gave Carrie her first glimpse at the back of his head. His gray hair matted, caked in black blood.

Ryan held his arm out to Carrie to say "stay back." He gave Gary's body a hard kick. The corpse gave way and began to roll over the cliff. Unfortunately, Ryan risked doing the same, losing his footing.

"Help!" he hollered.

As Gary's body disappeared from view, dropping down the face of the cliff, Carrie reached out and grabbed a flailing Ryan by the wrist.

"Got you!" she said.

Ryan landed hard to the ground on his side. Carrie kept hold. He was able to grab her wrist as well to secure himself. But his weight pulled her in his direction. Her shoes lost traction on the slick soil, taking her feet out from under her. She landed hard on her chest.

Dust caked her face.

Ryan twisted himself onto his stomach. The two of them now lay face-to-face, holding each other by the wrists, flat on the sandy ground. Ryan's legs dangling over the cliff.

"Phew! You okay?" he asked.

Carrie could only nod, having all the air punched from her lungs.

Ryan grimaced. "Keep holding. I'll work myself up, just don't let go."

It was in that moment, her eyes fixed on his, dust coating her nostrils and mouth, the sound of the surf pounding the beach below, that a most spontaneous, twisted thought bloomed.

What if she let go?

She could simply walk home. Get showered. Be ready for the movers to come and move her out of OB. She wouldn't have to worry about Ryan getting caught and implicating her, because there would be no more Ryan. He'd be the vanlifer who randomly killed a local apartment landlord, and tripped and fell to his death off Sunset Cliffs while concealing his crime.

All she had to do was let go.

Her grip must have loosened, because Ryan shouted, "Don't let go!"

She averted her eyes.

"Carrie!"

She loosened her hold incrementally.

"Carrie, don't let go of me!"

The terror in his tone snapped her out of it. What was she doing? She couldn't do this.

Carrie regained a tight grasp on Ryan's wrists, locking eyes with him again.

"Hold on. I've got you," she said.

"You scared me for a second."

She worked her way to her knees while maintaining her grasp on Ryan, straining her low back. She pulled anyway. The sound of scraping soil sent a surge of confidence through her. She was doing it. Saving them both.

"Keep pulling," Ryan said.

She smiled at him. He grinned back.

Then, without warning, Ryan tried to stand. The rapid movement caused the soil to shift. The ground shook suddenly. Then, the lip of the cliff broke off. Ryan's lower body dropped.

He screamed.

At the same time, Carrie was slammed to her chest again and sent careening into him.

Their heads collided.

She felt weightless. Saw stars. Then tumbling rock and sand.

Black ocean.

A dark wall.

Black sky.

Ocean one last time.

END

THE SLICK

by Kathryn E. McGee

Melody lies prone on her beach towel, damp hair spidering across her shoulders. She's propped on elbows, flipping through flash cards—*snowy plover, global warming, shark fin soup, passive thermal design*—her environmental studies midterm in a few hours.

She barely needs the cards, has all the content memorized. She flips anyway, tunnel vision, ignoring all the activity at Isla Vista beach. Preparation makes her feel good: a stress ball squeezed and released.

A snore interrupts her flow.

Her roommate Jen is passed out on the sand next to her, flopped and relaxed; probably doing yoga in her sleep, wiggling her toes. Always her move. The two share a bedroom, and even with the privacy curtains closed, Jen will have a foot come loose of the fabric at night, toes dancing, while Melody is packed in, grinding her teeth.

She sets the flash cards down, checks her phone. One o'clock in the afternoon. How did it get so late? She's got to leave soon: bike to campus, grab a coffee. Get her head on right for the midterm. She'll need a few extra minutes to clean off the tar, though. The natural oil slick in the ocean usually rubs smudges onto her feet.

"Hey, girl." She shuffles the cards. "Time for me to go." Jen keeps snoring, toes surely flailing with each in-out breath. Melody says her name, gives her a second to wake, and flips through a few more cards, reviewing a set of facts about sharks—*overexploitation, denticles, drowning.*

Jen finally groans, rolls over. "Jesus Christ. *That* was a morning." She brushes a tangle of hair from her cheek and laughs. "Still kinda got the spins."

"Seriously," Melody says, though she spent the morning at Gio's—the pizza place where they had a day-drinking pre-party for their other roommate's birthday—secretly sober, filled her beer glass with Diet Coke, said it was a Guinness. The last couple of hours, she's been studying while Jen's been sleeping off the booze like a narcoleptic sea cucumber.

Jen grunts a laugh. "You didn't fool me with your *beer* earlier."

"Ah, shit, sorry." Melody fake grimaces, cracks her neck again, but doesn't feel the usual relief: there's no fault left in her bones.

"It's all good." Jen's voice is gravelly. "You're going to do great things. Get rid of plastics in the ocean. Make clean energy. Save the sharks or whatever."

Melody nods. "At least, I hope so." Her eyes go to a group of college students playing frisbee, running in the surf. She stares past them, into the distance, toward the horizon. What if she can't change the world? What if all this time spent studying isn't worth anything? At least Jen is making art in her major, creating *something*.

"I'm just…saving the world with ceramics, you know." Jen laughs. She's been working on a bunch of sculptures that look like small ocean creatures and trying, she says, to capture a certain *feeling* that always seems beyond her grasp.

Sorority girls in white bikinis and see-through inner tubes run past, letters on their asses, singing some random song they all know. Melody looks to her right, watching them settle onto a beach blanket while laughing, woo-wooing, and secreting a box of wine beneath a web of tanned legs.

Jen cracks open a can to her left. "When in Rome. You want some?"

"As appealing as warm Natty Light is…" Melody shakes her head. "I can't. Drinking before a big test makes me anxious."

"I get it." Jen takes a gulp.

Melody frowns. Maybe she should be more like Jen, go with the flow.

Jen's situation is different, though. She's an art studio major. She can do her work drunk or hungover. Sometimes alcohol makes her art *better*. Melody's classes require constant focus and sacrifice. The stakes are high.

Reverse climate change. Save the world. She flips through a few more cards—*wildlife corridor, An Inconvenient Truth, peak oil crisis*—and sighs.

"You sure you don't want some?" Jen holds out her beer. "It's *light*."

"No, thanks." Melody's mind sinks into a watery gorge. Should she be drinking more alcohol? Going to more parties? Sleeping with more guys?

There was that one guy, Nathaniel. They talked at some parties, made out a few times, but he wanted to hang out *more*, so she stopped returning his texts. She didn't want to waste time. Studying was too important. He was hot, but there will be time for guys like him eventually.

The sorority girls are at it again, singing.

If she's been doing everything wrong by *not* dating Nathaniel, by putting that sort of thing off, then she's been wrong her whole life. She's already in her junior year; college will be over soon enough. What she's doing schoolwise really matters; it *does*.

She looks at the flash cards. *Shark fin soup* is on top like a Tarot pull. "Saving the sharks is important." She straightens the pile, nodding to herself.

Jen sips from her can. "Totally is."

"They're incredible creatures. And since you asked, they don't even have bone-bones, but *cartilaginous skeletons*."

"The name of my band."

"They're covered in *skin-teeth* called denticles. It's like a protective coating but made of individual little teeth."

"Their dental bills must be crazy." Jen takes another sip. "So why the skin-teeth?"

Melody looks to her right. The sorority girls have risen. They are playing frisbee with beach dudes: running, jumping, laughing, touching. "Nothing attaches to them that way."

"You know, 'Skin-Teeth' was our first CD single," Jen says. "Back in the day."

Melody smirks, turns onto her side, finally faces Jen. "Basically, it's shitty to kill them for their fins to make a stupid soup. They're at the top of the food chain but still as vulnerable as any other…" She pauses, staring. "Oh my god, is that *tar*?"

"What?" Jen looks down.

Large, black splotches cover Jen's shoulders and trail down the curve of her stomach, along her legs. Some are fingertip sized, and some are much bigger, several inches wide, staining her pink triangle top and bottoms, wrapping her limbs and toes.

Jen surveys the situation, then looks at Melody. "What the shit. You've got it too."

Spots dot Melody's arms, chest, and stomach, speckling her all the way to her feet. "Jesus." They're like Jen's, but smaller, not as many. Still *too many* though.

"If it's just tar, it looks fucking weird," Jen says.

Melody tries to pick at the edges of a spot but has an impossible time sliding her nail under. "It's not coming up."

"You got a flash card for *this?*" Jen frowns.

Melody shakes her head. "Must be from that natural oil slick in the water. That's why we always get tar on our feet on this beach."

"This is some Dalmatian shit though. How did we not see it when we got out?"

"I don't know. It's like it developed, or something."

"Developed? That's a thing?"

"You've got it a lot worse than me," Melody says. She only swam long enough to perk up her brain to be sharp for studying, but Jen bobbed around out there a *while*, at one point hooking up with a group on inner tubes tied to a floating keg.

She pushes herself up to sitting, looks toward the ocean. Her eyes lock on a wide swath of the deep that appears inky, not reflective or iridescent, but solidly black, the finish matte. The area seems dark and bottomless as if out of proportion, swelling and shrinking, moving in and out of plane. They were swimming in the same water an hour ago, legs dangling in that oily abyss, toes combing through god-knows-what in the waves.

"What the fuck," Jen says. "I can't even focus on it."

Melody squints, tries again, but gets vertigo, looks away. "Let's get out of here." She points upward, toward their apartment. Their unit is on the sixty-six-hundred block of Del Playa, about thirty feet above where they've been lying out, the rear balcony cantilevering over the sand. Columns are visible in the eroded cliffside, sticking out like ribs. Every few years, a balcony falls off into the ocean or onto the beach, depending on the tide.

She collects her stuff, working quickly, grabbing at everything and nothing, sand slipping through fingers. She stands. Her body feels heavy. She turns toward the black water. The world is off-balance, growing and shrinking.

"God, I feel *weird*," Jen says. "Kinda dizzy."

"Me too," Melody says. *And I didn't even drink.* She looks left and right and up and down as if on alert for a predator. She sees only college students drinking from red Solo cups, throwing a frisbee, so carefree it's like they're living in another timeline. The frisbee comes her way. She ducks. Then looks up.

The guy throwing it...

Shit. It looks like Nathaniel, emerging from the black waves.

"You ready?" Jen says.

Oh, god. Melody remembers her spots. She closes her eyes, squeezes her body rigid, holding herself together, focusing on her breathing. He can't see her like this.

"You okay?" Jen says.

"That's that guy, Nathaniel," she whispers. "The one.... Let's just go. I'm all spotty." She pivots toward the beach access, a long, wooden staircase leading up to the street.

"I don't see him." Jen hands her beer to Melody. "You're dehydrated, girl."

Melody is thirsty. Very thirsty. Another wave of dizziness hits. She stumbles. Her throat is dry. So dry. She coughs, takes the beer. She shouldn't drink, but coughs again, itches at the spots, and finally takes a long, long swallow.

The world steadies.

* * *

Cool ocean air rushes through the apartment. Doors and windows are splayed wide; the brine-scented breeze pulls Melody toward the rear balcony.

81

"I'll grab the baby oil," Jen says.

Melody walks onto the balcony, her footsteps unsteady, and flops onto a tattered old loveseat facing the ocean. A wetsuit hangs over the railing like a shed skin. Beyond, the slick spreads in a million directions, into infinity. The black is disarming, the absence of sheen unnatural. The waves crash *hard*, licking sand, coming in faster, higher, the darkness reaching.

Flash card words pulse in her mind—*dorsal fin, denticles, drowning*. She shakes her head.

Jen settles in next to her, placing a bottle of baby oil and cotton rounds on the coffee table beside a seashell-shaped ashtray she made in art class. The grooves in the seashell are uneven; the ashtray rattles in the breeze, threatening to slip through the railing and fall to the beach.

Melody steadies the ashtray with one hand, plucking a cotton round with the other. She soaks the cotton in baby oil, rubs it into one of the big, black spots on her arm. She holds the pad in place, hoping it will dissolve the splotch, but when she gently moves it side to side, the tar doesn't move. "It's not coming off."

Jen does the same, pushes hard, makes her skin red. "For me either."

They try for a while with the baby oil, then move on to canola oil. Then butter. Dish soap. Goo Gone. A dab of 409. A swipe of acetone.

Nothing. The tar won't budge.

Melody frowns. "I have to bike to campus soon, but I can't go like *this*."

"Maybe we should try to—" Jen grips the sides of her temples, bending forward, letting out a moan.

"You okay?" Melody says.

Jen groans louder, her back hunching, rolling. Tears pool oceans in her eyes. "Something's exploding in my head. Spots of bright light and…"

Melody puts an arm around her, swallows hard. "Did you drink any water when we got home?" She glances away from Jen, toward the waves, the crashing, the unfathomable blackness.

Jen manages to speak, hands on her temples. "I chugged a giant Gatorade. I need to take some migraine meds, chill out, I don't know." She gets up, turns her back to the ocean, and stumbles off, covered in splotches.

"You need help?" Melody calls after her.

Jen waves her off, staggers away, pressing the sides of her head as if carrying a stolen watermelon to a bathroom picnic.

"What about the tar?" Melody shouts.

"Gonna lay in the tub, soak it off." Jen disappears down the hallway.

Melody looks at her own spots of tar. They flood with detail, swirling in depths that go on forever and ever, pressing through her limbs, continuing. It's the strangest thing, like peering into an endless chasm. She loses herself, looking.

* * *

The shared bedroom is a whirlpool of clothes, books, shoes. Melody stumbles through, hunting for something to wear.

For what? She pauses. What is she doing? She can't remember. Then she reminds herself: *The test. The midterm. It's today. Now.* She needs to do well so she can get her degree. Do something important with her life. *Save the world.* The stakes are high.

She opens the privacy curtain that encircles her bed and searches for a clean top in the swirl of sheets, something that will cover the tar. She throws on a long-sleeved shirt, jeans, and boots up to the knee.

The spots are hidden now. Finally. She runs her hands along her arms, feeling the splotches of tar through her knit sleeves, and stands there, gently pressing. The spots are strangely soft. Her body is loose, too, like she just got out of a hot yoga class.

She needs to get going, to *leave*.

"I have to go to campus," she says, and spots her flash cards on the floor. She grabs them, throws them in her backpack—*wildlife corridor, coral reef, geothermal energy*. She walks into the hallway, passes the closed bathroom door. There's a faint splash on the other side. "You okay, Jen?" She presses her ear to the door.

"Fine." Her roommate sounds far away, as if pulled off by a riptide.

"You sound bad," Melody says.

"You worry too much," Jen says.

You're too rigid. This is what she means.

Melody sighs, tries to crack her neck, but nothing happens; her neck feels gummy, uncrackable, *cartilaginous*. That sensation again—loosening in her body—and she pauses there. Not moving. Only sensing. *Feeling.* She hears the ocean waves even though she's inside. Then a splash of flash card words—

dorsal fin

denticles

She breathes in sharply. "I've got to go. I'll see you tonight!" But her throat itches. Her thoughts scatter like fish food. Something about the sound of the bathwater. The feeling of having it over and around and *through* her, breathing it in…

She's thirsty.

Racing into the kitchen, she grabs a cup, fills it from the tap, chugs. Still thirsty, she chugs another. Another. The water tastes strange. She finds some old coffee sitting in the pot. She chugs that too. The coffee has an aftertaste. Salty, maybe.

What is wrong? I need to get out of—

I need to leave.

She should stay and return to the beach, lay out until the tide licks her feet. *No.* She has to go to campus. It's time for her midterm: the path to her dreams. Her parents told her a thousand times during all those late-night sessions as a kid, sitting beside her in the study nook while all her friends were already in bed wasting time resting—

You can be anything you want to be, Melody. She grabs her backpack, heads toward the door. The tar spots buzz and roll. The TV turns on, a reality show playing, a bachelor or bachelorette dating so many people. The screen pulses, waves of light swimming.

Stay and waste time…

the bathtub,

the water, the waves.

She races out the door, struggling to get herself down the stairs, gripping the rail to keep her clumsy limbs from falling. Finally at the bottom, she unlocks her bike, throws her weight onto her yellow beach cruiser. Riding toward campus is *hard,* every pedal, every movement a strain. Maybe she's getting the flu or something.

She pushes forward as if through a long study night. Her legs throb, joints ache. She manages onward, turns right on DP, left on Camino Pescadero, weaving through the bollards onto Pardall, past the Gio's patio where she drank Diet Coke while everyone else drank beer, and past the Gamma Phi house with the swimming pool and the Six Pak Shop with people stocking up for parties. Her body stiffens more; it *hurts.* She keeps biking.

Music pours from an open mic session at Java Jones; crowds of students sit at picnic tables, hanging out, lining the road. They're eating nachos at Freebirds and obliterating themselves at Dublin's and leaving backpacks on the ground while they drink from pitchers and plastic cups and laugh and laugh and laugh. Nothing is wrong. Someone shouts, "Who wants shots?" and the ocean waves are so loud, even here, even blocks from the water. Crashing. Slapping. Digging black nails through sand. Her spots pulse with fire all over her body. Her bones scream. She cracks her neck loudly without trying and flips through flash cards in her mind, again and again—

coastal erosion coral reef snowy plover peak oil
An Inconvenient Truth

passive thermal design

Now the tar spots itch. She keeps biking, tries to breathe. The itch is deep, coming from her bones, a wildfire spreading. She reaches the edge of campus and pulls over, pushing up sleeves, scratching. The spots on her forearm look different now. They've morphed into a patterned surface that feels rough, like her skin is made of a million ragged pieces. She thinks of skin-teeth. *Denticles. Drowning.* She starts shaking her head, scratching. She cracks her neck in every direction, little explosions firing as if bones are bursting. But there is no relief.

Some guy with dark hair stops his bike next to hers, asks if she's all right. He looks like Nathaniel. She pulls down her sleeves. Some shirtless dudes join him. One of them raises a beer, says, "Jack Johnson's playing at the Marley House right now!"

I'll be late for my midterm. She shakes her head furiously.

"You're missing out!" one of them shouts, and bikes away, leaves.

I know! she wants to scream. All of her joints crack and *itch*. She's scraping, clawing. She has maybe ten minutes to get to class. She gets off her bike. *You can be anything you want to be, Melody.* She inches onto campus one foot at a time. But she stops again, scratching her toothy arms raw, focusing on her neck, where it burns even more. All her bones are itching, begging to be scratched. An ocean of tears pours down her cheeks. *What the fuck is wrong?* She can't take the test like this. Maybe her TA will cut her some slack. She's never missed a class. *But what about her future? Has this all been for nothing? Is she ruining everything?*

She gets back on her bike, heading home, weaving until she turns right, rolling past the lagoon and Manzanita Village, toward the ocean. She takes a right on DP, biking west, faster and faster, tears streaming down her face. When she sees the beach access, she can finally breathe. Her neck moves side to side, a sail in the wind, the itch lessening. She leaves her bike unlocked at the bottom of her stairs—it'll be gone by sundown, she's sure—and walks up to her front door, throwing herself inside.

Shambling onto the balcony, she looks down at the surf, watching, listening. The ocean is soothing and loud, and she wants to eat the sound. Her joints start to ease up, relaxing, while the tide moves in, shimmying up the beach.

* * *

Melody throws her backpack on the bedroom floor, flash cards spilling out like sand. Words stare up, tossed at starfish angles, crooked and scattered. She can't make out any one phrase. She pulls out her laptop, heart racing. She'll tell her TA, *I'm sick. I'm sorry.*

But the feeling has returned, the looseness, especially in her neck. Her body is softening, a boat righting itself. She rubs her arms for a while… The toothy grit feels *good*. She collapses into bed, closes the privacy curtain, and drowns herself in blankets. She loses time.

Until she hears noises in the kitchen, realizes she's thirsty.

She slithers under the curtain, leaves her room, finds a crowd gathering. The keg is tapped, her roommates have started drinking. The music thumps, pulses in waves. Usher singing, "Yeah," over and over and over.

Melody drifts onto the balcony. One of her roommates, Heather, the birthday girl, leans against the railing, dressed as a sexy firefighter in a red pleather mini. She hands Melody a red Solo cup, overflowing. Another roommate, April, wades toward her as a sexy teacher with a black bra, necktie, and pencil bun. Another floats in as a sexy cop wearing a spangled badge on her negligee.

The dryness of Melody's throat catches up, constricts her voice. She chugs the beer and soaks in the relief. She pours another. The itch lessens the more she drinks.

The ocean breeze is rushing, whistling.

"Where is Jen?" someone says.

"In the bathroom," Melody says. "She had a migraine and…" *I had a midterm. I missed it. I need to send an email to my TA. I'm still thirsty.*

More people arriving. Night has fallen. The moon is full. Her roommates are letting everyone in, a crowd flooding the apartment, rushing onto the balcony. The career-day theme permeates; Melody sees a mathematician, a teacher, a guy in a white shirt that says *Consultant* scrawled in black marker.

She peers through the crowd, over the railing, down at the water, how it laps up across the sand, crashing against the bluffs, a faint spray reaching. The balcony creaks, old wood in conversation with the water. The rhythm of the waves, crashing. The rush from a few chugged beers, swirling. The spots, tingling, not so painful now.

A shift is occurring.

She whispers, "I have to email my TA."

Someone's turned the music up, the party raging, filling, no one listening. Bodies find each other in the darkness. She can't grab onto any one moment or song, only hears the crashing, the waves. The beer is hitting her. She imagines the black tar crawling up over the railing. Coming. She stumbles.

A man catches her hand.

Nathaniel, emerging from the balcony, wearing all black. He is dressed as a scuba diver in a wetsuit unzipped to the navel. "I saw you on the beach." He cocks his head, a curious octopus, and brushes brown hair from his brown eyes, holds out a hand. She likes the feel of his skin, cool and moist. She thinks of oyster pearls, sea urchin, lobster. *This is easy. You can be a normal person, Melody, do normal-person things.*

The rush again, the ocean, the waves.

She says, "I need to email my TA."

Nathaniel nods. "I'm glad it's Friday." He hands her another beer.

She drinks what he gives her, and starts feeling hungry, so hungry, hungrier than she's ever been. She looks down at his feet. He's wearing leather Reef sandals, toes exposed and tapping.

She moves around him like a circling hammerhead, hunting unseen. Eminem's "Shake That" comes on, and her arms are on his shoulders, bringing him closer, her stomach closing in. She grinds against him.

He asks where her costume is. She tells him she needs help and drags him down the hallway. Her bedroom swims in blackness. She finds a lamp, turns it on.

Nathaniel kisses her and she kisses him, stepping on her flash cards, floating them across the floor. His hand reaches under her shirt, touching her stomach, moving up. He lifts her shirt over her head and unbuttons her jeans. She remembers the spots. *All over.*

"I don't want you to see them," she says.

"See what?"

His hands are everywhere, feeling the spots, pressing them in circles, roaming as if with tentacle probes. It feels so, so good.

She scans her arms. The black spots have faded to flesh tone. Yet even in the dim light, they are everywhere, but now pulsing, thumping. No longer tar stains but fleshy, amorphous shapes bulging, pressing, flowing in and through her body.

Melody flings the privacy curtain open.

She's a wriggling fish slipping between fingers when she lies beneath him on the bed, moisture beading on the ceiling and dripping down onto her in the dark. She soaks in the salt water, tastes it on her tongue. A tide is rising, a tsunami building, freedom like swimming in open water, like the promise of endless eating…

what am I doing

The pulsing in her brain overriding, directing, and something rushes through her body from the spots. Morphing. *Changing.* All her energy floats into her teeth, an instinct, and she's biting into him, his neck soft and delicious while he flails as if tangled in seaweed. She clamps down, straining blood thorough broken flesh, lapping him whale-mouthed, her teeth the baleen.

* * *

Melody licks up the blood, senses it rolling through her body. Her joints loosening, her limbs stretching and elongating. She's doughy on a potting wheel, molding, reforming.

I need to email my TA

Relaxation, more and more. The taste of the blood still fresh. She feels it like floating. Music in the background, going. A slow song in the living room, the party singing loudly, drunkenly, "Jesus, take the wheel," and she is humming. Nathaniel does not know the lyrics, does not respond. He is curled beside her, a caught seal.

he needs help.

The waves are so loud. She is shrimp-served, tasting, *feeling*. The spots pulse all over her body. There is only sensation, food, music, and the quenching of deepest thirst.

"Melody?" A voice outside the privacy curtain, outside the door.

"Yes." Her voice is not her own. Breath enters her body along her cheeks and the sides of her torso instead of her throat. *What's happening?*

"I think Jen is really sick," someone says. *Who?*

Heather. Roommate. Birthday girl.

"She's making weird noises and won't come out of the bathroom. There's some kind of sticky ooze coming under the door. I'm worried she's vomiting or…"

Melody wades back through a watery doorway into the dry ship of reality. "I'm coming," she says, struggling with the words.

It feels as though she's swimming beside her own body, watching while she wipes her face with a floor towel, removes bloodstains, puts on a black minidress and heels, and finally her costume: a white lab coat. There is no prepackaged costume for an environmental scientist, so this is the closest she gets.

She sees Nathaniel's shriveling form.

I need to email my TA
call the paramedics
take the test
    don't drink don't
                    get distracted
            by stupid boys and stuff

I've been feeling really weird all day

"Hips Don't Lie" is playing. She whips the privacy curtain closed and straightens her lab coat. She shambles into the hallway while running her tongue along jagged teeth, catching herself on tilting walls. Everything is sensation, breathing through her skin, the whole place moving and lilting like a storm-rattled boat. The roommates have gathered, schooling outside the closed bathroom door, all of them drunk and leaning, unnoticing.

"She's moaning," April says.

"And gurgling," someone else says.

The music pulses, so loud, distorting, as if piped into a swimming pool.

"Maybe she needs some water," Heather says.

All Melody can think of is water, inside her, all around her. When she raises a hand to touch the closed door, it's cupped as if to propel her forward, to swim. Spots pulse all over her body, invisible to everyone but her. They throb with energy, spreading, growing larger; she can feel them changing her flesh, making it toothy and slick.

April has found the key; she's wriggling it in the lock, opening the door.

Melody peers into the bathroom. She doesn't see Jen. Not kneeling before the toilet or lying in the tub. *She's not here…* But now she hears Jen's voice, not in words, but a screech in her mind.

Someone turns on the lights.

The floor is a puddle of limbs and flesh. It takes a moment for Melody to understand what she is seeing. Jen has melted—turned gluey, dissolving, changing. Her arms and legs are fastened together, her body remolded into something oblong and loafy, flesh-toned and greening: cucumbered. The tar spots have erupted into spiny protrusions displacing appendages, pushing off toes, now pulsing with the strange offbeat rhythm of underwater antennae, reaching.

The roommates scream.

Jen's facial features remain visible, centered in the gooey log, melting into the mass. Her lips tremble when she opens and closes her mouth, gasping. She smiles slightly when she sees Melody, holding her gaze before her eyeballs drift and her mouth leaks. Threads of white shoot out from her spiny pieces, sliming the walls.

Melody watches with fascination, unmoving while her own tar spots pulse in unison. Her stomach rumbles. She wades into the puddle. Some of Jen's parts are detached and drifting. Her toes, displaced by pokey spines, float in the watery ooze. Everyone screams and screams while Melody watches, rumbles, *feels*. There is only instinct. Jen's screech makes the others cup hands over ears, but Melody bends down, slurping floating toes into her mouth.

"What are you doing?" April says.

Melody shakes her head, thoughts rapid firing—

green building peak oil

an inconvenient truth

coral

reef

shark

    fin

    shark fin shark fin

—until she swallows a few of the toes, swimming through screams into the hallway, toward the party, where the soundtrack changes. Amy Winehouse's "Back to Black" wails, bodies sweaty and warm and humping and swaying. She flops past them.

Someone sees her and shouts, "Doctor! I need help!" throwing back a beer.

Melody turns her head. *I'm a scientist, actually.* That feeling again: her body turning gummy, elongating. The flesh-toned spots spread, changing her skin. Her arms feel thicker and velvety like suede in one direction, toothy and rough in the other, the surface taking on a grayish pallor, little parts pulsing, moving…

She swims through the dancing bodies, mimicking forms and movements, toward the balcony, toward the waves. She is stretching, growing, and now something is sprouting on her back, penetrating upward. Jen's high-pitched squeal calls to her from the bathroom, from the ocean. It's hard to breathe.

The partygoers pack the balcony, playing beer pong beneath a blood moon. The tide is so high, crashing beneath, slapping the bluffs. So hard. They all hear it now, calling. Everyone rushes to the balcony and looks down into the abyss.

      do you see the waves?

        the blackness?

The sea churns, waves cresting and curling like fingers beckoning.

"I can't look at it," one guy says.

Beer pong continues; another guy taps another keg.

Jen's squeal echoes.

Melody gasps for breath, tries to find flash card words.

      the ocean the waves

        the ocean the waves.

"What is this?" A girl pulls back from the railing. Her palms are stained black.

"It's across the floor," someone else says. "It's *everywhere*."

"What the fuck!" Two guys pick up the stained upholstered love seat and chuck it into the ocean. More people rush to see. All of them, crowding the balcony.

Melody is on the floor now, thrashing, moving herself along like a caught fish pulling its own line forward, toward the railing, propelled by the side-to-side movement of her ankles and toes fusing, the large growth on her back bursting through, helping maintain her trajectory.

"What the fuck is that?" a woman screams.

change the
> *world*

sacrifice
> *it's up to*

>> *me*

Melody flips onto the rickety wood cantilever, adding her weight, which suddenly seems more substantial, as if she's grown muscle mass.

hungry

swimming

She bites the leg of a guy nearby. He shrieks.

Everyone crowds the balcony edge, peering out at the slick, the railing covered in black. Someone shouts, "It's breaking!"

Jen's seashell ashtray falls, slipping through rails into the ocean, splashing. The entire balcony is tilting, leaning downward at an impossible angle. The crowd plunges. A teacher, a mathematician, a zookeeper, all tossed and tumbling, hands in the air, screaming.

Melody slides toward the edge.

Her skin pulses and buzzes, undulating and melting into its final shape, relaxing into a new way to breathe. When the dorsal fin is large enough, she dives into the sea.

Fathoms of blackness and swimming and circling until she surfaces and scans the bluffs where black tar clings, reaching, spreading across balconies. Beside her in the water, people are bobbing, drifting, and screaming.

Costume parts and red Solo cups and ping-pong balls float past. Melody opens her mouth and gnashes teeth, severing a drifting frisbee.

Breathing deeply, snapping at a passing fish.

anything

I want

to

be

Diving under, gliding with lateral locomotion, forward propulsion. Circling bodies caught up in the slick, feet dangling in a wriggling buffet laid out deliciously. Swimming onward, mouth opening, clamping onto a flailing calf, the flavor sweet-sweet-sweet, no rush to swallow. Saw teeth. Piercing flesh. Chew. Bite. Nourish.

Hunger is infinite, a *reason*. Loose legs whirl the slick into a cocktail salty and stirred, a thirst-quenching drink in a wave-drunk dream.

END

MEMENTO MORI SYRENI

by Megan Jauregui Eccles

I'm halfway through a reread of *The Bell Jar* when the call comes in. I like to let it hit the fifth ring, but the new guy—some Ken wannabe named Darren—is annoyingly chipper and never lets it go beyond the second ring.

"County coroner's office, this is Darren speaking."

And he's smiling—like the person on the phone can see him—awaiting the news of the body. His blue eyes twinkle like he's campaigning for homecoming king.

He's not the first true crime wannabe with a well-worn high school letterman jacket who's seen one too many police procedurals and has rolled into the ME's office. Once they have a bad case—three-week-old body in a warm apartment, cartel dismemberment, high school kid wrapped around a tree—they always leave. This job is all guts, no glory.

But it's quiet.

I've always had an easier time around the dead than the living. Darren's sparkle will wear off after a while. And then he'll become a phlebotomist or dental assistant or vet tech. Back to warm bodies, where he belongs. And I'll still be here.

Living the dream.

"Mermaid!" Darren's practically vibrating. He writes down the address on a nice notepad he brought from home and grabs the keys. "We'll be there right away."

"Hold on, hotshot." I take the keys from his overeager hand. "You're still on probation. No way you're taking the rig."

The rig is an old white van stacked with a couple of gurneys and a pile of body bags. The vinyl floors are easy to spray out with a hose. She's been to hell and back—and as long as I don't stare at her too long, she stays running. Which is why I call her Eurydice. She's the only constant about this job besides death.

"Have you seen one?" Darren slides into the passenger seat and clicks his seat belt.

"We get a few a month. It's not news anymore."

"Oh." Darren looks like I just shot Bambi. "Shouldn't they be in some cool lab or something?"

"A body is a body," I say. "The first few rounds of washed-up mermaid corpses got ET treatment. The rest are just flesh-covered bones that need a place to go."

It's probably the thirtieth this year. The novelty and magic of mermaids actually existing has long since worn thin. But we haven't had a lot of bodies this week, and this is an excellent opportunity for training Darren. It's been a quiet month for us. Things always slow down in the fall. School starts, and people get busy before the grief of the holidays begins.

"I haven't seen one." Darren puts his hand on the dash. "I mean, I've seen pictures and stuff, but never seen one in real life." He's babbling. It's a thing he does, apparently. "As a kid, I was scared to go in the ocean because of them. Well, technically not mermaids, but Ursula, the Sea Witch. I'm not sure what exactly she counts as."

"Cool." I haven't been able to impart the value of silence to Darren, but I keep trying.

"We should think of a name for the rig, I think this old boy deserves it."

"*She* has a name."

Darren looks far too excited, and I immediately regret sharing even this tidbit with him. "What is it?"

"You haven't earned that information yet."

Instead of looking defeated, Darren takes it like a challenge. He squares his already square chest and looks out the windshield like he'll find the answers on the hazy horizon.

He won't.

There's really nothing he can do to make this job home. He just doesn't have the temperament for it. I've seen enough people come and go to know that. There's a fearlessness required for this job brought on by being beaten back. People don't spend time with the dead and the dark because they've had a happy childhood and easy life. They seek out the solace and the finality of jobs like this because they know what it's like to be dead to the world.

I'm happy to be out at the beach without the rush of tourists, even if it's to pick up a body. Darren chatters on about helping people and this job and some dream he carries in his pocket like a dime-store novel. I tune him out, let myself enjoy a brief moment of pleasure at the whisper of the ocean. The nostalgia of the sea has always been a comfort to me, long before I made death my job. I box up those feelings, tag them, and slide them into cold storage. I'll bury them later, when I don't have a real body on my hands.

There's a pair of squad cars parked near the pier. Biggs and Wedge—a couple of assholes—step out with Starbucks cups and breakfast sandwiches. Wedge gestures toward the pier. "She's down there. Need us to stay?"

"Sure!" Darren says.

"No," I say at the same time.

They exchange a glance and start to take Darren's cue. I hold up my badge for seniority and shake my head. Biggs shrugs and gets back into the car.

"Isn't the cot going to be hard to push on the sand?"

"We'll just use pro slider board and carry." I point to the back of Eurydice.

"Oh. Okay." He takes the board, a bag, and straps.

I slip off my boots and toss them onto the front seat. It's against protocol, but it's not like there's a crime scene to be tampered with. It's just another mermaid that we'll process, cremate, and put on a shelf. Darren sees what I'm doing but doesn't say anything, for once. I head toward the pier, trusting that he'll follow. He jogs to catch up to me, eager to see the mermaid.

"Oh, wow." Darren puts his hand to his mouth like he's going to get sick.

They're not pretty like in the fairy tales. More like nightmare fodder: spiny ridges down their backs; filmy, white eyes; and tiny, pointed breasts. They're all slick, gray, and hairless with fish mouths that open too wide with rows of shark teeth. Maybe people would have felt differently about the whole thing if they had been beautiful, like so much of the sea. But they are angular and ugly, like the things down at the deepest part of the ocean. Things the light won't even touch.

This one has shallow cuts up its arms, with inky blood that smells like copper and salt staining the sand. It's the first one that I've seen that's hurt, and there's a brief flash of feeling that I tamp down. It's just a body, and not even a human one.

The first round of mermaid bodies was national news, with labs and zoos fighting over the remains. But three years and hundreds of mermaids later, no one really gives a shit anymore. California passed some law about accepting the burden of processing the bodies, so it falls to the taxpayers to put them in the ground. There were all sorts of protests about that, religious groups and animal rights fighting over the definition of a soul. But then the next news cycle hit, and people got busy and bored, and it all fell away.

It always does.

Darren lays down the board and straps and bag, prepped for transfer. I snap on my gloves. Darren's face goes blank when he realizes he's forgotten to grab some. I sigh and toss him the extra pair I always carry—just in case. They're small on his big hands but better than nothing.

"On three." I reach for the shoulders. Darren tries to find the best position at the tail and settles on halfway. "One, two—"

The mermaid thrashes, making a mewling sound somewhere between a whale's cry and a banshee's shriek. Her dark, salty blood sluices down my gloves and she flicks her wide, flat tail, more eel than dolphin.

"Oh crap!" Darren falls back into the rising tide. "She's alive!"

"No shit."

Her mouth opens and closes, gasping like a fish. She looks at me with strange, milky eyes. They have some sort of mercurial shift to them, lovely enough that it catches me off guard.

"What do we do?"

I don't know what to do. Give me a body, and I know the process, the care, the boxes to tick. I know where to slice and what to weigh and exactly how to put a person back together. But with the living? I'm back in high school, uncomfortable in my own skin and unsure of my place in the world. And it's a terrible feeling. I try so hard not to care; I try not to give a fuck about anything. But the apathy is hard-won, nurtured and curated. I am a broken, shell of a thing. I am wounded, imaginary. Less real than this fantastical creature writhing in the sand.

And that's what I see in the mermaid's eyes—my whole life. For the first time in forever, I don't think. I pull off my glove and touch her cheek and wait for the answer. At first, my mind fills with the sea. Not the shore and shallows, but the deepest parts, filled with monstrous and beautiful things that fear the clarity of the light the way we fear the opacity of the dark. But then it changes back to my life, what I have done. And then it's just a litany of bodies, one after the other, flashing in my mind. Bodies I've had a hand in laying to rest.

I know what she needs.

"We have to help her. Go get the kit underneath my seat."

"What—"

"Just do it."

Darren runs like a fucking track star. Maybe he was one, once. He's back faster than I can process her wounds. There are just over a dozen, marked almost ritualistically up and down her arms. She's not hurt anywhere else. I open the black bag. There's makeup in there in various skin tones and shades, corpse wax, a comb, cotton balls, some needles and thread. Everything I need to help a body look like a person.

It dawns on Darren what this kit is. He looks at me like he used to know the answers to who I was and now he doesn't. "I thought we weren't supposed to tamper with the bodies."

"She's not a body. She's alive."

He hesitates. "Shouldn't we call someone?"

"Probably," I say. "But then what kind of life will she have?"

There have been enough movies and books and shows for even someone like Darren to know what it's like to be othered.

"They'll study her." Darren drops down beside her. He holds her skin together with unexpected tenderness. "She'll spend the rest of her life in a lab. That's no life at all."

She thrashes when the needle first pierces the skin. Darren whispers something to her, his voice as low and soothing as the sea. His voice is too soft to hear at first, but then I catch the rhythm and the words.

"'What the Water Gave Me.'" I look up, briefly at him. "I didn't take you for a Florence fan."

"This song got me through some hard times." Darren keeps his eyes trained on the wounds. "Thought it might help her, too."

It does seem to help, like a reverse siren song. She winces a few times when the needle pierces her skin; then she settles. Her tail shifts, making patterns in the sand. Darren's hands are steady. He looks up at me like he's seeing me for the first time.

"You've done this before." His voice is thick with awe.

I keep my eyes trained on her wounds, making careful stitches. I'm not sure how the nylon will hold up in the sea, but I have this feeling like everything is going to work out. I never feel this way, and so I lean into it.

"I don't work on the living."

He shakes his head. "That's not what I mean, and I think you know it."

"Sometimes when we find a body, we forget that they used to be people." I move to the next cut. "Sometimes it's more important the family sees the person they love instead of the tragedy. Sometimes it's more important that the person has a little dignity in death."

The mermaid's breathing is jagged. I see the problem immediately.

"Flip her around so her gills are in the water."

"Gills?"

I point to the lines under her ribs. I hadn't noticed them on the mermaid bodies before. I continue to stitch.

"The Huxton case, was that you? Because I heard it was a gruesome scene, but when I got there, you were already there, and it wasn't bad at all."

"Yes," I say, even though I don't mean to. The memories of Susanna Huxton come to me, unbidden. I can't unsee it, can't rewrite the story so she has a happy ending.

"Aren't there rules about this sort of thing, protocols?"

"The case had already been ruled a suicide. There was no evidence to gather, no one waiting for answers. I couldn't leave her like that." There's a cut that's too deep. I'm not sure how to stitch this. "There were pictures of her grandkids on the walls. She looked like she was kind. I didn't want her to be remembered by one final, terrible moment."

"And that John Doe?"

Darren sees my hesitation and takes the needle from my hand. To my surprise, I let him. He does something I would have never thought of—he does a double layer of stitches to close the wound inside and out. His stitches are quick and even. He moves down the line of her arm with the precision of a surgeon.

"He had a knee replacement and we found him: his name was Nolan Edwards. There wasn't much I could do."

"His hair was combed."

That strikes me. I didn't think anyone would pay any attention to that. No one but me.

"You're the medical examiner. You can separate the evidence from your own work?"

"Yeah," I say, a little bashful now that I've been caught.

"That's…really kind of you."

"Don't let it get around."

"Do you remember every name?"

I reach down and grasp the mermaid's hand, watching Darren work. "When we have names for things, for people, it helps it all be real."

"I was going to be a surgeon, you know. Went to one of the best medical schools and everything." I can see that he would have been good by his even stitches and careful hand. "But during my residency, I lost someone. It was my fault. It was a big important solo surgery, and I had gone out to celebrate the night before. I was tired going into it. I knew I shouldn't, but I got cocky, and someone died. I don't want to ever hurt someone like that again."

I suck in a breath. "George Descanso?"

Darren's mouth drops open. "How did you—"

"It was a conflict of interest for the hospital. They sent him to me—us." He'd been closed up so neatly, perfect stitches. Darren's work, I'm sure now. That was two years ago. I wonder what Darren did in the meantime.

The mermaid shrieks, as if to remind us that she is very much alive.

"Sorry," he whispers to her.

The weight of his confession settles on me. I don't know what he did in those lost years, but I understand why he's here. "You can't hurt the dead."

The corner of Darren's mouth twitches, and he continues onto the mermaid's other arm. I was wrong about him. He's exactly the kind of person who will make it in this industry. He's not afraid, because he's already lost it all. The ocean's foam laps against my bare feet. I wonder, briefly, about all the stories. I wish I could ask the mermaid. I wish I knew her so that she could be remembered.

The mermaid takes long, slow blinks.

"I don't know why I'm telling you this." Darren blinks a few too many times, his voice tight.

"It's the mermaid," I say, not knowing, at first, if it's true and then being absolutely certain. "There's something about her. It's like being drunk or high or up really late at night. All our walls are down."

"You're really pretty, but you scare me," Darren says, and I keep myself focused on waves lapping at the mermaid, because I'm blushing and I'm not sure which part of what he said is more flattering. "Which is exactly what I just thought I wanted to keep a secret, and there it is. Coming out of my mouth. Do you think this is what the Greeks meant when they wrote about sirens?"

"You don't seem like the type of person who know about the Greeks," I say, and I would've regretted it if I could remember how to regret, if all of that hadn't already slipped away.

Darren laughs, which is nice. It's a nice laugh, not the laugh of a homecoming king or jock asshole. He laughs with practice, like he's good at it. Like he's laughed before. "I know a lot about a lot of things. I didn't have a lot of friends growing up."

"Looking like you do?"

"Is that a compliment?"

"Yes and no," I say. "I expect beautiful faces to hide ugly things."

"Me, too." Darren is almost done stitching. "I'm sorry that has been your experience. I'm sorry it was mine. God, it's weird being like this. I feel like I could tell you anything and also that I should."

"She gets us vulnerable and then she strikes, I guess. It must be a predator-prey thing."

"She's not striking. But you are. Dammit, I wish I could stop complimenting you." Darren shakes his head. "What if it's more than that? What if in the deepest, darkest parts of the ocean, the mermaids need to feel each other? There's no need for light because they are the light."

"Fuck, Darren, that's… I love it. I really wanted to hate you. I really wanted you to hate me. It makes all of this easier."

"All of what?"

"Being alone and liking it."

"Do you like it?"

"No," I say. "I used to come out here, take off my combat boots, and let my troubles sink into the sea like the sun. I'd wait out the stars and imagine a different life for myself, sometimes scratching out poetry by the light of the moon. Alone has always been easier then, now. But at least back then, I had some semblance that I would matter, instead of just hanging my hat on the idea of a pension. That's growing up, I guess. You cash in checks of idealism in exchange for the overtaxed money of reality. But in all of that, in the grief and the bodies and the endless list of names that people forget, I just wanted to be remembered. I want to matter."

"You matter to me"—Darren starts on the last of her cuts—"Ellie."

And I'm not sure if it's the mermaid or the sound of my name on his lips or sweet, salt air, but I feel like I'm outside of my body, looking at the three of us: boy, girl, mermaid, and all the possibilities set out for us. The way we've compressed a lifetime of trust into thirteen strange and magical minutes and how I feel like I'm not the person I was before and I'll never be that person again. Because I want this, I want this connection. I want to exist in a world where Darren—or someone like Darren—likes me, knows me, and cares about whether I prefer raw or white sugar and where I forget my glasses and hears the sound of my breath at night.

I look up into those blue eyes. "You're the first person who's seen me in a long time."

"Like, you're a ghost?"

I laugh harder at that than I'm proud of. "Like, I'm not anyone to anybody. Like, I'm a shadow. I've been in the dark for a long time."

"Like her." Darren ties off the last stitch and inspects his handiwork. Some of the color has returned to the mermaid's skin. "This might be the mermaid talking, but I think I might be in love with you."

"It is the mermaid talking, and I think I love you, too."

"We can't tell anyone about her, about this. I think if people knew, they'd do bad things to have her power." Darren looks between me and the mermaid. Her body flutters in the water.

"This secret dies with us," I say. "And I want you to take me to dinner."

"Oh. I mean, yes. I would love to do that. I'd love to take you anywhere." His face turns red. "This is too much, isn't it?"

"Probably," I say. "But does it matter?"

The mermaid gives us one last, long glance, and for a moment I'm sure she'll slither back into the sea, to whatever dark places mermaids go. But instead she spasms, her fish mouth gasping open and closed three times before she goes limp.

Another body. Another life lost.

A knot forms in my throat. Maybe I would have cried fifteen seconds before, poured open like I was. But the walls around my heart snap up, and I just stand there, heart pounding in my ears, waves lapping at my feet.

We stitched up her wounds. We got her back into the water. We did everything that seemed right. But still, we couldn't save her.

Darren lets out of a cry of anguish. He pulls her strange body toward his and cradles her. Her head lolls back, her spiny hand falls into the foam. I clear my throat and turn away, allowing him a moment. Allowing myself one. I wipe away the salt that burns my eyes and open the body bag. He places her inside with such tenderness, like an awakening of all my fears.

There are tears on Darren's face. "She needs a name."

He looks to me for something I cannot give. Who she is, who she was, I can't say. I can barely wrap my mind around the tense change. It's the worst part of living, dying. Moving from present to past. From *is* to *was*. This is beyond me.

Or it was, before.

I clear my throat. "Florence."

Darren nods and says thickly, "Florence."

We take her body up the beach and to the rig. Once she's secure, we sit inside, silent. The waves crash on the shore. Seagulls fight over someone's lost ice-cream cone. Fishermen cast their lines over the side of the pier, hoping and wishing and wanting something deep below, something they may never see.

I twist the keys. The engine turns over, once, twice, then starts. The mermaid smells of brine and copper and something intangible. Another dead body for us to process and bury. Another form to be filled out. Another hole to fill.

"Her name is Eurydice."

"What?"

"The rig." I put my hand on the dash. "She's been to the underworld and came to life because I didn't look back."

"Are you telling me this because of the mermaid magic?"

I look at Darren. The love is gone from his eyes. The madness of the mermaid's power has left us both. But I remember, and that's enough, for now. It's a start.

"I'm telling you this because you earned it."

DRIFT

by Jeff Kronenfeld

Like a shark, if I stop, I drown. Gliding down the face of a wave. Gliding over asphalt. All I have left is moving…and the dog.

I've run out of west, which is why I turn south. From one campsite to the next, I limp down the coast toward my contact in Mexico. With almost a thousand miles to go, I keep a low profile, or try to.

Early morning. Everything swathed in darkness and fog. I've been driving all night. The dog whines from the back seat. He needs to crap. I pull off at the next exit. Some small coast town, the idyllic kind that gets you thinking what your life would be like if…

I pull into a happily deserted beach parking lot. I let the dog do his business and throw on a pot of water. My home is a V-dub Westy I bought off a gray belly for too much cash. Orange. Little stove built right in. For another arm and a leg, he made the fake ID match the name on the title. Now I look like countless other beach bums living the van life, invisible through my conspicuousness.

The dog comes back as the water whistles. I pour it in the French press and step back into the driver's seat. The coffee steeps. I roll two joints.

A deep drag. A thick bank of fog rolls over the waves as heavy, narcotic smoke spills out the window. Out goes all pain. A warm blanket falls over my consciousness. The sweet-sour stank of bud. The earth-rich scent of steeping coffee. Through the cracked window, the cold clean of morning sea. My soul becomes as placid as the ocean on a windless day.

The sun peeks over the mountains. I pour muddy fluid into a dinged aluminum cup. Swell from the northwest. The winds are offshore and mellow. I cough and toss out the tarry roach. I whip out my tide chart. It's rising. I squint through thinning fog. The waves look about a head-and-a-half-high. It's some Goldilocks shit. Everything just right.

I should keep driving, but instead I slip into my wetsuit and grab the board. The only thing that trumps the restless power of the road is the force of a wave. Pure energy. I whistle and the dog comes bounding out. We start down the beach.

We follow jagged boulders and rocks toward a point at the headland's end. I swear I smell more of that perfect pungent odor, like a forest of cannabis lies just out of sight, but it's probably just my own weed-soaked reek. The ocean drums the shore to our right, churning and mashing and pulling in and out. Seals play in the surf. Gulls bob easily in wakening thermals, gliding over the dark metallic tint of the surface, staring curiously at their reflections. We trek through the mist.

Roar. Liquid thunder. That jet engine sound. I hear before seeing. I stand dumb and awed by the rippling curl, the wild, tossing mane of Poseidon's steeds. My hands shake from cold or fear or both.

I tell the dog to hang out. He will wait patiently till I return, no matter how long. No one loves me like that dog. No one ever.

I walk in water until the pull is too strong. I get on my belly. Long, steady strokes. Foam and spray lash my bearded face. I grit my teeth. This is what Northmen felt straddling the prows of long ships. Walls of white water. They're bigger than I thought, two-head-high-plus, maybe three. Maybe twenty footers.

Too far out, it rolls right past. Too far inside, it's bath time. Position is key.

The first wave lifts me high. Not quite right. I drop down the backside. My gut twists and balls ache. Next one isn't right either. I get over it, and the third one is on top of me. A big boy, the one in the set that rises above the rest. I wheel my board around. Paddle, paddle, paddle. Don't look back.

Fuck. I'm inside.

A liquid mountain pile drives me, ripping the board from my hands as easily as my old man tore away toys when he was lit.

In the washing machine. Spinning. Trying to fight. Ice-cream headache. The sea steals my warmth. I'm under it. The churning center of force passes over, pinning me. The Earth's pulse. If land is bone, sea is blood. The roar is oddly quiet, faint like a storm's distant echo.

I once heard drowning feels like falling asleep. If I die down here, would it really be so bad?

But what about the dog?

I push off the rocks, thrusting upward and breaching the surface. A deep mammal breath.

Life.

I turn. Impossibly, a breaker even bigger than the last barrels right for me. There is no time. Everything goes black.

After what feels like eons, I crawl out of the sea, onto land, like that ancestor four hundred million years past. I'm cold and miserable and smiling. The dog is waiting. He gets up, stretching, then shakes his way over, licking beads of salt water from my face with his warm, rough tongue. Good boy.

We got company. I pop up, a stupid grin on my face. First time in I don't know how long, I'm happy to see other people. Two of them, tall and tan with boards tucked under their arms. Long, windswept hair and clean-shaved chins. They're cut and pasted out of a faded photo from the sixties. They're everything I'm not.

"She's throwing today," I say.

They give me this hard look before bursting out in laughter. I laugh too. When all that dies down, the one with the pearliest whites you've ever seen asks, "Where you from?"

I toss him the name of a city too far north for him to know too well. They trade skeptical looks.

"This spot is dangerous. Shallow reefs and a major undertow. There's a sheltered cove, thirty miles south. You might find it more congenial there."

They laugh again. I reach for the pouch hanging from the dog's collar and whip out the other joint and a lighter. I flash it.

"Break bread?"

They grin and pull out blunts.

"We'll potlatch if you make like a tree."

We sit facing the Point. I trade an alias for nicknames. Puff, puff, pass. Their shit is good, real good. It hits heavy and tastes like a pristine sea breeze. They start talking place.

"Before we whites came, the natives believed dead souls went to an island over the horizon. This being the furthest point west for hundreds of miles, it seemed the logical launching point for the journey. The Point is an old burial ground, a sacred place. We're its keepers." It's the one with the bleached-looking teeth speaking, Jaws he said they call him.

"Haunted," the taller one called Pipeline says, oohing for emphasis. He laughs, but not Jaws and me.

"What are you, some kind of guru?" I ask real glib.

Pipeline stops laughing. It's quiet save for the pounding swell.

"Just sharing the lore, stranger," Jaws answers while puffing out a cloud of smoke.

We finish the session without further incident. We sit awhile. They get up and start heading out. I get up, too, telling the dog to stay.

"Where you think you're going?" Pipeline asks.

"Back out."

"The swell is building. You may want to sit this one out," Jaws says, still friendly, though not quite.

"Yeah, it's heavy, but I'll manage."

"Like your last set?" Pipeline says, snickering.

The aggression trends more active than passive. This old feeling lights up. Rage I thought I'd left behind. My free hand balls into a fist.

"Look," Jaws says, taking a step closer, away from his snickering pal, "it isn't personal. The Point is some serious shit. The last thing we need is a dead body bringing undue attention to our secret spot. I'm sure you can understand. If you cruise on down to the cove, we'll be along in a couple hours with nice ladies and more smoke."

I know I should listen. My mission isn't waves but distance. Low profile. Months on the road. Everything I own in the van. Everything else a fading memory. As much as I've shed, I'm still me. Still stupid.

"Appreciate the offer, but if it's all the same, I'd like to catch one before I roll on."

Jaws shakes his head and worries a rock with his foot. Pipeline, who was hanging back, takes a step closer. Jaws turns to face his boy. I glance over my shoulder. The hairs on the dog's back bristle as he growls under his breath.

Lights. Pain. I'm horizontal, my board sprawled on rocks. The side of my face throbs. He fucking roundhoused me. It's one of the hardest hits I've ever felt. I blink and try to stand.

"Stay down," he whispers.

"Fuck you," I shoot back.

Fists and feet fly at me. Pipeline shouts, "Fucking kook!" and "Beach-bum poser!" and that sort of thing. The blood tastes like salt water in my mouth. Pipeline leans in real close, grabs my wetsuit, and is about to deliver a heavy right when, through a blurry left eye, I see the dog latch on to his face. They go down, the dog on top.

Jaws rushes over, booting the dog hard in the side. I manage to half stand and throw myself into it. I grab the dog's collar with both hands, pulling him back as he barks and foams and snaps his jaws at the air.

Pipeline is sprawled on the rocks, moaning. Jaws stoops down and pulls his friend's hands away. A good chunk of the cheek is torn off, leaving this gashed half smile of teeth and gums and blood.

Jaws keeps one eye on me as he tends to his fallen buddy, telling him to stay calm and all that. Then, Jaws stands and whips a gun out his board bag. Me and the dog run, full-bore sprinting into the woods. I don't even try to recover my board. I hear shouts from behind, things like "This ain't done," and "You're fucking dead." This isn't my idea of laying low.

As I crash through the thick undergrowth of ferns and shrubs, I stumble on a clearing in the stand of towering Sitka spruces. It's a sprawling field of the greenest-green cannabis plants I've ever seen, and I've seen a lot. They are at least ten feet tall and covered in heavy, trichome-laden branches.

I hear Jaws gnashing his way through the forest, so the dog and I plunge into the sea of green. Resin clings to my wetsuit and fingers and burns my eyes, but I keep pushing.

I stumble on a camp in the center. There's a tent, gardening tools, a pair of dirt bikes, a gas can, and a fire pit where coals smolder. I grab the can and douse the dirt bikes, tent, and some cannabis plants before shoveling on coals. The fire explodes in an acrid miasma of burning plastic and pineapple and skunk. I smile as flames snap in my eyes.

The dog and I dart into the field, sprinting as fire nips at our heels. I hear Jaws screaming and frantically fighting the inferno, desperate to save his crop.

We run and run until emerging into the parking lot, my van still the only vehicle in sight. In classic Volkswagen style, it takes a few cranks for the old girl to roll over. I'm sweating and flashing cold, muttering curses under my breath. This is why V-dubs don't make good getaway cars. Finally, she purrs to life. I flip her in reverse and get as close to peeling out as the four underpowered cylinders allow.

I pull onto the highway and head south. It's more or less physically impossible to speed in the van, especially uphill, and from the coast, everything is uphill. I'm maybe ten miles down the highway when I hear the siren. Fuck, I think. The flashing lights come barreling into my rearview. A high-speed chase is out of the question.

I grind the van to a halt on the gravel embankment. As I pull out the fake ID, I pray it's straight. I see the cop jump out of his car. My face throbs, and I feel like I'm going to puke. This is as shitty a spot as I've ever been in, which is saying something. The dog growls lowly in the back. I roll down the window and find myself face-to-face with a revolver.

"Get the fuck out."

The guy is off script. I comply, instinctively raising my hands.

"That way."

He motions with the gun to the other side of the van. I lead the way.

"Stop there and turn around real slow," he says. Behind is a thin patch of forest and a long drop to the sea.

"That's my cousin your dog nearly killed."

After everything I've been through, all the near misses and close calls, this is it. Done in by a Podunk deputy because the dog needed to shit. I wonder how long it'll take them to sort out who I really am.

"You blacktop gypsy punk," he yells, the gun shaking. I'd give anything to get out of this one. This time it'll be different, I promise. I'll really keep my head down and help old ladies and pick up hitchhikers and all that. I can't tell if it's rain or tears in my eyes.

From inside the van, the dog leaps for him. The cop whirls around, squeezing out bullet after bullet. I hit dirt. My ears ring with the sound of gunshots and shattering glass. I look up and see the deputy's panting back. The passenger window is busted out. He turns slowly, lowering the gun until it's level with my eyes. I stare down the long, black hole, and it's as good as a tunnel of light.

Click.

Another siren screams over the highway. I look into the deputy's eyes. They're wet too. Puffy and red. In what seems like slow motion, a jittery hand pops the cylinder open and slides in a single shell. Wheels on gravel. He snaps shut the cylinder. Another cop, older and huskier, rushes up.

"What the hell's going on?" He looks at his deputy, then me, then peers in the car. He shakes his head.

"Mike, put that thing away."

He cocks back the hammer.

"Don't throw it away over that goddamn cousin of yours and his acidhead partner."

The deputy doesn't seem to hear. I feel cold steel press against my forehead. I close my eyes, breathe through my teeth. I flinch when I feel the gun jump.

I open my eyes and find I'm not dead, my soul not a west wind racing over the sea. The sheriff's holding the revolver. The deputy is staring away from me, breathing like he's just been dunked in cold water.

"Get in your car. I'll handle this now and you later."

The deputy walks to his car without looking back. I'm still on hands and knees in the gravel and mud.

"Get up," the sheriff says.

I do.

"So, this is what's going to happen. You get in your car and drive south. Don't so much as look back, and don't even think of calling anyone. You got that?"

I nod and stagger to my feet, somehow manage to walk around the car. The driver-side window is punctured by little holes radiating spider webs. Covered in a thin glaze of blood. I get in. Everything else is covered too. The car starts easily. I drive until I think I'm safe. Eyes dead ahead.

I pull over and cut the engine.

I keep picturing the dog. I see his life all at once, flashing before my eyes like flipping through channels. He is a puppy, barreling around a corner and assaulting my shoelaces. He is a little older. Our first hike through the hills east of town, lopping and dragging, too tired to go on, so I scoop him up in my arms and carry him. I see all the times I neglected him, leaving him too long in the house because I was partying, the times I scolded him for shitting inside even though it was my fault for not letting him out, punishing his innocence for my guilt. Those sweet, terrible moments that make up life and our memory of it.

I stoop my head and fold my arms around him. There's blood everywhere. I press my face against his shoulders and neck. I pray not for him to be brought back, not that kind of prayer, but rather that his death was quick, peaceful, like drifting to sleep.

He isn't dead. I hear a faint wheezing, a labored breath.

I try to envelope him. To absorb his pain with my body. I shut my eyes and bite hard into my lip. I know what I have to do. I open one of the cabinets and pull it from behind the false back. I check that it's loaded. I look into his eyes, his kind, quiet eyes, and see fear and pain in the place of love. I press it against his temple.

THE WALK STREET

by Hoda Mallone

"**B**ut did he die though?"

"That is so not the point."

I sighed at the dismissal of my heeded caution, terrified of another close call. I slid my arms into my black zip hoodie as Luna swiped through her phone. Luna always used the most dire outcome as her baseline. She had a much bigger appetite for risk than I did. And I worried that would end this forever. We were doing this every other week, it seemed now. It started to become too easy, too lucrative, too accessible—a compulsion, a habit.

"You always get like this, you know? Right before a night."

"Get like what? I don't get, like, anything."

"Okay, Chloe."

"We've been at this a while. I don't want to get complacent. Or messy. That's all."

Luna looked up from her phone and studied me a moment. "We should slow down. Maybe take a break. After tonight." Her tone was warm now.

"Seriously? I've been saying that for months."

"And I finally agree with you."

"But just a break, right?"

"Obviously." Luna laughed, breaking the tension, and went back to her scrolling. She was, of course, right. I did get nervous. Every time. The only thing I could do to fight against it was overprepare. Luna worked more on instinct. Which had served us well more than once. Same as my overpreparedness had. I saw these two characteristics as holding the same value. Our partnership was complicated. For better or worse.

The lights were bright from the street, streaming into Luna's vintage Mercedes as we examined a paper map we printed out at the university library. We were parked off the walk streets of Manhattan Beach, fresh off a slurry of cocktails and chicken wings from the brewery. A needed boost of bravery for what was planned for tonight.

"This bitch is insufferable," Luna said as she watched story after story of her on Instagram.

I stared out at calm streets and watched the clock tick on the dashboard. The homes on the walk streets were the pinnacle of California beach living. Every way you looked featured a different kind of palm tree. Every home was unique. From tangy-terra-cotta-detailed Mediterranean bungalows to sky-high modern glass structures, row by row they rested—situated feet from the beach, the glow of the golden coast a constant comfort from the reality of a world that could easily be ignored while in the proximity of its warmth. Generational wealth. Tech wealth. Celebrity wealth.

Here, houses were always empty and almost always open, or at least unlocked. We studied the mistakes the "Bling Ring" made in the aughts so thoroughly, we could have taught a class on it. We weren't looking for fame. The opposite. We wanted anonymity through financial security. Those people were children. Photos of them wearing stolen goods all over social media, mugging for security cameras, looping in random friends, turning on each other. A whole mess. The main difference: we weren't going to get caught.

First, pick your mark. Second, locate the address. Next, Google Maps—survey the house from all the angles. Case the house prior. Establish the dates that the home will be empty. Then locate all cameras. Don't look suspicious. Most importantly, act like a man. We wore baseball caps, hair tucked in. Kept our nails clean and short. We dressed in oversized clothing. We changed our gait and walk. In and out in under fifteen minutes was the rule. And above *all* else: stick to the plan.

Part of the plan was planning for contingencies. We took not getting caught to heart. We kept a few crucial things on hand: digital decoder tool,

Xyrem, zip ties, tasers, just in case. And there were several cases where they came in handy. We were not naive to the fact that what we were engaged in was dangerous. Our caution was to mitigate that where we could.

Forget side hustles, forget influencing, forget digital goods. If you knew what to look for, if you studied, if you were professional—which I was—and if what I did was legal, I'd make more than most of the boys fucking it up on Wall Street. Some of the handbags we stole were worth six figures. The safes full of jewelry, no one even remembers, held more value than most people could even dream of. Shoes, coats, gowns. Mint condition Chanel and Saint Laurent. Vintage Versace and Dolce & Gabbana. And cash. Fistfuls of cash were always scattered about.

We were extremely careful about what we took and rarely ever kept any of it. We had our buyers who didn't ask questions. We invested our money. But, in a safe deposit box, in a bank far, far away, I did have a few favorites that I couldn't bear to part with. Every criminal has their Achilles' heel. Mine happened to be Hermès.

Despite all these years, celebrities haven't changed much. Even with the added security of doorbell cams and motion sensor lights, they still think they're untouchable, and are very unserious about safety. They are unserious in general, but especially about safety. Specifically, the ones who aren't *really* that famous, but think they are. Those idiots were the bread and butter of this little operation.

On the west side is where athletes reside. Lakers, Dodgers, Clippers, Rams, Chargers, and Kings all keep homes in this cozy little neighborhood, houses starting at $3 million. So quaint. When you walk down the streets with no car access, the houses practically echo with lack of life. No children running through their open halls, no dinner being made, no silly arguments being had. Just the dark and hollowness of the rich.

We cased the next hit the weekend before. There are no gates here. No security checkpoint. Only the arrogance of wealth. We walked lazily by the house, dodging pastel-clad tourists and Inland Empire escapees. Luna's eyes never left the place as she methodically licked hazelnut gelato off a cone. The large, square concrete tiles of the walk street felt warm under my leather sandals squeaking with every step. We knew Luke Hunter would be out of town the next week. He was set to start in the big game to be played three thousand miles away. And more importantly, so would his girlfriend. The one with all the things. The things she posted every single day online from this very house.

We rang the doorbell twice. Nothing. So we tried the door handle, and it clicked right open. Bingo. We walked through the entry slowly and into the great room. It was very dark, but the light from the beach shined in, so we could see just enough. I fumbled in my pocket for my mini flashlight. Luna whispered something inaudible to me. An unfamiliar panic rose in my chest. Luna giggled a little for some reason.

A voice from the dark said, "Hey."

We jumped. My heart in my throat, I saw Luna reach for the Xyrem-soaked gauze in her pocket. *Fuck, not again.* I touched her elbow lightly, eyes wide with caution. She eased.

"Hey," Luna said.

"Why are you in my house?" he said, unmoved by our presence, then clicked on the lamp on the side table next to him.

Why wasn't Luke on a court in Madison Square Garden right now? How did we miss this? I went into default plan B mode.

"Sorry, we thought this was our friend's house. So, so, sorry," I said, and motioned toward the door. But Luna stood and stared at Luke, head cocked to the side like a labradoodle.

"Why are you sitting in the dark?" she asked.

He sipped his rocks glass slowly, the brown liquor disappearing between his lips. He didn't take his eyes off us and thought about his response. Then he took another quick sip.

"I'm lonely."

Luna huffed. Didn't get the response she imagined, I guess.

"Everyone's lonely," Luna said.

"Sorry, sir, we didn't mean to bother you. Let's go," I said more forcefully this time.

"Why don't you not go?" Luke said.

Luna and I locked eyes for the first time since we walked in. I was screaming inside, *No! No! No!* But before I could protest, Luna said, "Sure. As long as you're not going to kill us."

"I thought you were here to kill me."

I looked from her to him, and from him to her as they studied each other, suddenly aware of the third wheel I'd become in this fucked-up game of sidestepping truths.

Luke stood up. I thought about his stats that I had memorized: twenty-nine years old, six-eight, 240 pounds, palms the size of a dinner plate, born in Milwaukee, only child, dating the insufferable girlfriend for one year and eight months. I knew I couldn't leave her here. I was on Luna's side now.

"You look familiar. Do we know you?" I said.

"You might know my name, but you don't know me."

"What are you? Like *infamous* or something?" Luna had a knack for making an insult sound sexual.

"I play basketball."

"Wait…shouldn't you be playing basketball right now? Isn't there a game on or something?" I said, trying to casually move past this awkward part as quickly as possible. If I had to be here, at least I could get a drink out of it.

"I'm suspended," Luke said, and downed his drink. "Happened this morning."

"Were you bad?" Luna asked, again, too sexually.

"More like infamous," Luke said. "Drink?"

"Yes," Luna and I said in unison.

Luke moved across the room to the bar. He was wearing a snug, black V-neck sweater and casual dress pants with red socks. He kept fussing with his normally slick curls that had become slightly unruly under his constant touch. I recalled all the research I did on him. Photo after photo of him on the court, him with his parents, him with the painfully insufferable, but admittedly smoking hot girlfriend. We sat on the stools across from him. Luna took off her sweatshirt and slung it over the barstool. Her tank top had rhinestone straps, sparkling through strands of sleek, blond hair. He took down two rocks glasses like his from the top shelf and poured us two whiskeys. With his back to us, he said, "I'm Luke."

"Ella," Luna said.

"Lisa," I said.

"Luke, your house is beautiful, do we get the grand tour?" Luna asked.

"But of course," Luke said with an oddly placed French accent, turned with a whirl, and put down the glasses in front of us. We all clinked glasses. *Salud!*

His demeanor shift threw me. I looked to Luna for confirmation of this absurdity, but she seemed pleased. We sipped and pretended to like the burn.

"Follow me," he said. We took our drinks and did as we were told.

"Living room, bathroom, den, and down there is the TV room."

It was perfunctory, but we continued to "oooh" and "ahhh" as expected at the kaleidoscope of navy, brown, and gray modular furniture. He started to ascend the stairs; we followed, weirdly obedient.

"The guest rooms. Guest bath. And my room."

We walked into the sprawling bedroom with walls saturated in textured, dark-gray grass cloth, a marble fireplace took up one entire wall in the room, and a giant bed against a wall of windows facing the crashing sea.

"But I know what you're here to see."

He opened a small door next to the bathroom and clicked the light on. This was unlike anything else in the house. A pearly white, girly, little jewel box at the heart of the hypermasculine space. A chandelier sparkled bright in the round room, the walls lined floor to ceiling with clothes. An elaborate shelving system of shoes and handbags stood to attention as we glared. Designer shopping bags spilled over with things across most of the floor space.

I had to catch my breath.

Luna sat on the ivory, bouclé, tufted ottoman in the center of the room. Luke stood just outside the door and sipped his drink, watching our reactions. It felt like a move he'd done before—showing the poors what real opulence is.

"This your girlfriend's closet? The blond with the tits, yeah? The model," Luna asked, being just as much a blond with the tits.

He stared at her a beat too long. She was unfazed. I felt myself blush.

"Yeah, that's the one."

"She's, like, a feminist or something?" Luna goaded.

"Something like that."

"There's the book and a podcast and stuff about women not being objectified?"

"She uses her platform for that, yes." Luke was going with it.

"Every other picture she posts is of her naked, right?"

He looked at her, incredulous to her mocking.

"Maybe you don't understand feminism?" he said.

"Maybe," I said, hoping to ease over this bump.

"Doesn't matter, we broke up."

"Oh? Shame," Luna said.

"I don't know about that," he said. "Now you won't have to feel bad when you steal her shit."

Without missing a beat, Luna said, "What?" and truly looked offended and confused. A goddamn professional.

"I know who you are," Luke said, continuing to sip his seemingly never-ending drink. "You can take whatever you want. I don't give a fuck. Just don't be obvious about it."

It was so silent, the crashing waves outside soothed us like a sound machine in the room, dutifully working to lull us to sleep. He walked away, and we heard him land on the bed across the room. We looked at each other and whispered.

"We have to go. Right now."

"No fucking way. This is a gold mine!" Luna whisper yelled at me.

"He knows who we are? We have to get out of here and figure out what that means. This isn't a game, Luna. What if he's calling the cops right now?"

"Of course it's a game. Look at him. But we're better at it. He doesn't know shit."

"How the fuck do you know that?" Controlling my rising rage within the unsatisfying whisper.

"I just need to get close enough to him to drug him. We take what we want. And he'll think this was all a bad dream." She finished her drink.

That was the stupidest thing I'd ever heard. I finished my drink too.

"How do you expect to do that, exactly?"

"He's lonely, remember?"

"I'm leaving. This is not what we agreed to. Ever."

"What? No!" she whisper yelled.

I stood up to go. Then I saw her. Tucked away in the back of the second-to-the-top shelf, next to three Chanel flap bags. The Hermès Birkin 30 Diamond Himalaya Matte Niloticus in alligator leather. A bag so rare, I'd only ever seen one once. When I'd held her, wearing white cashmere gloves that day at the dealer, I thought I would faint. When he pointed out that the hardware was 18-karat white gold and studded with white diamonds—the cadena lock alone is comprised of 68.4 grams of 18-karat white gold and encrusted with forty white, round, brilliant diamonds totaling 1.64 carats, and the touret, the pontets, and the plaques de sanglons featured more than two hundred diamonds for a total of 8.2 carats—my mouth went dry. He repeated what it was worth to me four times before I heard him. And there she was. In the exotic flesh. Not six feet away from me.

"Fine. But this is the last time we do this bullshit. I'm done."

Luna smiled and got up quickly; we both walked out of the closet to see Luke lying facedown on his bed. We looked at each other and walked over to him. Luna sat next to him, and I sat on the end of the bed. My hand was in my pocket poised on the taser. She lightly placed her hand between his shoulders and whispered, "Luke, you okay?" her voice genuinely kind.

He lifted his head and smiled at her sweetly. He moved a bit of hair from her face. I wondered for a second if they knew one another. He slid his hand to the side of her face and lifted his head to hers and kissed her. I slid off the bed to the floor. They continued to kiss. I felt all the booze hit me then. I watched them, completely oblivious to my gaze, and couldn't understand the flurry of emotions that consumed me. But one stood tall among them. A revelation I did not enjoy. A pang of jealously so hot, I could have evaporated. I wish I had.

I could swipe the bag and run out of here… Luna is smart… And I didn't know what planet she was on right now, let alone the game she was playing… I could go and initiate my exit plan… But what if something happens to her? What if she's in over her head here? People know we're friends... The police would look for me.

The mental deductions came fast and relentless, but my mind was sloshy and slow. Luna was on the bed with Luke now, everything intensifying. I needed to make a move. I tried to walk toward the closet. *Whoa.* My head spun. The room spun. I stumbled and felt nauseous. I put my hands on my hips and leaned over slightly, trying to breathe, to regulate. Again, the mental mathematics pelleted my soggy mind. *I've only had three drinks... They're still kissing... Something's off... This feels more than drunk... Oh fuck.*

I turned and looked at them on the bed. The moonlight through the glass practically blinded me, and I staggered a few steps backward. Luna sat up finally and looked at me, more confused than concerned. She smiled softly. "Chloe, are you feeling all right?"

Am I all right? Are you?! I thought but couldn't speak. My heart started to pound harder and louder. She rushed over to me and caught me as I fell to the floor, her arms wrapped around me, her face hidden in darkness. My vision blurred as I desperately tried to cling on to consciousness. Luke was looming behind Luna. Unhurried, unbothered. His dark silhouette etched a shadow over us in the moonlit room. *Why did you say my real name?*

"You're okay. Chloe, you're okay," Luna kept repeating in singsong.

Stop saying my name. Stop saying my name. The corners of my vision closed in. Stop saying my na—

END

BLOOD IN THE WATER

by Craig Clevenger

Everyone thought Father Martin had drowned until a piece of him washed up on the beach. I'm not sure which piece. Lot of blanks in my memory from that afternoon.

We'd been in California for two years, and I hadn't learned to surf, only went swimming when Mom dragged us to the beach for *family day* after church. I was barely sixteen, all rib cage and bird-wing shoulder blades. Other guys tossed footballs and Frisbees, had grown-up muscles, and they seemed so much taller than they were. And the girls were swelling out of their bikinis. When they'd catch me staring, they'd just look away, forget I was there.

But then Mom would snap, "Get your ass in the water," start in about how our dad didn't drive us all the way out here so we could sit on our asses, that I needed to get some sun, and so on. Mom always wanted me to "get some sun." Sure enough, a group of girls would pass right when I took off my shirt. I could smell their coconut oil, count the water beads on their brown-sugar skin. They'd keep walking.

Truth was, I loved the ocean. I mean when Father Martin was still alive and before *Jaws* came to theaters. I still can't fathom ever being as lucky as I was that day, or as naive. Maybe it wasn't luck, but I was just too damned skinny. And *naive* is the wrong word, because the ocean was still safer than home. I saw shapes beneath the surface sometimes, like seeing a face in the clouds. Always a trick of the shadows, a low-flying bird or a passing helicopter. I'd learned to tune them out, even after I saw the same one twice.

The tide would splash over my ankles, and fresh quicksand sucked at my feet. When the water reached my shins, I'd pull my knees high like I was stomping on grapes, push against the crashing surf until I was waist-deep, then chest-deep, then swimming into a gray-green wall rising from the surface. It was all about timing, gauging a wave's speed and distance, when to inhale and how long to hold my breath. Once the waves were small enough to ride over the top, I'd keep going.

Beyond the last island of floating kelp, the beach was a pale strip of sand full of stick figures and flecks of bright color. I couldn't hear Mom hissing or yelling, wasn't consumed with hating her. I didn't resent Dad for having no will or opinions of his own, or for being resigned to his role as Mom's silent enforcer. I didn't think about the priests and nuns and phys ed coaches who ran St. Alexius High School like a cattle ranch, didn't think about the girls who didn't think about me. I wasn't skinny and pale and weak. I was just floating with the current, not thinking my legs were strips of bait dangling above the miles darkness filled with silent circling teeth.

* * *

We went to Father Martin's noon Mass on Sundays. Father Martin had replaced Father Ripley, who had replaced someone I don't remember. I once thought priests rotated parishes the way military personnel were shuffled among bases. I know different now.

Father Martin was from Florida. He was younger than the other priests, had a tennis player's tan and what people called baby fat. When he hugged me or put his arm around me, I didn't smell coffee breath or that fake Irish soap Dad used. With Dad, touch was about control. Holding the back of my neck to guide me to a pew before Mass or taking my elbow when he wanted my attention. Mom was affectionate mostly in public, but her hand on my skin made me shiver, like an insect creeping across me in the dark.

Father Martin took over as the parish youth minister. He was the first priest I'd seen wear street clothes. At youth group, he wore sandals and jeans with T-shirts from Christian concerts. On field trips, he let us play whatever music we wanted on the drive. Yeah, I was in our youth ministry group, went to meetings every Saturday night. I was an altar boy, too. Those things allowed me to leave the house without suspicion, wouldn't lead to getting screamed at or hit.

Like the night a cop stopped me for not having a light on my bike. Mom was big on having dinner *as a family*, and because of that stop, I was late.

"Where the hell have you been?"

I took the citation from my pocket, and she snatched it from my hands before I said a word. She went to the table and slapped my dinner onto a plate—chicken, instant mashed potatoes, and canned green beans—then slammed it to the floor.

"Go to your room, boy." Dad's voice was cool, measured.

"Not until he cleans that shit up," Mom said.

My disbelief led to a flicker of hesitation that brought a flurry of slapping at my face and head. I scurried to pick up the shards of ceramic, dropped them into the kitchen garbage.

"And I told you to get rid of that goddamned shirt."

My Molly Hatchet T-shirt, the one with the Frazetta painting. I wasn't allowed to play their music in the house, but she'd never said anything about the shirt.

"Yes, ma'am." I kept cleaning, shoveled the green beans off the linoleum with my bare hands and threw them out.

The belt slashed me across the back. I hadn't even heard the warning jangling of the buckle.

Mom screamed, told me again to lose the shirt, so I took it off. Then she screamed at me for wasting the green beans, said that she'd cooked dinner, and so I was going to goddamned eat it, and if I didn't want to eat my dinner the way she served it, then I could damn well be on time, and on and on and on.

On my knees, shirtless, I felt the air on my skin and the whole world staring. No sound anymore but the scraping of knives and forks or Dad clearing his throat. The chicken leg had landed at the baseboard beneath the counter, with all the crumbs and bits of dried noodle and strands of hair. I wiped it against my pants before taking a bite, then scraped the potatoes together and licked them from my palm. I needed something to drink but didn't want to ask.

* * *

The ocean gurgled about my ears, and I could taste the salt. I'd matched this distance twice before but wasn't tired this time. I kept going, a burst of light in my eyes every time I turned my head for a breath, until I lost track of my strokes. Then I stopped to look back.

The beach was a pale scratch behind the rolling waterline, the hills and palm trees all flattened by the distance. The breaking waves, that background noise like slow-pulsing radio static was gone. No seagulls shrieking, no parents and kids shouting back and forth or squealing when the cold struck their ankles. No dogs barking, chasing tennis balls or Frisbees. The breeze whispered across my wet ears, then faded. Nothing but the horizon behind me and quiet all around.

* * *

Ernie and I helped clean up after youth group one night. We stacked the chairs, put the tables away, all that. Then he was gone. I didn't see him outside, hadn't heard his dad pull up. I found him in Father Martin's office, the two of them sitting in the corner beanbag chairs, with Ernie holding a half-pint flask. I knew I shouldn't have seen it—just an instinct—so I looked away, pretended I hadn't, and almost missed Father Martin's expression.

"Hey," and Father Martin said my name, but I'm not putting it here. "We thought you'd left." He waved me in and said, "Close the door." He took the bottle from Ernie and handed it to me. Didn't ask, just held it out until I accepted.

I'd never tasted alcohol, so I had to keep from breathing through my nose to take more than a sip. I made a face and they both laughed. Later, Father Martin offered us both a lift. I had my bike, so I told him I was okay to get home. He gave me some peanut butter candy and a look that said, *This stays here, with us.*

128

I didn't need any look. Time spent with Father Martin, with any priest, guaranteed I wouldn't be punished. Ernie climbed into his passenger seat, and I pedaled home.

* * *

The Steps are about coming clean with yourself and those around you. A searching and fearless moral inventory. A willingness to make amends and then making them. Steps Four, Eight, and Nine. If I'm being honest, which I am (Step Four), I'm the one who's owed amends. But that's not how the program works, and I want this to work. This is my first time beyond Step Six. Last time I made it this far was my first time past Step Three, and my longest clean stretch to date. Two years, four months, and eleven days. On day twelve, a cop woke me on someone's front lawn. My nose was broken and my wallet was gone. So here I am again, and the person I need to make amends to, I can't.

Ernie never came back to youth group, and I didn't see him at school the next week. When he finally showed up for third-period health class, I asked where he'd been, but he acted like he didn't hear me. Then the bell rang, and Sister Baines launched into roll call, said we'd be watching a film that day.

Muffled laughter swept the room—we knew what a *film* meant in health class—but Sister Baines froze us with a look. The nuns could do that. She stood in back while the film played, a pad of detention slips at the ready. The narrator talked us through a close-up of some dude checking his balls for lumps, and I think that was then Ernie wet himself.

Sister Baines sent him to the nurse's office. She'd tried to be discreet, whispered to Ernie beneath the projector's thrumming, the voiceover skips, and the music stretching in and out of tune. But this was high school. Rumors were faster than radio.

Ernie was excused from health class for the semester, and you can probably fill in the rest. No takers for lab partner, lunch by himself in the quad. But so much more, and so much worse. You know, high school. I wasn't part of that collective cruelty, and for a long time, I told myself that was enough. That I had done the right thing, that I was a good person.

Freshman year, our phys ed coach assigned team captains, who chose the strongest and fastest players first. The leftover kids, like me and Ernie, were divvied up as a formality. Softball, we played outfield. Always. Touch football, we had the same play in every game: *go long.* So when Ernie and I had both showed up at youth group one night, both wearing identical Van Halen T-shirts, we became friends. It was still that simple. But he'd stopped coming to the group, and he avoided me at school. That was my excuse, anyway. We both lived on the social sidelines with the other dorks, sure, but Ernie was radioactive. He finished his miserable sophomore year, and I never saw him again.

Ernesto, I am sorry. I turned my back on you and lied to myself that I didn't.

In a darkened confessional booth—mandatory once a month, per Mom and Dad—I confessed to "not being a good friend," a sugarcoated country mile from the truth and the closest I ever came to it, until now. Father Dupont—I recognized his voice through the curtain—ordered ten Hail Marys, and that was good enough for God, the Vatican, and me. But it wasn't good *enough*.

Senior year, I went to Ernie's funeral. Besides me, his parents, and his brother, there were seven people there. They all said the overdose was an accident, but I still carried that for a long time after.

Yeah, you've already put it together. Me, I was still a kid who, for the first time, had a place where an adult didn't berate, threaten, or physically hurt me. And all those headlines and lawsuits, that reckoning was years out. This one now, this is mine.

* * *

My longest swim to date. The coast stretched farther than I'd ever seen from land, both directions vanishing in the afternoon haze. The sun was heavier than when I'd started, a slight cast of amber to the sky, but I still had the energy to make it back. When I was close enough to ride the waves, I'd be feeling winded. When my feet touched sand, I'd be heaving for air. That's how it was every time, but I always made it.

I took long, lazy strokes and kept my face in the water, only turning for a slow inhale. Told myself to keep moving, don't think about the distance, because if I did, I'd fixate on my breath, on the strain. And if I didn't shake that, then I'd fixate on what might be swimming below me in the dark.

Maybe it was the current, or I'd kept my head down for too long. When I checked my distance, I was still a long way out, and the afternoon light had deepened to a warm gold. I was closing in on the Whaleback, a hump of rock about two feet high at low tide but still hard to see from shore. I'd need to stop there and catch my breath before going the rest of the way. I caught the shape just before I pulled myself out, but didn't bother looking up for the bird or whatever might have thrown a shadow.

When it was really choppy out, I might see a fin. That was what I'd think, at first. Sometimes a submerged rock or mass of seaweed looked like a dolphin or a seal, maybe something else. But it never was, really. Almost never. Forcing those thoughts out of my head was how I checked my panic. But the thing was, really, the harder I worked to push those thoughts away, those shapes and shadows in my imagination, the less I thought about home.

* * *

Sometimes the youth group would go for pancakes, or a couple of us would just hang out after the meeting with Father Martin. Yeah, I know. What I'm saying is, my parents—my mom—didn't care how late I was out, because I was with Father Martin and the youth group. So when I turned sixteen, earned my license, and bought a used piece-of-shit Corolla with my savings, I went to my first high school party.

Danny from the youth group had invited me. Danny went to public school, knew the guy whose parents were gone for the weekend. I took his directions to a neighborhood in the hills. The cramped street parking told me I was close, and the opening riff of "London Calling" led me to someone's porch. I stood there, listening to The Clash through someone's front door, wondering if I should knock. It felt weird to just walk into a stranger's house, but I did. Someone I didn't know shouted something I couldn't hear, handed me a red Solo cup, and pointed to the keg. Danny was nowhere to be seen.

I filled my cup and faded into the background. A few students from St. Alexius were there, kids who didn't know my name but I knew theirs. The girls wore denim skirts, spaghetti-strap tops, vacuum-tight jeans, and undersized T-shirts. The first time I'd seen them out of school uniform. I took long, shallow sips, feeling more conspicuous the longer I stood in one place, nursing a warm beer and talking to nobody. I chugged the rest—god, it tasted terrible—just to go for a refill, to move with a purpose and use my voice.

The ring of dudes at the keg greeted me with chin juts and cup salutes. Like I belonged. One of them said, "Refill?" I nodded, *yeah, thanks*, and when the foam had spilled over the top of my cup and down my fingers, they were chanting for me to chug. I mean, cheering me on, like that never happened in phys ed or anywhere, so I knocked the whole thing back without a breath. They slapped me high fives and whooped like I'd just won a rodeo or something.

Three or four light beers wouldn't hit me at all these days. Back then, my liver was still new, and a few watery beers made me happy and confident enough to talk to new people, even make some new friends. And then drive home.

* * *

The cop lit up my rearview mirror, and that hot vibration hit my guts, that same fear-hum like when a belt buckle jangled in Mom's hands. I pulled over, but the cruiser kept going. That sobered me up fast, but still, Mom would know where I'd been, what I'd been doing. I was certain.

I found a pay phone and called Father Martin.

Our church didn't have a rectory. Father Martin lived in a one bedroom with a couch, TV, and a tiny kitchen. His bookshelves were packed full of theology books and religious biographies, with ceramic saints or votive candles in every spare nook. But mostly it looked normal, like he was just any other dude with his own place. Father Martin saw my surprise and made a joke, like I thought he lived in a bell tower or under a bridge.

Of course he'd drive me back to my car. Of course he'd call my parents, say I was staying the night. Of course he'd tell them I'd be at noon Mass on time, since it was his service. Of course they trusted him. Of course I did, too. It was a night away from home.

He set me up on the couch, and we stayed up late, talking. After a pause Father Martin said, "Things aren't good at home?" It sounded like a question, but it wasn't. He knew.

Growing up in the Catholic church, going to Mass every Sunday and holiday, plus attending Catholic school, you learn to take blame. Our mom didn't beat us; we were just unhappy. She wasn't abusive; we just didn't like rules. I needed to think less about myself, needed to learn patience and understanding. I needed to pray more, especially for my parents.

Ask God for the wisdom to see your parents for who they are, as human beings doing their best without a book on how to be a good father or mother.

When you're an adult with children of your own, you'll understand how much you are loved, how profound that love between a parent and their child truly is.

I'd heard it all, but Father Martin didn't say any of those things. He put his arm around me, rested his free hand on my leg. He'd never done that before, and I think I stopped for a second because with his one arm around me, he pulled me closer, just a little.

"Go on," he said.

And I did, told him about the names Mom called us, about the belt and my dinner on the floor while Father Martin ran his thumb across the hole in the knee of my pants.

"That's not discipline," he said. "That's cruelty."

I'd never cried harder than that first time I cried with relief.

I'm not ready to talk about this. Maybe someday, but not now. It's all a blur, anyway. Not my memory, but what was happening. Like, what I thought was supposed to be normal and what I was comfortable with. What I said, what I didn't say, what I wanted to say, and what I thought I should have said. Not knowing what affection was, but knowing what it wasn't. And not wanting to hurt his feelings. A blur.

The oven clock read *2:30*. Father Martin had gone to sleep, and I was standing in his darkened kitchen with a glass of water, staring at the snapshot collage on his refrigerator. Father Martin and my friends from church, even a few I knew from school. Weekend retreats, youth ministry meetings, and other events. A shot of me from the group's mountain hike, another from the previous year's winter camp, my face half out of frame. A row of kids with Ernie at the center, beaming with this big dopey grin, everyone cracking up just as the picture was taken. Another shot from a different event. A fundraiser, I think. Ernie was smiling again, not spontaneous like the first photo but just as big and real.

I'd forgotten about his smile. The Ernie in those pictures looked exactly like the sullen kid who'd stopped talking to me, who wouldn't look at me anymore. Exactly like the kid who'd wet himself during a sex ed film and was bullied savagely for the rest of his sophomore year. The resemblance was uncanny, but it wasn't the same kid. Both had disappeared. Last time I saw the smiling, happy Ernie, he was getting into Father Martin's car.

The next morning, Father Martin drove me back to where I'd parked; then I followed him to church and filled in for an absent altar boy. We met Mom and Dad after Mass and lingered so they could thank him, so Mom could use her glittery social face. She asked how my night was. Whenever Mom asked me about my day or night somewhere, I always said, "Fine." It wasn't an answer, but it wasn't a lie, either. It meant school, work, or whatever was over, that I'd already forgotten about it, so there was nothing to tell.

"Fine," I said. I lied.

My sister wasn't there and I said something—I don't remember exactly. If you didn't know what to look for, you'd miss it, but Mom's laughing and sparkly public face switched off for a blink. There was never an excuse for missing church, which meant my sister was in trouble. Mom just said she couldn't make it, and that was the end of it. She switched back to laughing and sparkling, thanking Father Martin for taking me off their hands and giving her a break for the night. She kept lightly stroking my arm with her fingers, the same way Father Martin had touched my knee. It reminded me of brushing past seaweed.

Mom had found a pack of smokes in my sister's dresser, I learned later. She was grounded to her room for a week, couldn't even come out for meals. I brought her dinner a few times, but she kept the lights out and her back to the door. Mom said she couldn't use the bathroom until she'd cleaned her plate. The day of her eighteenth birthday, she left for school that morning but didn't go to class, and she never came home.

* * *

My sophomore year ended two weeks later. I didn't go to youth group for the next two Saturdays but didn't tell Mom or Dad. On the first Sunday of summer, we went to the beach after church, where Mom urged me to get in the water as soon as we settled. She was gentle at first, like it was just a suggestion, but when I shrugged it off, she kept at it.

"We did not come all the way out here..." she started up, speaking through clenched teeth. Something about how pale I was, that I needed some sun, that I shouldn't be sitting on my towel sulking—her favorite accusation after berating one of us—on such a beautiful day, and on and on until the veins and tendons on her neck stood out.

"What's our famous marathon swimmer doing on dry land?" Father Martin stood behind us, zinc oxide down his nose and swim goggles around his neck. The West Coast water was too cold for him, I guess, because he wore a black wetsuit, unzipped, the top half hanging about his waist. The sight of his bare torso and dough belly made my hands shake.

Mom hit the Fairy Godmother switch, offered Father Martin a soda from the cooler and told Dad to make room on their blanket.

"I'm going in." I took off my shirt.

"I scare you off?"

At first, I thought he meant the youth group, and I felt a strange flush of shame mixed with panic.

"Nah." I took off my sandals. "Just taking a swim."

"How about a buddy?" he said. "Safer that way."

I should have said *no*, but I couldn't, not to his face and not in front of Mom. For years I replayed that exchange in my head and *should have* won, every time.

"Fine."

I had just stepped into the tide when he touched my shoulder from behind. I pulled away.

"Whoa," he said.

I felt bad, right then. Still don't know why but I couldn't help it. I wanted to protect his feelings.

"You okay?"

"Yeah."

We just stood there until he said, "No goggles or anything, huh?"

"Nah."

"What, you Aquaman or something?"

"No, I just, I don't know." I kept going, the water up to my knees. Father Martin sloshed behind me. "How far you go?"

"Just past that rock out there." Mom had set us up at the Whaleback.

"Where?"

I pointed, kept walking. The water was up to my waist.

"Still don't see it," he said. "You sure?"

"It's not that far."

"You sure—"

Maybe he was going to ask if I could really swim that far, or if I was messing with him, pointing to a rock that wasn't there. Or maybe he was going say, *You sure you're okay?* I dove forward and swam.

* * *

By my third semester in college, I was on academic probation. College was just a tool to help me leave home anyway, a stepping stone to cut contact with my parents. So that third semester was my last.

I never married, had a long chain of shitty relationships that I endured because I was grateful for the affection. More than grateful, but surprised by it. Every time. And I howled at the moon over breakups, my heartache always out of proportion with the actual loss. Eight weeks of dating, maybe a little more, but I'd carry the hurt for a year. Yeah, there were plenty of good relationships. I fucked those up, too.

I drank, wrecked my car, sobered up, and started drinking again. I've sobered up for good more than once. Two decades passed before I had any perspective on this, and I didn't come to it alone. There were friends, therapists, groups, counselors, and sponsors. But they came after years of wreckage.

I think about my sister sometimes, hope she's okay. Maybe someday I'll be able to find her.

* * *

Twice, I paused to ask Father Martin if he wanted to turn back, but he said, "No." When we made it to the Whaleback, he pulled himself up, put his hands on his head to stretch out his lungs, and breathe.

"You're trying to drown me, aren't you?"

No sounded like a lie, even in my head.

"What happened to Ernie?" I was still treading water. And no, I don't know where the question came from. Maybe it was being in the ocean. I felt safe.

"What?" He squinted at me, heaving for air. With his big dumpling body squeezed into the black wetsuit, he looked like a seal.

"Ernie," I repeated, trying to say it clearly, from my chest, like the name alone would have Father Martin against the ropes. But I was suddenly thirsty, my tongue sticking to the bottom of my mouth.

"Hey, buddy, if you're upset about something, we can talk about it, okay? Just come out of the water."

"I'm fine." Like talking with a mouthful of cotton. I couldn't breathe.

Father Martin smiled and said, "I think I know what this is really about."

What this is really about.

It was about him wanting me to see us as friends, but not equals. It was about me being too ashamed to make an accusation that I didn't want to believe.

The night at Father Martin's place, he'd spoken softly, like he was trusting me with something. He kept asking me questions, each one narrowing how I could answer the next. I can't remember anything I said, just that I was talking really fast, mostly mumbling. I sat there in my boxers, coiled tight like bracing for a plane crash while he worked his thumbs around my neck and shoulders, but I couldn't relax. I was too afraid to follow his questions all the way to the end, where I might ask for something I didn't want, something that wasn't my idea but would still sound like it. He finally said, "Good night," and went to his room.

I knew *what this is really all about*, but I couldn't put it into words, not for another twenty years. If I said anything at all right then, his questions would corral my answers into whatever conclusion he wanted, and I'd somehow end up apologizing.

I couldn't say anything and didn't want him to touch me. I pushed off the Whaleback and started back to shore. Father Martin called out; then I heard the splash, so I swam faster, afraid to look back. Like those nights when I biked home after watching a horror movie with Ernie. The more I forced myself to look ahead, the more my imagination ran amok, and the unseen thing behind me was closer and more monstrous with every second.

I could swear I heard Father Martin shouting, close enough to grab my ankle, but it was just the noise of my own arms and legs cutting through the water, the sloshing about my ears when I came up for air. Until I heard him for real, not yelling after me but full-on screaming, just for a second, and then he stopped, quick as switching off the radio.

* * *

His funeral was packed. Everyone said over and over that Father Martin had given his life for mine, that his sacrifice had saved me. Just like Jesus. It made me sick and angry and guilty, so I just cried. Mom hugged me, a lot. It didn't bother me so much at the funeral. But that was the last time she touched me. And I never went back into the ocean. I just left Father Martin behind while he called after me, and I just kept swimming to safety.

THE RIOT AT THE END OF THE WORLD

by Sara Marchant

#1

The coffee shop where we sit looks familiar, but it must be brand new. It smells of fresh paint and plastic torn off vinyl seats. Our flip-flops stick to the unscuffed, orange laminate flooring. But the building is ancient, or as old as the Mission Beach boardwalk anyway. From the open door, we can hear the creak of the wooden roller coaster as a carload of children rattles by, not all of their terrified shrieks in fun.

"I've been here before," I say after a minute. But when? My tongue strokes my molars, trying to dig out the memory.

Patrick, his blond surfer curls hanging in his eyes, looks over from the women's room door. He's been watching it since his girlfriend, Belinda, went in. She's almost, but not quite, my best friend. He doesn't turn his gaze back to me; instead he looks over my head at the framed print on the wall. Travel posters, sparkling fresh, dot the wall over every booth. Like a half-assed theme. Our poster is from China.

"The Forbidden City?" he asks.

"No," I say. "Well, yes—I have been there. But I meant this café. Where we sit."

"Belinda said your parents send you guys away," he says. He's back to staring at the restroom door. "You and Nora."

"Yep," I say. They did it once, sent us away for an entire summer. We still don't know why. Why do parents do anything? Patrick doesn't care either way.

"She said you came back from China sick," he says. "Lost a lot of weight."

Now he looks at me, or rather at my tits, which didn't suffer in the slightest from the weight loss. He meets my eyes after and has the grace to blush. I smile in forgiveness. Who could resist such bounty? I am leaning on the table, my tank gaping so my blue lace bra shows, as an offering. A little gift. Belinda is almost breastless. She has what my mother, who detests Belinda, calls "fried eggs."

"You're pretty," Patrick says now. "You should learn to surf."

"What?" I laugh. "No."

"You don't think you're pretty?"

"I don't want to surf."

"She's afraid of the water," Belinda says as she joins us. She must have snuck out of the bathroom when Patrick finally focused on me.

"Seriously?" Patrick takes Belinda's hand, but his eyes don't leave mine. His gaze is soft. He feels sorry for me, for my fear. I could use this against him, if I wished. Against Belinda's hold on him.

"I can swim," I say. "I just prefer to keep my head out of it. My sister used to waterboard me."

"I thought you were twins," he says. As if twins can't be homicidal.

"I meant our elder sister," I say. "Naomi." But I'm distracted because now I remember why this place feels familiar. I don't know why Naomi knocked the memory loose.

"I've been here before." I interrupt their silent communication. Patrick asked Belinda a question with his eyebrows, and she mouthed, "Wait," back. "I was here when it was a burrito place. With Bob."

"Oh, him." Belinda's upper lip does that sneering thing that makes my mom want to slap her. This time the sneer is justified. My lip doesn't curl at the thought of Bob. The heavy heat of shame and fear sits low in my belly; I cradle it only for a moment, then shove it away.

"He was her boyfriend," she tells Patrick, and he shrugs. Big deal.

"Tell him," Belinda says to me. "About your ages."

"We were here," I say instead. "Really late, like out all night because my parents were away and my sisters were out, so no one cared where I was. Bob was high, and he bit into his burrito, and it went 'crunch,' and he spit out half a cockroach."

I pause for them to finish their choked gasps of disgust.

"But he was so high," I say. "He merely shrugged and finished eating the burrito."

"And you kissed this guy?" Patrick asks, laughing.

"No," I say. "Not if I could help it."

Patrick laughs harder, but Belinda merely nods before checking her Swatch. She knows all this. It must be over five minutes because she gets to her feet once more. She hasn't touched her coffee, which is now cold with scum on top.

"Be right back," she says before disappearing into the bathroom. I would have put the plastic test in my purse, even pee-soaked. What if the janitor cleaned while she sat out here not drinking coffee and judging my life choices?

"I've never been to China," Patrick says. He reaches out and clutches my hand. I remember my mother advising me, as I dressed for this outing, to steal Patrick away from Belinda. Save him from that flat-chested, overperfumed snot. I could do it; I would enjoy doing it. I could take him up on his surfing offer and accidentally seduce him in the sea. It would be so easy. But he's currently seeking comfort from me. And besides, there's a code.

"Yes," the voice of my mother whispers in my ear now. "The code is 'every man for himself.'"

"One of my mother's boyfriends took us to Iceland, though," Patrick is saying when I once more tune in. The fingers of his other hand are tracing over our entwined ones on the table, over and over like that trick with a pencil until soon you can't tell if you are flesh or wood. I shiver. "Iceland was… It scared me. What do you think the end of the world will be like?"

"A riot," I say. The noise of it in my head.

Patrick nods, pleased. "Yeah, people all freaking out."

That isn't what I meant at all, but Belinda is exiting the bathroom. She's smiling, but here are fresh tears of relief on her face. Patrick drops my hands and runs to hug her. I walk to the counter and order new coffees to go, carefully watching for roaches.

Outside, across the street, the roar of the ocean's waves is momentarily drowned out by the screams of the foolhardy souls riding the wooden roller coaster, so I don't hear what Belinda says to Patrick that makes him throw open his arms wide enough to embrace us both. But when his hand lands at the top of my butt, I quickly pull it up and off. If Belinda notices, she says nothing, only takes the coffee I hold and wipes her eyes on the napkin I offer.

"Let's go," she says, and we follow her out.

Another carload rattles by on the rickety track above us, the joists and joints older than our grandmothers, and the passengers' screams sound like a riot.

#2

When a car runs out of gas, it makes sputtering noises before it gently coasts to a stop. It is exactly like in the movies. For some reason, this pleases me. I don't even mind that Patrick tells me to climb into the driver's seat and lock the doors and lower the seats so we're not visible, before he runs in his long-legged lope down the dark highway to find a gas station.

"Does he have enough money?" I ask too late. He's already gone.

"He has his grandmother's credit card." Belinda yawns. "For emergencies."

Patrick lives with his grandmother and her youngest child, a woman who has Down syndrome, in an eerily large house, more like a cold barracks than a home. Two long hallways are connected by a large, round dining room containing the biggest round table I've ever seen, topped by the world's largest lazy Susan. The grandmother raised fourteen Catholic children here—yet it is hard to believe the house ever rang with the young voices. Now a cult laboring under a vow of silence as they prepare for a spacecraft to come lift them away, that I can envision.

Patrick seemed to agree. He only whispered when he gave me a tour after introducing me to what family remained. I pulled my hand from his grip in the girls' dorm hallway. His grandmother was an elderly, stern presence and only nodded when he'd presented me. Patrick left me in his room, with his aunt Patty, to join Belinda in the bathroom. She'd beckoned him from the doorway, an odd look on her face. I assumed they were about to fight.

Patrick's aunt had very little language, but she brought out a thick photo album that we flipped through on Patrick's cot-like bed in his concrete-floored cell. Patty pointed out everything edible with one stubby finger and muttered, "Lunch." I liked her priorities and appreciated her keeping me company while her nephew and his girlfriend didn't argue after all but had quietly noisy sex in the bathroom marked *Boys*.

"Where is Patrick's mom?" I ask Belinda in the car, as the passing headlights create a strobe light effect. My astigmatism makes it extra fancy.

"He's not sure," she says. "Don't ask. She takes off with her latest man. She's always done it. That's why his grandmother got custody."

"But he's over eighteen now?" I've never liked younger men.

"Yeah." Belinda sighs. "He likes it there. She needs him, he says."

"Is his mom pretty?" I ask once I finish shuddering.

"She looks like Patrick." Belinda giggles softly. She's nervous here on the side of the road. "Only, you know, girly. So yeah, really pretty."

"I heard you earlier," I say. "In the bathroom. Patty did too. She mimicked the grunts."

"She won't tell." Belinda dismisses Patty with a wave of her hand. "She only knows food words."

"Seems risky," I venture.

"We used a condom," Belinda says. "I'm pretty sure we did. Sex is…sex with Patrick is so good. I didn't know it could be good, you know? And he is…he is everything."

"It's dangerous," I say. "Letting someone matter that much."

"Oh, you." Belinda hits what part of me she can find in the dark of the car. "Someday you'll fall. Although I never understood…"

"What?" I ask when she doesn't go on. "Understand what?"

"Bob was a grown man," Belinda says. "And you were too young. I get it, so I mean I understand why at first you didn't want to. But he was so crazy about you. He did anything you asked and weren't you even tempted?"

"Never," I say, shuddering again. "I didn't want him to even touch me, because he wanted too much. It's like Patrick staying in that big cold house because he feels needed. I couldn't stand that."

"Do you ever think…" Belinda stops, and she doesn't start again even after the car no longer rocks from the closeness of a passing truck. Maybe we should turn the flashing emergency lights on.

"What now?" I ask. "Think what?"

"Do you ever think there's something wrong with you?"

"No," I say. I laugh even though I know she's serious. She obviously thinks there's something wrong with me. "And I don't care if there is. I like me this way. I don't know who I'd be otherwise."

"You'd be Nora," she says. She means my sister, my twin. Some people call her my other half, but we don't even look alike. Nora is taller and prettier than I am; she's an athlete who gets perfect grades. Nora is everything a parent wants. Aside from her few peccadilloes, as my mother calls them.

"No," I argue. "Nora doesn't want to be needed either."

Nora wouldn't have sat with Patty on that hard, narrow bed, listening to a litany of "lunch, dinner, fish," for fifteen minutes while the boy she had a crush on audibly screwed her best friend in a bathroom sink.

"But Nora wants to be loved," Belinda says. "We run in the same circles, you know. I see her out more often than I do you."

Belinda sees Nora at parties, at clubs, at the underage venues they frequent. Belinda is my friend because she, too, likes reading and talking about films and going to museums and sewing her own clothes, but she's a social animal like Nora—they drink from the same kegs, know the same dealers. Like Bob, he was a dealer. That's why he was able to lavish money on me. Belinda knows public Nora; I know private Nora. I hold my twin's hair while she vomits up the alcohol and wipe the blood from the sink once her nose finishes bleeding out the drugs. Nora wants to be loved all right; I hate it.

"That's why your mom hates me," Belinda says, and I jerk at her honesty.

Because it's true. My mom hates Belinda because she narced that Nora drank until she blacked out, she snorted until her nose bled. Nora needed to be stopped. But our mother refused to believe it until she saw it herself the night Nora's buddies brought her home unconscious, and that made our mother feel guilty. Guilt is another one I don't understand.

"You had to do it," I tell her, the smell of the night highway all around us. "You did the right thing."

"Nora hates me too," she whispers.

"But she's alive," I say. "And she goes to therapy, and I haven't had to clean blood from the sink in months, so I thank you."

"You're welcome." Belinda is still whispering. It must be hell wanting people to like you.

"Did Patrick run all the way to Santee?" I complain. "I have to pee. And we aren't going to make it to the show on time."

"How did you break up with Bob?" Belinda asks. She strokes my forearm with two fingers over and over, skipping on my skin, and it feels good, so I shift in the reclined driver's seat until she loses me. "You never said."

"It was just a fight," I say, remembering how my head barely came to his shoulder, the way he held my hand in his large, calloused palm when I was scared of the dark. "A normal fight, and I realized I was done."

This isn't the entire truth, but no outsider needs to know about that night. After what he did, and how I said I never wanted to see him again. The way he tried to hold me down, how glad I was that my brother had taught me to fight dirty, the sight of Bob's fist in the air, and my relief that when one screams in my house, at least three siblings come running. Belinda is an only child.

"Not why," she says. "How?"

"I just told him no," I say. My throat is sore now from how loudly I yelled then. "I told him to leave and never come back. But the funny part was afterwards. He wrote my mom a letter."

The memory makes me laugh, and in relief, I let it go until I can't speak. Belinda pats around in the dark car—it's late enough now that traffic is slowing and the lights are dim—finds my arm and pinches.

"Ow," I say. "He wrote my mom a letter demanding she make me take him back."

"What?" Belinda laughs too. "How did he think that would work?"

"She read the letter that night, at the dinner table, and we all cracked up until we choked on the spaghetti. Well, except Norton, but he doesn't have a sense of humor, and the whole thing is his fault anyway."

Belinda stops laughing.

"Mom said, 'I can't even make Nora clean her bedroom, and he thinks I can make Nell take him back?'"

"Wait, wait," Belinda says. "Your family discussed his love letter at the dinner table? God, you're all weird."

"Not a love letter," I argue. "More like a ransom demand. But he had no leverage. Bob had nothing I wanted."

"That was the problem," Belinda says.

"Yes," I say. "That was always his problem."

Of course, Belinda doesn't really understand, because she dates boys like Patrick, with his inherent sweetness. I was attracted to Bob's wildness, his crazy eyes, his utter ignorance of proper behavior, and his willingness to do anything to be with me. To break literal laws. What made him exciting was what made him dangerous. Even at fifteen I recognized this. I thought that recognition would protect me. It didn't.

Running footsteps thump up to the car, and Patrick presses a hot hand to the window as he peers inside to check on our welfare. Soon gurgling gas fills the tank, and Belinda only has time to say, "Thank you for not stealing my boyfriend," before Patrick joins us, and our private time is over.

"You're welcome," I say as I crawl over the console into the back seat.

"For what?" Patrick asks. I can feel his gaze on my upturned bottom.

"Never mind," Belinda and I carol in unison.

And the night doesn't end, but our intimacy does.

#3

This hot afternoon, standing in the driveway of our family home, Nora is angry that I'm wearing our elderly grandmother's dress. No, it goes back further than that. Nora is angry that I stole the vibrantly colored, snap-front housecoat off the laundry line behind our grandmother's brown brick house, smuggled it out of Denver back to San Diego, and have been wearing it all summer long with my Doc Martens Mary Janes. Sometimes my bikini is underneath Grandma's housecoat. Mostly, it isn't. The suspense is the fun part, according to my boyfriend, Bob.

This makes Nora especially angry. She hasn't said a word to me all day, only shoulder checked me as she climbed into the back of the two-door Accord coupe we inherited on our sixteenth birthday when our father bought himself a Lexus. Bob looks mystified by my sister's behavior, but when I explain that she hadn't wanted to come on our excursion but was forced by our mother because it wasn't seemly that I spent the day with two adult men all by myself—Bob's eyes light with an evil delight, and he follows Nora into the back seat.

"Ugh, give me those fish," she says in disdain. "You're going to smash them." I hear the slosh of the water-filled plastic bag as she takes the feeder fish from Bob's grasp. Then all is quiet.

Bob's sidekick, Jiro, slides into the passenger seat. Nora and I have only just turned sixteen, and I need more driving practice. Normally, I prefer to let Nora ferry me around whenever I can. But Bob isn't allowed to "instruct" me since the incident with the school bus, so Jiro is riding shotgun today. He gives me an apologetic look, and once more I wonder at their relationship.

Bob is casually hateful to Jiro, constantly dragging him into fistfights Bob starts and then promptly loses so thoroughly, Jiro has to step in and save Bob from death or maiming. Once, at an impromptu beach concert, an inebriated NASA scientist—no joke, I went through his wallet after Bob knocked him unconscious with a Coors stubby bottle—became enraged over Bob's taunts about the "staged" moon landing, and the scrawny guy gut tackled Bob into the bioluminescent-lit surf. Jiro knocked the scientist over before Bob drowned.

Usually, during his fights, I would leave with others, figuring Bob would eventually notice my absence or be murdered. Either way, it had nothing to do with me. At least he didn't expect me to jump in the fight or "have his back" with more gusto, as I'd heard him bitterly complain to Jiro after the NASA debacle. Bob felt Jiro's energy was lackluster.

"I don't know how you put up with him," I mutter to Jiro now.

"I say the same to you," he replies as he pops the cassette out of the stereo, examines it, and then throws it out the open window.

"Well, I don't," I say. I don't protest the treatment of the cassette; it's Nora's mix. We don't share a taste in music. "You're the one who lives with him."

"I don't have to have sex with him," Jiro says, and because he's Japanese, it takes me a moment to determine he's serious. He doesn't do sarcasm much.

"Yuck," I say. "I don't either."

"Not what he says," Jiro tells me quietly. He's angling the rearview mirror to look in the back seat, where an ominous silence holds. Nora must be really pissed, although she's not a big talker on a good day. I'm afraid to take my eyes off the road, my hands off the wheel; I'm afraid to look in the back seat.

"Then he's a fucking liar." But why is Bob equally quiet? Normally, my conversation with Jiro, these accusations, would be fighting words.

We're speeding down the 8 freeway, Jiro's window open, so it's not until I re-angle the rearview mirror as I navigate the interchange to the 5 west that I catch a glimpse of the situation in the back seat. My boyfriend, my grown-adult, inappropriately aged boyfriend, is kissing—I mean tongues involved, deep, wet, noisy kissing—my twin sister. And my sister is kissing him back.

In shock, I turn back to the traffic, steering through the crowded freeways off to the narrow surface streets of the beach cities, all of our lives in my hands. I ignore my pounding heart, my sweaty palms, and Jiro's concern as he sits sideways, studying what he can see of my face. And they haven't stopped by the time I drive into the pedestrian-choked streets of downtown La Jolla, and I don't actually know where I'm going, because I'm only sixteen for god's sake. Jiro is too polite or scared to speak, and Bob was the instigator of this particular field trip. The car is idling at a stop sign across from the Catholic church surrounded by a short chain-link fence covered with sturdy, dirty ivy when I snap. I can hear the smacking noises of their wet lips.

"Are you kidding me?" I yell. "Are you seriously kidding me right now? You assholes?"

In my fury, I get the pedals mixed up and slam on the accelerator, drive up the curb and over the sidewalk. The car is only stopped by the dusty ivy, which is tough and filled with trash. There is a moment of stunned quiet before the absolute cacophony of Bob and Jiro screaming blame at each other, half of it in Japanese, and Nora shrieking at me for damaging "her" car.

But I'm not listening, because there's a nun tapping on my window glass, twice only, as if hesitant to disturb me as I'm being yelled at by pervert traitors. At least, I think she's a nun. She's dressed in a gray pinafore, her hair is covered by a hood, and her kind eyes are surrounded by smile wrinkles. She uses her gold ring to rap once more on the glass, so I lower the window.

"You're blocking the sidewalk, dear," she says. This dulls the impression of kindness but serves to shock the yellers into silence. "You cannot park here."

"My boyfriend was kissing my sister in front of me," I tell her, and she shakes her head in disapproval.

"You definitely cannot park here," she repeats.

Then we're all laughing; even Nora is yelping her seldom-heard belly laugh. I can't help but laugh harder; my sister's laugh has always ignited instant joy. Once, while we were playing Barbies, her laugh made me lose control of tears and bladder. We'd laughed harder when she'd realized I'd peed my pants. Nora is only young, even younger than me by twenty-two minutes. It's not her fault my stupid boyfriend is using her to try and make me jealous. To manipulate me into sleeping with him. I can forgive Nora. But Bob is a dead man.

I put the window back up, slowly reverse off the sidewalk with a few vines dragging from my bumper as evidence, and listen to Jiro's directions to our destination, the tide pools. Nora still holds the bag of feeder goldfish Bob brought to the house earlier. I hate to think of what those creatures suffered during the illicit clench, perhaps held between Nora's knees in her ragged jeans.

By the time we trek to the pools, I'm newly angry and can't speak to anyone. Wordlessly, I take my sister's hand not clutching the rubber band–secured fish bag, and she allows me to drag her to the farthest-away pool uncovered by the tide. Together, we crouch and offer the golden-scaled bounty to the scuttling crabs and gently undulating sea anemones, whose soft tentacles wave open and closed in creaturely delight when we hand them a fish.

A little crab places one delicate leg on my palm to snatch a fish flopping in misery as it drowns in the air, and Nora looks away when the crab rips off a bite-size piece and stuffs it into the tiny aperture of his mouth. But I don't look away even as Nora shudders, sitting so close our shoulders touch, her long legs dangling over the side of the sharp rock into the sea proper. I refuse to look away from the miniature carnage.

"I'm not angry at you," I whisper. You'd be forgiven if you thought she couldn't hear me over the pounding of the waves and the roar of the wind, but she is my twin. We grew in the same salt water and listened to the same heart beat above us. She turns to meet my eyes, and she nods.

She knows I will always forgive her. And she stays by my side as I continue to hand little fish to hungry crabs and watch them be consumed. She hadn't wanted to come today; the kissing was her revenge. But she went too far and she knows it. Nora accepts her punishment.

On the drive home, Nora sits in front with me. She acknowledges the back seat with one dirty look when she finds her mixtape is gone. She plays Violent Femmes at top volume all the way home so that no one is tempted to speak, to try and defend himself. Even Bob knows there's nothing left to say, however. If you refuse to fight him, he simply gives up. There's a certain triumph in surrender.

#4

"Are you wearing that out of the house?" Nora asks as she lounges in the doorway of my bedroom, still dressed in her sweaty soccer uniform. She has dried mud over her left eyebrow.

"Leave her alone." Naomi pops off from her position on my bed. She's waiting to put my eyeliner on. I can't bring myself to hold the match-warmed black point that close to my vulnerable eyeball. "Normally she dresses like Sophie B. Hawkins."

"What's wrong with that?" Nora and I screech in tandem. Naomi laughs even as she covers her ears. Disgusted at agreeing with me, Nora throws me the stink eye and prepares to steal the en suite bathroom we share.

"A little black dress is the perfect first-date look," Naomi says, going back to chipping the polish off her nails. She brushes the mess off my bedspread when I point to it.

"This weirdo looks like a cross between Darla and Bonnie Parker." Nora waves a hand at my vintage baby doll dress.

"A hat!" I am inspired by Bonnie's famous cloche and run to the walk-in closet, where my extensive collection is displayed on cup hooks screwed into the wall. Nora helped me set it up on a day she didn't completely hate me.

"Now see what you've done," Naomi says to Nora. Her tone is resigned even as she throws this month's *Sassy* magazine at my twin, who is sneering at the black straw beret with dotted swiss net I attach to my hair with its vintage, only slightly rusty comb.

I preen in front of the full-length mirror, struggling to see my outfit through the E.E. Cummings poem I've written on the glass. Nora slams the bathroom door. We hear the gush of the shower.

"Come here, you little freak," Naomi says. She strikes her lighter to rewarm the eyeliner. "Let's get this over with."

"There's nothing wrong with my outfit," I huff as I submit.

"Everything about this is wrong," my eldest sister murmurs as she holds my chin with one hand and balances the heel of the other on my cheek. She runs the heated black goo on my lower waterline. "But no one asks my opinion, so I say nothing."

"Except now," I say.

"Shut up." She removes the stick from my eye only long enough to slap my bared thigh. "And sit like a lady in your dress, not like the hoyden you are."

"Hoyden," I whisper. "Good word."

She only slaps me again, so I quiet until she finishes dragging the warm, sticky black line around my fifteen-year-old eyes.

When Bob and Jiro pick me up that night, there is a girl with them. Well, a woman. She's wearing a bronze-colored pantsuit, high-heeled sandals over white lace socks, and holding Jiro's hand when he introduces her as Cherry.

I didn't know women could be named for fruit, but she doesn't like it when I share this with the group. Bob laughs, but I wasn't trying to be funny.

The restaurant is Cajun, and there are white tablecloths and candlelight, and I'm glad I'm wearing what will forever be known as my Bonnie Parker dress, even if Cherry looked startled when I adjusted the lace of my hat to cover one eye. She openly snickered when I tripped in my spectator pumps. But the maître d' sent her a chastising look as he caught my elbow. I like this place even though it turns out they have octopus on the menu—maybe they don't realize eating an animal with enough self-awareness to keep a garden lessens their humanity.

The waiter isn't swayed by my argument, though, and Cherry mutters, "For god's sake," so I stop midstory of the cephalopod who left his tank to turn off a forgotten light, and order the alligator tenders to start and seafood salad for main.

Looking relieved, the waiter retreats. Cherry heaves another sigh, but before I can ask what her problem is, exactly, Jiro hurriedly tells a complicated and unintelligible work story about a car wash.

"I thought you worked at a grocery store," I interrupt.

"Not anymore," he says, throwing a dark look at Bob.

"Here's our drinks," Bob says brightly, and Cherry turns her beady eyes on him.

Bob ordered a clear soda for me, which I resented—did he think I was a child who couldn't read the menu?—but he waits until the waiter leaves to slosh a glug of his sauvignon blanc into my glass. The glass is now overly full, and I lean down to sip it to safety before I am able to join the others in a toast. Cherry rolls her eyes at Jiro, and I decide the game is on.

The smile I bestow upon her is so vivid, she blinks. One of my sisters would know to look for the weapon in my hand when I smile like that, but Cherry seems like a bit of an idiot as well as judgmental, so she cluelessly smiles back before she launches into a sob story of her recent breakup. Of course, Jiro is her rebound; he's so polite and stoic. Women like Cherry probably read that as shit eating. I nod in better understanding. Cherry nods back.

"A relationship based on a shared love of cocaine was never going to work," she says. It's the first time she's been interesting.

"May I see up your nose?" I ask. All movement ceases after their heads swing to face me. The couple at the next table are staring as well.

"Are you…" Cherry starts, stops, then starts over. "What?"

"In health class they said excessive cocaine use erodes the frenulum inside your nose," I explain. "I've always wanted to see it."

"I think you mean septum," Bob says. He raises his wineglass to toast me, not at all disappointed in my request. "The frenulum is elsewhere."

Cherry's hand has crept up to carefully touch her—rather pointed—nose, but now it slaps down on the white-clothed table. The glasses rattle. The white candle tilts in its holder, spilling wax onto the flowers surrounding it.

"Health class?" Cherry asks. "Are you still in high school?"

"Here is the food." Jiro beckons to the approaching waiter to hurry.

My alligator tenders accompany my salad, which is not what I was expecting. But everything is odd now, and the service seems rushed, and I have to wiggle my fingers at the waiter to stop him from leaving.

"Could I have a dish of ranch?"

"Ranch?" The man repeats it back like he must have misheard. No one in this restaurant sounds Cajun; they don't even sound French. This guy, probably as old as my PE teacher, sounds like the guy who services our pool. Chad is from New Jersey.

"Ranch dressing," I prompt. "For my salad."

"We have a sweet mustard." He stops speaking as I feel my lips curl in disgust.

"Never mind. Thanks," I say, shaking my head. "You may go."

He looks to the rest of the table a bit blankly before walking back to the kitchen. The others are settling into their meals without conversation, so I munch an alligator strip as I evaluate the salad situation. Despite my lecture on the evils of octopus predation, a tiny little guy is draped artfully across the romaine on my plate, a whole crawdad lying next to him like a marine-themed crime scene. Everything glistens with a vinegar-scented oil.

"Have we learned nothing?" I murmur to my octopus as I lift her tenderly between two fingers. With the other hand, I walk the crawdad to meet his little pal.

"Another fine mess we find ourselves in," the crawdad says to the octopus in my best Tom Waits impersonation.

"Easy for you to say," the octopus speaks in falsetto. "I'm just a baby, I had my whole life ahead of me."

Metal clinks against china as Cherry puts down her silverware. Pleased with the attention of my companions, I continue the puppet show. Octi and Tom are plotting to escape until one of Bob's oysters, which are indescribably nasty, gently points out that they are both dead. Octi is still weeping, her little legs shaking in a puddle of oil, when Jiro points his fork at Bob.

"I told you she's too young," he says. He looks to Cherry for validation.

"You're just jealous because yours is boring." Bob jerks his head toward Cherry, who reacts like a struck cat.

"Excuse me." She stands and leaves for the ladies'.

Tom the crawdad buries the octopus under a lettuce leaf, humming a dirge, and is burying himself when Cherry finally returns. She leans into Bob's personal space to whisper, "You belong in jail." Then she walks out of our lives.

The maître d' magnificently bows to her back before assuring me, "I called her a cab, mademoiselle."

#5

We are in the pool, Nora swimming butterfly laps holding water-filled milk jugs in each hand while I lounge on a raft out of her way, when our elder brother appears from the side of the house. There's a man his own age following him.

My brother shoots me with his finger in acknowledgment, then yells, "Where is everyone?" over Nora's splashing. He goes inside when I cup my hand behind my ear and shake my head. I can't hear him. His friend is passably good-looking, and Nora won't speak to me until she's finished her water polo coach's required program, so I roll off the raft to swim to the steps for a better look.

Norton exits the house, two beer cans in hand. His friend takes a beverage before squatting on the concrete lip of the pool next to me. His eyes linger on my bikini the way men have been looking at me with frequency the last two years. I like it; it makes them a little stupid. They think they're powerful, in control, but the way they don't even see the person behind the breasts says differently. As long as I didn't hold the shiv between my titties, they'd never see it coming.

"Well?" Norton says. "Where is everyone?"

"Dunno." I shrug elaborately. The friend moves his entire head as he follows the movement. "Out?"

"What's for dinner?" Norton asks. "I've brought a friend."

The friend drops to sit cross-legged next to me, offers a hand to shake and a grin that makes me understand the word *lascivious* for the first time. But I like the way his eyes light up when he looks at me. And he's looking at me, not my taller, thinner, prettier sister churning through the water like some kind of scary mermaid.

"I'm Bob," says Bob.

"Cool," I say. I swipe the beer from his hand as I push off the pool wall and, beer in hand over my head, swim back to my raft. The men can't reclaim the can without a full immersion. "Thanks."

"Dammit," Norton yells. He smacks Bob's shoulder. "You can't do that."

"Do what?" Bob says. He's laughing as I drink the beer from the safety of the raft. I save half for Nora, who pauses to swig it while I hold one gallon jug for her. She one-handedly crushes the empty can before handing it back to me and returning to her laps. She never speaks a word.

Norton and Bob are conferring poolside, heads together.

"Forget about it," Norton finishes. He makes a chopping motion of negation at his own neck before he expertly ducks the crushed can I chuck at them. The aluminum missile bounces off Bob's head.

"Get out and come talk to me," Bob says. He extends a hand as if I'll do as he tells me.

"Nah," I say, treading water, holding the raft like a shield.

"Good girl," Norton says, so I swim to the steps and pose in baby cobra. Bob nods approvingly at my closeness and what the position does to my chest. My brother scowls.

"Remember that tape I gave you?" Norton asks me. "It's his band."

"Oh yeah," I say. "That was awful. Like elk screaming, with drums."

"Awful?" Bob looks genuinely distraught. "Elk?"

He reaches out quicker than I can jerk away. He cups the back of my wet-slicked head to pull my face up to his. I scramble to find purchase in this awkward position, my breasts about to pop out of my bikini top, and all I can grab is his forearm. He's almost kissing me. Nora stops splashing, and I hear the jugs thunk as they hit bottom.

"Girl, you need soul," Bob says before he puts his mouth on mine.

"Get away from her," Norton is yelling. I hear Nora speeding toward us. "She's just a little girl."

Bob's is the first tongue passed my lips ever, and I gag at the sensation. Bob quickly pulls his face away, then laughs when he realizes why I'm sickened. He seems pleased, happy with penetrating my virgin mouth, so I dive at him. He opens his mouth again, his triumph cut short when I sink my teeth into his face, and I bite his lower lip bloody.

He screams, tries to pull away, and the tension of the retreating flesh between my teeth makes me nauseous again, so I release him. Norton grabs his friend from behind, lifts him bodily, and hurls him headfirst into the pool. There's an audible thump when his skull hits a step. Nora grabs my arm, and we scramble back, splashing maniacally as we swim in reverse to the other side of the pool.

"Spit it out, out," Nora says, throwing handfuls of chlorinated water in my bloody mouth. My rinsing and spitting doesn't satisfy her, and she pushes my entire head under as I fight her. She knows I've always hated that. Naomi not only scrubbed us like potatoes in the bath, she was positively brutal with the hair washing.

"Stop," I sputter when she pulls me back up by the hair. "I didn't swallow it."

Bob laughs again, holding his lip, where he sits on the pool steps with Norton crouching above him, and temperate Nora tells him to go fuck himself. Norton slaps the back of his friend's wet head in annoyance. Bob grabs his arm, and Norton goes underwater as well.

"Don't be nasty," Norton says to Bob when he emerges. He checks to make sure his watch still functions.

"What?" I ask. "I don't get it."

Our mother chooses this moment to appear.

"Oh roughhousing," she clucks. "Aren't you all a little old for this? Everyone out of the pool. We'll have to eat on the patio to avoid a wet mess in the dining room. It's brisket tonight."

She doesn't wait for a response but goes inside, and soon she and Naomi are bringing plates and platters and utensils outside. Norton is told to cover the patio chairs with towels and introduce his friend properly. Bob sets out to charm Mother, and we're all shocked when it works.

What would it take, I wonder as I sit trying to avoid Bob's gaze and hands, to jolt my mother out of her complacency? How far could I go before she noticed and stopped me? Deep in thought, I fail to prevent Bob from wiping the brisket au jus from my still-damp face with his thumb. When he then sticks that thumb into his mouth to suck it clean, I gag so cartoonishly that Naomi flicks me with Nora's discarded towel.

Mother finally agrees with Bob that in order to apologize for our "little contretemps" earlier, he should be allowed to take us girls to the movies with him and Norton.

"Not too late, though, boys," Mother says. "And girls, get dressed properly. Dry your hair and take a sweater. And no more roughhousing! Don't embarrass your brother in public."

Nora silently gets up, goes inside the house, and locks herself in our bathroom, I assume until after we are gone and the danger is over.

At the theater, I sit between my brother and Bob; I don't know how he finagles this. He buys me candy and popcorn and a cherry slushy and holds my hand when Jodie Foster is trapped in the basement with the serial killer. Norton leans over and pointedly removes my hand from Bob's. But it's too late; the damage is done. They say the best way to survive a rip current is to stay afloat and shout for help. But if no one is listening, all you can do is swim parallel to the shore.

When Bob puts his arm around me and squeezes my shoulder, I turn my head and bite the back of his hand. He shakes me off his hand but whispers into my ear, "You're a riot."

I am, I think. *I am a riot*. And I start swimming parallel to shore.

BIG PINK

by David Zimmerle

The sunsets I remember hit different up there. Like I was surrounded in pink. Swimming in it. Slicks of blush and streaks of black, everywhere. Lonely me all buoyant and alone with the grand Golden Gate just around the Lands End hook, shining auspicious shades of it, too. That marvelous color change. So different than down south. Different than home. How quickly and unassuming the shift. Sandy, emerald-green caverns to pink waters and pink skies. Just like that. Enough pink for a lifetime. A real good kind of pink.

Which is to say I had no room in my life for Nikki. Not really, anyway. Not then. Not with the learning curve of *that* wave. Its goddamn dangerous seduction. Its seasonal mystique that canceled out her long, blond ambitions, the large handfuls hiding underneath her fuzzy sweaters, and her fair skin, wild San Francisco blushing that would always be at odds. Because she was a sorority girl who had bubbleheaded plans for us. And it would be too complicating. That, and other fretful things. But what I didn't realize is how there would be brilliance in what she left me.

That first year, I lived on the third floor with most of the frat pledges even though I wasn't rushing, often jarred awake post-midnight to bodies crashing in the hallway just outside my door. They'd leave broken imprints of themselves in the drywall. Some battered their desk chairs into kindling. One guy threw his TV from the dorm window four flights up. Another drove all night to Santa Barbara and came back the next morning with a stolen daiquiri machine from his local diner. They were animals finally unleashed to run amok.

Toward the end of first semester, around the time the bathroom stall doors went missing and the toilets all clogged, a pledge from San Diego clutched my face with still-freezing hands and stopped me on my way to the stairwell in my desperate search for a working commode.

"Just got back from surfing, man—you have to go," he said, salted-red eyes gleaming under fluorescent light. "Gotta get out there while we're here. Unlike anything you've ever seen."

I was not ready though. Just an OC kid up north and all mixed-up confusion. Didn't stop my imagination's spin en route to the eighth floor though. Because maybe I could be ready. Soon. And suddenly Nikki right there in the hallway. Fresh from the shower, in her pink bathrobe and matching hair towel. At the time, she was dating that floor's RA. And I'd seen her about a week prior in this same pinch, only looking morning-tossed with a bag of bagels and a messy ponytail. Eyes that met mine more than halfway. Side glances of lust and flirtation. She caught me when I turned my head for a better look. Smirked over her shoulder and shook her head.

But there was no time for any Nikkis. Only time for recon, studies, and surf. So it began. Bus rides up Fulton through the Richmond to the Sunset. Just to see. Watching dark mountains roll under pink-gray skies. Capped out and heaving. Sheer and impossible. Just enough leeway between sets to make it out. A shoeless, shin-high dip for some semblance of bravery. One day. To feel *it*. I figured to drive back after summer for sophomore year, better served with wheels. The trusty 6'3" riding shotgun with my unfortunate 3/2. Which would have to be enough because I was broke.

Fall and its good fortunes though. Not a hint of the slump. Finally got my feet under me in what I'd considered a temperate chill. Found the green room. Felt the wall. All forward and go. Nothing too unwieldy until winter, when a Santa Cruz friend I'd made called early one morning.

"We could probably make a go of it," he said. I could feel his nervous laugh, and it didn't sit well. "Let's head out."

There was no report then. What the hell was *online* anyway? And if some nascent version did exist, I had no idea. So when no one was at the beach, it didn't initially strike me as odd that the whole gray stretch was empty. Even with the outside a fortress of walls. We made it out somehow in the slack, totally out of our element. That first taste of real cold. My stupid suit. Cold enough—big enough—where bad things happen. That first drop, a messy pearl. Drove me deeper than I'd ever been. Darkest I'd ever seen. Sucked me back out—way far out—and across the beach. A clip so fast, I couldn't believe I was on the other side of the windmill. It was too big, and I was a fool with numb limbs. Some pink opened in the sky though. Some sweet grace pushed me in, even if I was thrashing head over heels the whole time. I coughed up water on the sand. Down the beach I found Santa Cruz supine on the shoreline. He stared into the overcast.

"Not smart," he said, still trying to catch his breath. "What were we thinking."

I looked to the wild sea, humbled in a way I'd never been. Thinking of all the disastrous ways this wave might not be worth it.

In Latin American studies class later that morning, Nikki sat next to me at a long table.

"You know, it's great being single again," she said as we settled in to critique *The Old Gringo*. "Nice to know *we* can finally go out."

She squeezed my knee. I was stunned. She was so forward. A girl who knew exactly what she wanted and how to get it. She grabbed my hand.

"You're freezing!"

Maybe it was the idea of the old gringo going into Mexico for his death song. Maybe it was how just an hour earlier it'd felt like I'd almost cashed my chips. But something suddenly seemed right about Nikki.

"Sure," I said. My tongue tripped me up, so it sounded more like a question.

"You know, you should be my date to the sorority ball next weekend. How 'bout it?"

I struggled to form an answer.

"Sounds like a great idea" seemed like the right thing to say.

"So it's settled," Nikki said, now squeezing the top of my thigh—crinkling her nose a little. "More details later, 'kay."

Now, I'd been wrestling with this idea of her pinkness for a while—and when she began to sit closer, it was evident that my intuitions were correct. Her perfume reminded me of what pink smelled like. The backs and sides of her arms were this kind of blotchy pink whenever she took off those sweaters. Her lip gloss always a shade of pink. I caught the meshy upper edge of a pink G-string once when she leaned over to grab a book from her bag. One friend joked that she probably still had her Barbie dolls. It was becoming more difficult to accept the insistence of that color and the ways it almost conspired against the pink out there. I didn't have the guts to ask her why that color. And there I was, swimming in pink. Suffocating in it.

It was on my mind that whole week—these undercooked thoughts of her. And when Nikki didn't show up for class on Thursday, I'd found a reprieve from my obsession. My negative associations stalling out, since she wasn't around to remind me of them. I hit up a dive favorite with friends and my fake ID on Saturday night, drinking in the starry charms of Columbus Avenue. Frothy pitchers arrived and disappeared soon as they came. The night all smoke and haze. Inside I felt an unraveling, unfurling lust—this seed of an idea that Nikki might not be so bad after all. That pink could be okay. Maybe better than the big pink out there. Just fine, actually. What's a color anyway? I left the bar and hailed a cab, intent on calling Nikki once I got back to the dorms.

When she picked up the phone, her voice was scratchier—stuffed up.

"A booty call!?" she said, sounding like she was talking through an empty roll of paper towels.

"Kind of. Maybe, I guess."

"I'm just getting over a head cold. Plus, my roommate's here. What's the deal with yours?"

I looked over at Jack, who'd probably been asleep since eight or nine. He was a responsible student majoring in architecture, whose nonstop schedule was a bird's-eye view of eternal damnation.

"Yeah, he's here," I said, flicking at the phone cord. "Some other time, then."

"Tell you what," Nikki said, "come meet me in our lounge. Hang out for a little."

The room was empty when I walked in, except for Nikki on the couch in her pink pajamas—the glow from the TV our only source of light in the room. She patted at the cushion next to her on the couch.

"Saved this spot just for you," she said. "What do you feel like watching?"

I didn't care and said so. Then I leaned in and started kissing her neck, blunted by the courage of my night on the town. She pushed my head down closer to her handfuls. And after a minute or so of making out with her chest, brought me back up to eye level. I didn't care about the pink anymore for some reason—sated in part by the soft velour of her. Underneath, inside, throughout…we're all pink anyway. Shades of it, really. Pink nipples and tongues. Pinkish palms. Pink flesh. Ubiquitous pink. Pink that hides. Pink is pink and nothing more.

"Not here," she said. "But tomorrow night I'll make sure my roommate's gone—we'll totally get it on."

"Okay," I said, a weird flow of confidence brimming over. "That's cool."

"I'll wear my special panties, too," she said.

"Special?"

"Oh, yeah," Nikki said with the utmost nonchalance. "The ones my dad made. They're *real* nice. You'll see."

I could have gone white, and I may have. But I'm sure she couldn't tell because we were already that color from TV's glow. My brimming reserves dropping back down to empty.

"Your dad…made them?"

"Uh-huh. He likes that sort of thing."

She said this easily, casually—revealing so much of herself with such indifference—like panties could very well have been replaced with him making her a dollhouse or a birdfeeder.

"You'll see, I promise—I know you're really going to like them," she said.

I had the same feeling like when I'd fallen from the lip, totally bowled over by this sordid father-daughter connection—and the intimacy they shared in creating just the right fit. Did he bring out the measuring tape and loop it high up there by her inner thigh, paying special attention to her iliac crests—connecting those precious points of reference with a line that ran across the soft land below her navel? Did she model them when he'd finished the painstaking process of threading every stitch? With love? Being into "that sort of thing" sounded more like a hobby than a profession like fashion designer or tailor, and she confirmed this when I asked, saying he sold insurance. I thought about how the wave maybe was worth it after all. Definitely not something like this. If anything, just to see those pure pink skies. Nikki pulled me over her like a blanket as she lay down on her side, and we watched the last hour of *Saturday Night Live*.

When she called me on Sunday afternoon, I told her I'd come down with something and we'd have to wait.

"Oh, no!" she said. "I didn't get you sick, did I?"

"It's fine," I said, doing my best impersonation of a head cold. "We'll just play it by ear."

"There's always the dance…and then after. Get better, babes."

I missed class on Tuesday. If I saw her, I wouldn't know what to say. I purposely went to class late on Thursday, sat in the back of the lecture hall, and left early to avoid her. When she called that night, I said I still wasn't feeling good.

"But you'll be fine for the dance though, right?" she asked.

"Oh, yeah—getting better day by day. I'll wait for you in the lobby."

"And I'll be wearing them, you know."

I laid out my nicest clothes that Saturday morning, hung them over the back of my desk chair. A reminder that I had committed, and that later, surely, they'd be on the floor in my room or hers while we tossed into each other under the covers. My best clothes weren't much. Cheap slacks and a sateen button-down. I didn't even have dress shoes. And wouldn't you know, the gray sky parted and the pink came in. I must have hit thirty or more green lights to the coast. A-frames for miles. Soon the pink was everywhere, and I even stayed until I could have sworn I saw shark fins.

After that, I left for the bars. By eight it was clear that I wasn't going anywhere—better staying put, blunting my edges, playing pool, and erasing any thought I ever had of Nikki. I sat at the back of class from then on, and we didn't talk for the rest of the year—barely acknowledging each other for the rest of undergrad. Throughout that time, the whole pink stretch became a second home where I notched waves of consequence. Caverns were mastered and bonfires raged. I soothed a dying gray whale lolling in the night's low tide. I broke the nose of a big San Fran psycho with the point of my elbow, spilling him into Geary Street, just before he and a few others were about to jump me over surfing their waves and how they hated my Volcom T-shirt. A friend filleted his foot on a fin, and we rushed him to the hospital, blood all over the truck's bed. There was magic in every direction. You could strike sparks.

Several years later I rummaged through a forgotten box of college things while packing for my first big move from home to some jerkwater town up north for a newspaper job. The box contained books mostly and other artifacts, like that tobacco pipe I'd puff sometimes when the foghorn sounded. Found it next to a disposable camera that didn't have any pictures left to take. Scrawled on it was *Sophomore Year*. The lady at CVS gave me dirty looks when I picked up my photos later that week. On the loveseat in the living room, I opened the envelope and settled in for my retrospective. Somebody took one of me playing chess wearing an Indian headdress on Halloween. I found one of Jack crouched over a pool of beer foam on the floor, pointing at it and looking back at the camera in the middle of a big-mouth laugh. There was a series of photos that captured the fog sweeping in across pink skies—always hovering just below the red lights of the Sutro Tower.

Then the girl seated at my desk, neck down, so I couldn't see her face. She wore a tight, pink evening dress, breasts all pushed up. Pinkish-white, flesh so firm. *Familiar handfuls.* I flipped to the next picture, and there she was again, still faceless—this time toying with a strap at her shoulder. *Patchy traces of blotchy pink.* The next photo she'd pulled down the dress's top half to expose her pink satin bra, a graze of pink areola peeking above the edge of a single cup. *A girl who knew exactly what she wanted.* I flipped again, and she was standing up now, using the seat of my desk chair like a footstool. Conquering it. She'd lifted up her dress to reveal the most couture panties I'd ever seen—to this day, even, so far removed. Lines of pink- and white-colored fabric, edged with pink doily lace, crisscrossing each other in patterned harmony—the camera's flash giving its silken sheen arresting emphasis against enough labial curve. *And how to get it.* The last photo was a note on the chair in black marker—a simple message, *Surfing? Really? Over this?*

VESSELS

by Ioannis Argiris

"Adrian, the kids won't be able to make it up there this summer," his sister says.

"Why not?" He leans against the railing on the upper deck of a Bay Area Ferry heading to Oakland.

"The kids have summer camps and stay overs, and it's just too much to drive up," she says.

He flips his sunglasses onto his face. It's always sunnier on this side of the bay. The brighter side. He tucks his hand into his life jacket. But no matter how sunny it gets, the wind still gets him on that bay water. Hands will crack, dry out. He forgot his gloves at home, next to his reading glasses on the nightstand. He woke up too late. He always forgets them.

"How about I come down there?" Adrian suggests.

"I don't know."

Adrian spots some kids playing on the railing on the opposite side of where he's posted up. He watches them fight for position to get the last views of the San Francisco skyline before it disappears. He can't figure out whose kids they are, but then notices a single father fumbling through backpacks and lunch boxes a few rows back.

"Sis, maybe we can get together again at the end of August."

"Okay, let's try that."

Adrian ends the call and walks over to the father. He stops short and changes direction to the kids as one of them leans over the railing a bit too far. Adrian grabs the kid's foot just before it loses traction on the railing.

"No playing on the railings," Adrian says. The kids are terrified. Maybe they're not used to such an authority figure so direct.

"I'm so sorry, sir," the father says.

"Please just watch them until the ride ends."

The kids continue to run around on the upper deck and into the interior of the ferry.

Adrian heads back to his spot against the railing. The ferry passes cargo ship after cargo ship. Large ships that go back and forth from Asia to the West Coast. Chipped, rusted paint on wide steel bodies. Giant letters painted on their sides. Initials of shipping tycoons or dead presidents. Up top are cargo containers stacked ten to fifteen high. It's a busy week at the port terminals in Oakland, with all berths filled up. Tugboats prepare to maneuver the horizontal skyscrapers out into open waters. Opposite of the Oakland port is Alameda Island. The abandoned military base from WWII. It was also used by those crazy scientists who bust myths with all those wild experiments. Nowadays, Adrian feels it's a wasteland on the edge of the bay. Dirt mounds with vents on top of old military storage bunkers. Graffitied-out watch posts. A few landing strips. Nature taking it back.

Today, the waters are so calm in the estuary and inner harbor that it feels like he's flying. Other days, the waves feel like Adrian has had the spins from an all-night bender. They're getting close to docking now. About five minutes out from Jack London ferry landing. It's his shift to help off-load the customers. He heads down to the lower deck and ropes off the sliding-gate area. The signal to the patrons to get their stuff ready. People wait with their foldable bikes, tech workers in their jacket vests, lawyers, teachers, and stadium vendors, all waiting to disembark. Every time that rope goes up, it's clockwork. And Adrian realizes his life is one routine after the other. Probably until he can't do this anymore. Until the wind gets him, or maybe he falls into the chilly waters of the bay and gives up. Or he decides to leave the Bay Area altogether and head south to be closer to his sister and nephews.

An Amtrak train blows its horn on the second street tracks. Passengers anxiously wait to have it go by. The ferry always waits for them, but they don't know that. They're just lucky it wasn't one of those Union Pacific cargo trains that go on for thirty minutes. The ferry leaves at that point. The next rush of customers makes their way onto the ferry, and he counts how many come onboard. Congestion occurs at the ticketing area like always. People confused on badging in, trying to validate their parking, bikes trampling people, out-of-breath runners trying to make it—clockwork. Adrian tucks his hand into his life vest, the other one clicking the counter. Always got to have a manual count of passengers to make sure they are offboard. Can't have anyone staying on for a free ride, or worse, someone has fallen into the bay. Seaweed carpets the rocks on the banks of Jack London. Next to them is the old USS *Potamic*, the one FDR used as a floating White House. His hand tucks farther into his vest because no one ever tells you how cold it gets on the bay water. Hand so dry, you'd think it's a catcher's mitt. Adrian goes through so much lotion, the CVS clerks must think he's jerking it way more than he should as a forty-something-year-old.

Leaving the Jack London ferry landing, Adrian watches the crowd head inside because the scrap metal company burns nonstop. That shit can't be good for any of them. He stays outside though—the quiet eases his thoughts about what he'll do alone for the summer now that his nephews can't visit him. He loves taking them to the ball game or the California Academy of Sciences museum and walking across the Golden Gate Bridge—it's the only time he's really ever on that beautiful bridge. He tells them about all the crab fishing and sea lions. And how if they look over the edge of the Golden Gate Bridge, the bay waters are deep enough for great white sharks too.

"Excuse me, how do I validate my parking?" a customer asks him, breaking his soothing trance.

"First floor, by the café," he says. "Look for the computer."

He looks back out toward the port terminals. Semi-trucks waiting for their cargo to line up under cranes. Cranes that morph into those mechanical creatures from those 1970s space films. That's what he told his nephews once they were old enough to watch those films. Dockworkers are so busy, they can't even eat lunch. He spots a few hanging out near a berth, taking a break.

Wish he could take a break. His shift doesn't end until nine. Just beyond the dockworkers, he sees a few smaller shadows running between containers. Are those children? The thought of young kids running around heavy machinery and large containers worries him. He decides to text his on-and-off-again girlfriend, Em. She's a clerk at one of the terminals. Maybe she'll call it in. Maybe not. He sends her the details anyways. He hopes it was just his tired eyes playing tricks.

The ferry picks up speed once they pass the levees. The air gets colder on the open bay water. Saltier too. Cargo ships anchored randomly in the bay, waiting their turn, their orders, or hiding stuff—drugs, stolen cars, people too—before border patrol or customs review their shipments. Across the bay, naval ships are docked near the large porcelain-looking basketball stadium. He realizes how many people forget how busy the bay waters are. The fog still creeps behind those San Francisco hills, waiting to blanket the region at night—calming everything down. Traversing under the Bay Bridge, Adrian forgets how big things are. How men constructed such wonders. And how that bridge survived a 6.9 earthquake. And they still haven't rebuilt the SF side like Oakland did. Instead, they dress it up with lights for the wealthy to look at. On the other side of that bright steel curtain is another world, a stage composed of tech and money. Skyscrapers so large, each one bulging into the sky. Tech buildings, Alcatraz, Golden Gate Bridge, Fisherman's Wharf, and the Ferry Building all come into view. They even built new condos on the once-radioactive Treasure Island to give people this multimillion-dollar view. Sometimes it's all too much for him. So he focuses on the water and his job. To ferry people back and forth. Job to home and back again. Clockwork.

Later that evening, Adrian meets Em at Jack London ferry landing. He usually can't be let out on the Oakland side, but the captain owes him a favor.

"Thanks, Em," Adrian says.

"Are you sure about what you saw?" Em asks.

Adrian stays quiet. The question sways in his body. Was he just overreacting to the conversation with his sister? That he wouldn't be able to see his nephews until late summer? Did he manifest some kids playing at the docks? No, he knows what he saw. He's confident in that. Two kids playing or maybe running around cargo containers.

"Yes," Adrian says.

Em pulls off to the side of the road a few hundred feet away from the terminal entrance. "I don't like this."

"I know what I saw," Adrian says.

"We have protocols for trespassers," Em says.

He figures that Em doesn't want to lose her job. That she'll call security regardless of the situation.

"But what if security is in on it?" Adrian says.

"They might be, but it's the right thing to do," Em says. "There'll be a record of it."

Adrian opens the door. Em follows.

"Records can be manipulated," Adrian says. "And I thought you hated Port Authority because they wouldn't reprimand one of their own for what he did to you?"

Em stops walking; she looks back at her car.

"I didn't mean to—" he says.

"But you just did," Em says, looking at the terminal. "I fucking hate Dell. They still let him work nights. Fucking creep."

"Go ahead and call it in," Adrian says. "Let's see if he's in on it. Call him."

Em pulls out her phone and puts it on speaker.

"Dispatch. Who's calling?" the phone says.

"This is Em from Oakland international terminals, berths number fifty-five to fifty-nine," Em says, looking at Adrian. "I need to get a hold of the Port Authority."

"One moment." The line cuts out and then switches over with some buzzing and proceeds to ring.

"How else can kids run around at night?" Adrian says under his breath, his hands in the air.

"Shut up!" Em says.

"Hello?" a voice on the phone says.

"Dell?" Em asks.

"Yeah, this is Dell," he says. "Who's speaking?"

"It's Em."

"Hey, how's it going, cutie?" Dell says.

Em covers the phone and mouths, *Fuck you*! She glares at Adrian. He feels like shit.

"I wanted to check if you saw anything odd on the cameras?" she asks.

"It's been quiet tonight," Dell says. "Why, what's up?"

"Oh, I was leaving the terminal, and some cars seemed to be rolling in for a sideshow down the road."

"Didn't hear anything on my end."

"Well, I thought I saw a few teens trying to hop a fence by the entrance," Em says, struggling to come up with a lie, waving her hand at Adrian to give her something. "You know, they've tried to break in before to steal stuff."

"Em, this isn't one of those fast-car films," Dell says.

Adrian places his hand over the phone's mic. "He's fucking lying."

"Is someone with you?" Dell asks.

"Yeah…um, I'm outside of a bar on the west side," Em says, shrugging.

"Which one? Maybe I'll stop by after my shift, and we can finish what we started," Dell says.

"What? No—" Em says. "It's getting loud here."

Adrian grabs the phone from Em, screams gibberish, and then spits out white noise before ending the call. "Fuck that creep."

Em walks away from Adrian. She leans against the car. He upset her with this crazy request. Adrian meets her at the car door.

"I'm sorry you had to talk to him."

"I hate that guy." She shivers.

"What do you need right now?" he asks. He can see she may not be up for this. Was he really going to break his relationship with Em over what he believes he saw?

"Show me on the map where you saw them," Em says.

Adrenaline kicks in, and he opens up Google Maps on his phone. "Over here, by the water."

"Berth number fifty-nine. I'm not surprised."

"Why's that?" he asks.

"It's near a storage area, and it's in between both terminal companies," Em says. "These companies hate each other. They sabotage containers with rotten fish or nasty oil spills near each other like a weird fuck-you. They confiscate containers when ships can't pay their fees. Most of the time, the area usually has empty containers."

"But why would there be kids there?" he asks.

"It's also a great spot to hide things." Em opens the car door and grabs something from the console. Adrian spots that she has her badge in hand, and she's strutting toward the terminal entrance. He follows quickly.

Inside the terminal, they walk to the far end of the berths, to number fifty-nine. The closer they get, the colder it gets. Water slaps at the docks. The bay waters have turned.

"You think he'll catch us on the cameras?" Adrian asks.

"Maybe, but he's probably watching porn," Em says. "Hasn't been the first time he's been caught doing it."

"Scumbag," Adrian says.

"Plus there's only one camera on this side that I can recall from the security station."

They sneak up against a container, dodging spotlights from above. The cold steel burns his hands. He wishes he had his gloves. The air is saltier as they edge closer to the water.

"Let's just hope you're—" Em says.

"Wait. You hear that?"

Adrian hears kids crying nearby. It's faint, but just enough to break through the cold breeze. Adrian takes off running toward the cries. Running between containers. The cries getting louder. The area getting darker. Colder. And closer to the water. The waves now crashing up onto the docks. The cries are closer now. There's an intensity to them, like when one of his nephews fell from their bed and he came rushing in to comfort him. He could feel his nephew's head pulsating with each cry. A bump emerging on the skull. That same bump catching his throat because he's out of breath. His limbs pulsate because he hasn't run that hard in years. He stops. A wail of a cry comes from around a container. Then the cries stop altogether. He turns around and realizes he's lost Em. In front of him, a refrigerated container hums. Spray-painted Greek letters and a fish symbol repeat themselves on the side of it. The door seems to be partially opened. He spots a small shadow near it. A neon-blue light peeks at the edges and from between the doors. The closer he gets to the figure on the ground, the more he realizes it's a child. But a much larger figure emerges from the other side of the container and holds the kid down to the ground. He's in a security uniform.

"Who are you?" Adrian asks. "Wait, are you Dell?"

"How the fuck do you know my name?"

The kid on the ground gasps for air and continues weeping. Dell shakes him to stop. The kid quiets a little.

"Stop that," Adrian says.

"You shouldn't be here," Dell says.

"There was another one," Adrian says, ignoring him.

"I said, who are you?" Dell asks.

Adrian looks around. He can't find the other kid. Maybe he went back into the container? He twists around, searching. He spots a small silhouette against the neon-blue light at the edge of the door. Cold air escapes from the container, engulfing the second child.

"What the hell is going on here?" Adrian asks. What's Dell doing to these kids? He looks at the one on the ground. "Is this man hurting you?"

The kids don't respond. They don't even receive his words. He sees the wide eyes on the one being held down by Dell. The kid must be frightened beyond anything Adrian can think of. They look dirty. Their clothes torn up with holes. The neon-blue light bathes the one peeking around the container door. He has no shirt on. What the hell is happening? Adrian sidesteps Dell and approaches the door.

"Back the fuck up," Dell says, his hand to his hip, on his gun.

Adrian continues to the container door. He's frightened for the kid. There's a sadness to him, like he's been roughed up. The face of his nephew morphs onto the kid's. Adrian shakes it off. His hands wipe his face, like *Please let this be a dream.*

"Stop." Dell draws his gun on Adrian.

Adrian freezes. He's never had a gun on him. Not even when he got mugged in Oakland a few years back. No, that time it was with a nine-inch blade up against his back as they stole his wallet, watch, and phone. He had struggled stupidly like he had a chance maybe. This was different. With the threat of a bullet a few feet away, memories with Em flooded his thoughts—them at Alameda beach, watching horror films together, their first kiss. He wondered what was preventing him from settling down.

"Everyone follows me," Dell says. He pulls at the kid's collar. "Up. Up." The kid drags his feet to stand. The other kid creeps back into the container. Back into the neon blue. Adrian steps closer to the container. His hand on the steel door. His icy fingers neon blue from the light and cold air. Just beyond, machines hiss and pop—they spit out beeps and static.

"Stop! You don't know what you're doing," Dell says.

Adrian looks back at the man holding the gun in one hand, the kid's torn collar in the other. To the left of them, an engine revs in the darkness. They both look in its direction. Bright spotlights shine on them. A forklift accelerates. Adrian pushes Dell in front of the forklift. Dell raises his gun, but it's too late. The forklift slams Dell up against another container. Dell's body sandwiched like a steel hamburger. Em hops out of the forklift.

"Corrupt piece of shit," Em yells at the meat bag. Whatever's left of Dell goes limp.

"Em," Adrian says, pulling her away from the gory mess. He turns her away from it and hugs her. "Are you okay?"

Dell groans behind them. Em steps toward him and grabs the gun from off the ground. "Are these the kids? Are they okay?" she asks Adrian.

He realizes that she's visibly upset through those words. Her lip is quivering. Her eyes are welled up. She's shook. He can't believe what Em just did to save his life. To save these kids. But these kids don't look shook at all. Instead, they're crawling slowly back to the container doors, to the neon-blue light, to the hisses, pops, and beeps of what's inside. They disappear. Adrian turns his head to Em. She glares back like *What the fuck?*

"What's inside?" Em asks.

"I don't know, but we got to get them out," Adrian says.

"No! Wait, let's call it in."

"The cops have to be paid off for this type of stuff."

"Not them," Em Says, "the fire department."

"Whatever." Adrian waves the cautionary words off to the side. He opens the container door and is immediately drenched in neon blue. The cacophony of machine noises makes it difficult to hear Em telling him to stop. One of the kids grabs his hand and walks him over to a person lying on the ground. Adrian crouches, and his hand touches the icy steel floor. He leans into the old man. He's wrinkly, dirty, and part of his head is shaved. The old man is wrapped in a thermal sleeping bag. Tubes and wires are hooked up all over the old man. Little ports all over his exposed body. Fluids pumping in and out. The tubes and wires lead to a little box emitting a neon-blue light. Adrian stares at the little box and touches a few tubes. It seems to be taking measurements and regulating the flow of the liquids. What the hell is flowing through them? He reaches for a button, but the kid stops him.

"Forces," the kid says.

Adrian doesn't understand the word the kid says. Instead, he looks around and sees twenty other old men wrapped in thermal sleeping bags and hooked up to little boxes with neon-blue lights emitting hisses and pops and static white noise. He steps forward to another man but stops short at the crunch underneath his feet. He lifts his boot and picks off a purple-onion-sized fish scale. Fish scales are littered all over the icy steel floor.

"Who are they?" Adrian asks the kid.

The child doesn't respond.

"What is this?"

The kid grabs Adrian's wrist and leads him through the container. The tubes flowing in and out of the little boxes and toward the back of the container. It gets colder. Like it's one of those foggy winter nights on the San Francisco streets. Adrian stops. He can't stop staring at the dark-blue creature propped up against the steel wall. The human-looking shape is strapped down. Arms hang off the straps, legs bound together like a fin, and its scale-like body is hooked up to all the tubes flowing from the little boxes from the old men. Neon-blue liquid flows into the creature through multiple ports.

At the front of the container, Em paces near the doors, trying to get phone reception. "What did the kid say?" Em asks.

"Forces," the other kid repeats, and runs past Em to the back of the container. Em follows the kid.

"I can't get through to the fire department for some reason," Em says.

At the back of the container, Adrian continues to glare at the dark-blue creature.

"Em, come here," Adrian says.

Em walks over and stands by his side, the phone to her ear. They both stare as the kids crouch at the bottom of the dark-blue creature. Adrian feels subtle vibrations on his skin. Vibrations from the tubes and wires coming from the figure in front of them. Em's fingers interlock with his. He can't move. He can feel her struggling as well. Their bodies are pulsating. The dark-blue creature moves fishlike. Spazzing left and right. Its eyes open, neon-blue light emits. Adrian can't stop looking. His ear twitches at the sound of the steel doors screeching to a close behind them. He still can't move. He wants to run away but can't. He wants to get closer but can't. His head won't move. Warmth drapes over him. Em mumbles something. He glances her way. Em's eyes roll into the back of her skull. He looks at the dark-blue creature. Its face now inches away from his. Its mouth opens slowly.

"I am Ceto," the creature says.

Adrian struggles, and the creature stops speaking. Adrian's ears twitch at the low primordial frequency of words. He feels liquid running from his ears.

It speaks again. "I am Ceto, wife of Phorcys, mother of Medusa. Now where is Phorcys?"

His voice is muted. His mouth dry. And Adrian can't stop looking at the creature's neon-blue eyes.

They burn his retinas.

Everything around him turns to neon blue.

The container walls turn blue.

The little boxes turn blue.

The kids turn blue.

His pulse slows.

The creature's neon-blue eyes engulf him.

His vision tunnels into the depths of the bay water like he's looking up at the Golden Gate Bridge. The outline of steel fading, blurring through the dark-blue waters. The container sways. Then it rises into the air. Stacking onto a pile of other containers. Neon blue edges their lining. Boxes among boxes. They're now just another vessel for the bay.

DEAD CALM

by Ruthie Marlenèe

Even in the calmest waters, a journey out to sea can turn deadly. Penelope's husband wanted to upgrade to a new model, a bigger, sleeker yacht, and so his plan was to travel to Point Loma to make the trade. But at four a.m., when the *Gilligan's Island* ringtone sounded in their bedroom at home, she sensed a glitch. Denny, the deckhand, wasn't going to make it on this leg of the journey. That's when she came up with a plan of her own, one last-ditch effort to salvage their marriage. *Phil will be so surprised*, she thought, throwing some things into her backpack and scrambling to be out the door before he got out of the shower. *He'll think I've gone for a run.*

At the docks in Marina Del Rey, Phil climbed aboard his boat, went into the pilothouse, flipped on the generator, and turned just as Penelope walked in from the salon carrying two cups of coffee and a box from Dunkin' Donuts. "Surprise!"

"What the fuck!" He looked surprised indeed. "What are you doing here? You tryin' to give me a heart attack?"

"You mean the donuts." She giggled. "You used to love it when I cruised along as your first mate. Said I was the best mate ever. Anyway, I don't want you going alone. It's too dangerous."

"Nothing I haven't done before."

"Even brought my deck knife," she said, jutting a hip forward to show him the "gift of steel" you give your spouse when it's your eleventh anniversary. She'd given him the Rolex Submariner because his older model

179

didn't have the Rolex crown featured at six o'clock, which he said made all the difference.

He looked at his watch, his lips pursing tight, his nostrils flaring. The impatient look he gave her more and more lately. "There's no time to argue," he said, eyeing the donuts. "Go handle the lines."

They should have been farther along past San Pedro, but even the best-laid plans go awry, like Denny flaking or the plan to love and cherish each other till death do us part. The plan had been to leave just before sunrise and return before nightfall with the new 101-foot Italian Arno Leopard that had been shipped across the Atlantic to Florida and then delivered via Ensenada to the marina in Point Loma. Phil hadn't figured on spending so much time coaxing half a dozen stinky sea lions off the boat deck before departing. Domesticated, the lions acted as if they owned the place. A big, fat bull held out, barking at her, reminding Penelope of someone she lived with. She felt the pain as her husband jabbed at the animal hard with a boat hook until it roared and slithered into the water.

"Penny, what's taking you? Quick, pull the fenders," he yelled. "Let's get the hell out of here!"

What's the hurry? And suddenly she remembered the main reason she didn't like coming along. The second reason was that she really never liked the ocean, except to look at it from the shore. Rather, she was afraid of it ever since she'd gone on a fishing trip with her dad when she was a little girl. The fishing boat had rocked from side to side on choppy seas. She thought she'd throw up, but then her dad, excited to reel in a stupid fish, accidentally knocked her overboard. No floaties or life vest. The shock of the frigid water was as sobering as the thought of dying. Of course, Dad had dived in to save her from drowning, but still. She'd swallowed an ocean of water that she threw up all over the deck. The nightmares still haunted her.

Now, she would suck it up for Phil in an attempt to resuscitate their dead marriage. Always a quiet, studious type, she was terrified of a lot of things, people, and places. But Phil had always urged her to face her fears, and she used to love how he challenged her. Oh, she even learned to swim all right, and had taken a basic safety-training course for boaters, but out in the ocean, you were always in the deep end with no shallow places to stand. Out here in the middle of the sea in a midlife crisis, the waters could turn violent. You might get too tired, and you might drown before you ever made it to shore.

When she'd first met Phil, he wasn't yet into yachting. He was a sandy-haired surfer turned Realtor into flipping real estate; she, a landscape designer into flipping soil—the soil of her Indigenous roots, the land of the Tongva. His office had hired her to design a small garden with low native plants that wouldn't block the view from one of the Santa Monica properties he'd scooped up. He loved that she wasn't afraid of getting dirty. She loved how he talked dirty during their lovemaking.

The sun scratched its way up over the Los Angeles International Airport. Funny how the rising sun made even the El Segundo Refinery look luminescent as the sun splayed its hand, sending fiery-fingered claw marks across the South Bay like the claw marks she'd left on his back, the kind of rough sex he used to relish with her. She slipped on her aviator sunglasses and then took a sip of sour-tasting coffee from Dunkin's that by now had cooled just like her marriage. *If only I could get the sun to shine on me like that every morning*, she thought, *maybe then he wouldn't notice my flaws. Maybe, he'd want me.*

She'd always considered herself a sort of plain-Juana-looking type; a "blank, tawny canvas," her grandmother used to say. Tomboyish, she was athletically toned; her best features were her arms and long legs. She had a farmer's tan from living in her T-shirt and jean cutoffs. She didn't like to wear makeup, but when she had to, she could clean up nicely, like she had their first time.

One balmy evening after an open house event in Mar Vista, she'd shown up just as Phil was locking up. In a casual, flowery summer dress with just a swipe of raspberry lip gloss across her canvas, she'd brushed out her long hair, usually in a ponytail or braid, until it gleamed like deeply polished teak. She felt him watching her as she sashayed through, pretending to own the place, straight out into the backyard garden he'd hired her to design. This is the one. *It's time*, she thought, sprinkling some wilting purple begonias while scanning her creation filled with pygmy date palms, olive trees, and snake cholla. All that was missing was the proverbial apple tree.

Startled when he came up behind her, she'd turned and accidentally hosed him down. Snatching the garden hose from her, he sprayed her back, quickly apologizing and offering to run in to get her a towel. But when she started drowning in his ocean-colored eyes, she latched onto his lips as if his mouth were a life preserver, the taste of peppermint on his tongue, such a classic salesman's tool. "There are three bedrooms inside," he offered, but instead she lured him farther into the garden she'd created.

Still wet, they'd slipped and slid and slithered over each other until they ended up wrestling playfully in the mud, and then they landed on a small patch of lawn where they tugged at each other's clothing, exposing those parts that hadn't yet been soiled. "You like it nasty, you little temptress," he whispered, tugging her hair. "You little freakin' flora, fucking fauna." Her whole body convulsing as she fumbled with his pants zipper.

And as the moon shown through a fog blanket of twinkling stars, the smell of earth in her nostrils, the feel of him inside, her nails digging into his back, she knew she'd finally found a home and a garden for them both. "I plan to buy this place," she whispered into his clay-caked ear.

Her offer was accepted almost immediately.

But then years into a marriage she'd invested in, a relationship she'd nurtured, the passion started to die, their intimacy never growing into anything more than a garden of dandelions. She couldn't understand the change in him, the sudden bursts of anger. Her hands would become calloused trying to pull all the weeds, but Phil's clients would never find so much as a speck of earth beneath his manicured nails.

Penelope stuck her cup into the small galley microwave to heat it up and then joined him up in the pilothouse, where she rested a hand on his shoulder, flooded suddenly with ideas about putting the boat on autopilot. She remembered, when the boat was new, the thrill of making love on the bow's sun pad as they bounced along—the boat on autopilot at six knots. She gave him a tender squeeze now, and he shrugged her off, leaving her with erotic thoughts that drifted off in bubbles out beyond the hypnotic horizon, across the shimmering swathes of sunlight and into the sky. She sipped her soured coffee and wondered why he needed a new yacht. But the bigger question was, how could he afford a bigger one? The Los Angeles real estate market sales had sunk because of a severe shortage of homes for sale, but Phil was buying a new boat? *What next, a newer model of me?*

Now, she wished she'd stayed home—the newer, bigger one he'd bought in Playa Del Rey—to dig around in her garden, a new design of indigenous plants that really didn't need much tending or water. She'd named her plants as if they were her children—according to Phil, the time was never right to have kids. Phil, she'd named one of the heartier, thorny plants that wouldn't hurt you unless you got too close. Really, she should have stayed home to study some more for an upcoming continuing education exam in order to maintain her landscape license, but here she was at six thirty in the morning, cruising along in the Hampton as they rounded the bend where multimillion-dollar homes perched precariously along the cliffs, where the Point Vicente Lighthouse flashed night and day. But even with so much light, she felt lost at sea without a compass home.

And then, through a straggling patch of morning fog, a cluster of colorful Mylar balloons bobbed along like hungover party girls, reminding her of the party she'd thrown for him last Saturday. He'd gotten so drunk. That was his excuse for leaving with the stripper one of his buddies had hired for his forty-fifth. Unbelievable to think that in this day and age of #MeToo, this was still happening. Boys will be boys. And girls will be girls, too, she knew. He'd apologized. He was drunk. It didn't mean anything. *We might have had more fun had he invited me along.* Yes, Phil's little woman, still in her prime, his little "squaw" had always been a trooper—a good sport—like now as she acted more like a first mate than his playmate.

Here she was sitting at the helm, already nauseous from the smell of diesel and a bit groggier than usual from the seasick patch she'd put on earlier. Clammy, needing air, she walked out onto the catwalk on the port side and inhaled a deep breath of clean salt air, the sea spray like a gentle lover's kisses on a restless brow.

Full of promise, it was the stunning sort of morning a bride might like for her wedding day or a sailor would like for a day of sailing, or an old person might like for their funeral. Denny, Phil's surfing buddy from Santa Monica High, had certainly missed out on this journey, citing something about "personal matters," Phil had told her. Probably, more like *Mutiny on the Bounty*, she thought, at once recalling Elias, the yacht broker Denny had brought along to Phil's party. He'd reminded her of a steamy Marlon Brando with his earthy, chocolate-colored eyes. Visceral and ominous with wavy, dark hair combed back and a broad, muscular chest with the iconic macho chest hairs bulging out of a Hawaiian Reyn Spooner shirt, he'd shaken her hand and taken her breath away like a rogue gust of Old Spice–scented trade wind.

She breathed in now as if she could conjure up his smell again. Instead, she whiffed something different about Elias, as if he'd been trying too hard to look like someone he wasn't—like a cross between Simon, the car salesman in *True Lies*, and maybe Christian Fletcher. Oh, she wouldn't have minded taking the Elias character as a lover like they do in those romance novels. She wouldn't mind letting him fuck her blind while whispering dirty sweet nothings in her ear. And then she remembered that striptease scene in *True Lies* with Jamie Lee Curtis. She imagined herself role-playing, like she used to before they were married. Or maybe he was more like that *Pirates of Caribbean* actor, before he was accused of spousal abuse.

Shaking her head to clear it, she walked back in and took her place next to her husband. "Water is dead calm," he said. "Should be smooth sailing. Looks like we'll pull into port on time, after all." She sat straight as a fishing rod, blinking like a nighttime buoy and trying to focus. "Just like I charted," he said, swelling his chest, all puffed up like a blowfish.

"Looks like…" she answered quietly, staring out toward land. "Just like you charted." Of course, he's always right. Out here, without her land legs she felt vulnerable, crippled, at the mercy of the sea and her husband. They'd been drifting apart, like a boat without a rudder and nothing to anchor her. No one to make her feel she was enough. No purpose—just floating along until life's final pull of gravity brought her home. The effects of the scopolamine were really getting to her. She could barely keep her eyes open and couldn't help nodding off in her chair. She was plummeting to the bottom, to the dead calm.

They were just passing Angels Gate at the entrance to the Port of Los Angeles. "I've got this. Why don't you go down and take a nap?" Phil said. "You're no good to me zoned out."

I'm no good to you awake. She staggered down to the main stateroom and plopped onto the bed, but not before pushing a heavy, khaki-colored duffel bag to the floor. *What's he got in there? A dead body?* She chuckled, too tired to even care to open it—sleep was calling her. But she opened it anyway. It was full of cash, cold hard cash, in bundles of hundreds. *For the new boat?* she wondered before passing out.

Her eyes sprang open to the sound of an alarm and then a sudden decrease in speed. Dizzy, she climbed up to find Phil on his phone, studying the radar. She rubbed her eyes, noting the time on the screen was a few minutes past noon, and they were just about ten miles off Encinitas. They'd been making good time at eighteen knots.

"We lost an engine," he said into the phone. "We'll have to limp in on only one the rest of the way."

She peered a little closer at the radar, and then she noticed a mark, a spot like a mote in her eye that needed casting out. She pointed. "What's that?"

He narrowed his eyes, scrunching his brow into the shape of an 11. "Probably just a speck of dirt."

She wet her finger with her tongue and then tried to wipe off the smudge. "Well looks like that piece of dirt is going to cross the bow starboard side pretty soon," she said.

"Not sure."

Batting her eyes, she shook her head and then reached for the binoculars. Adjusting the focus wheel until everything became just a little more clear. "It looks like a panga boat," she said, her heart pounding. She'd seen them before, heard about them. She knew that meant drug runners, harmless for the most part with only the goal of delivery on their mind, but they seemed to be headed toward them. Her husband pulled back on the throttle even more.

"Why are you slowing down?" she asked.

With a look of determination, he answered her. "I'm going to let them cross."

She was confused and growing more nervous. When the little boat got closer and it didn't look like they'd cross the bow, Phil waved them off.

"Go down and hide," he told her.

"What? Why?"

"Just do it!"

She knew he kept a Glock 19 handgun in a drawer behind the sink in the head. She rushed down, and that's when she noticed the duffel bag was gone. She grabbed the gun, and then as she ascended the steps, she heard the annoying *Gilligan's Island* ringtone on his cell phone. "Got it," Phil said into the phone and then quickly throttled up, causing her to crash-land back onto the floor.

"What's going on?" she asked, rubbing her sore hip as she returned to the pilothouse, holding the gun.

"Nothing. Put that away."

She'd put the gun away when she went back down, she thought, as she looked back to see the little boat rocking back and forth behind in their wake. But then, there on the table on the aft deck sat the duffel bag.

Only twelve miles left to Point Loma, and the stupid *Gilligan* theme song sounded again on Phil's cell phone. "Tomorrow. Got it," he said, and she suddenly recalled the first time she heard that ringtone.

She'd prepared a romantic anniversary dinner at home one evening and they were seated at the dining table when Phil's phone rang. She thought Denny's ringtone was so cliché. "I need to take this call," Phil said, pulling away from the table. "Business." The dinner got cold. She had finished the bottle of Champagne by herself.

Without taking his eyes off the horizon, he told her, "Change in plans."

Even the best-laid plans.

As they pulled into Point Loma, he slowed the boat to idle in front of the Best Western. "I got you a room at the hotel," he told her. "I've got it from here. Besides, there'll be others at the dock to help me bring her in." He cleared his throat. "Seems things are running just a little behind with all the paperwork. I'll stay aboard tonight," he said. "Get a good night's rest, and I'll see you in the morning." He pulled up to an end tie at the side of the dock. She picked up the gun to take down and put away, but for some reason, she stuffed it into her pack. *He won't be needing it in the safety of the harbor.*

She was glad to be back on land, and when he phoned her early the next morning to let her know the plans had changed again—something about the weather and the need for more training on the electronics and that they'd try again later that night. Now, she'd get to linger a little longer, get a late checkout, and perhaps take a run. The hotel on Shelter Island was the closest she'd been to a vacation for a long time, even if she was alone.

Rifling through her pack for her running shorts, she felt the gun. *How stupid. I should have left it.* She put on her running shoes and hit the trail along the marina, a border between what she loved, the flora and fauna of the land, and what she feared the most, just about everything to do with the ocean. Hibiscus and fragrant tuberose dotted the path. Purple morning glory trailed along the tennis fence. She cheered up a bit as she passed a row of birds of paradise with their orange-colored Mohawks and violet tongues sticking out at her. The tall jelly palms and squat sago and pygmy date palms—so many things in life and on land to love.

Looking out toward the water, she chuckled at the clever names of some of the boats moored along the docks. *Fishy Business*, *The Cod Father*, *Baits Motel*, *Forget-Me-Knot*, *Knot Again*, and *Lady Kriller*. Phil had used their first initials to christen their boat *Two Peas in a Pod*, but they were nothing alike and, more and more lately, had nothing in common.

The boatyard was within walking distance, and so after her run and a shower, without waiting for his call, she decided to head on over. She clipped her deckhand knife onto her jeans, grabbed her backpack and then left her room. Only a hundred yards away, Penelope looked up and gasped. There she loomed, his latest lover, so dazzling in the sun, all 101 feet of her screaming sexy in a Sophia Loren sort of way, her engines already purring. Penelope noticed a couple of men standing at the helm, and then she heard Phil's ringtone on her phone.

"I'm here at the bank," she heard him say, but she could clearly see him standing on the bow, practically yelling. "There was trouble with the wire transfer." *Who yells in a bank? Trouble with the wire? So, what was that duffel bag full of cash for?* "We'll need to push things off until tomorrow. I'll let you know. In the meanwhile, I got you another night at the hotel."

She watched Phil go back into the cockpit, and when Denny, the deckhand, stepped out onto the deck, she was confounded. *What's he doing here?* And then, he climbed down onto the dock to unplug the shore tie. *Why's he doing that?* Back on the aft side of the deck, he pulled the lines aboard before heading up to pull the lines from the bow. Within minutes, the yacht started slipping away. *They're leaving—without me!*

Penelope ran up and jumped onto the swim step and then tried to open the tender garage behind the Jet Ski to hide, but it was locked.

Phil, Denny, and another dark-haired man were in the cockpit, settled into creamy leather, snakeskin-striped, racing-style bucket seats. Everything was so bright, even all the high-gloss acrylic paneling, including the ceiling, was shock white. She didn't think anyone noticed as she stepped into the main cabin and then down into the crew's quarters, where she took a seat on a bottom bunk. What was her plan? She looked up when she saw the shadow of someone coming down the steps, and she jumped up quickly to hide behind the door, where she took a peek.

It was Elias, the yacht salesman from last Saturday, the man she wouldn't have minded taking as a lover. What was he doing here? Her heart raced, and then the door swung open, smacking her on the forehead. He had his hand over her mouth before she could even think about screaming. "You shouldn't be here," he said, duct-taping her mouth as she kicked and punched before he taped her hands behind her back and then her feet. He then laid her down gently onto the bunk. "I'm so sorry to do this, Penelope." *He remembered my name.*

As he walked away, memories of the birthday party bubbled to the surface. She'd watched her husband leave the party with a stripper. Elias walked up and handed her a drink. "If you were my wife, I'd never leave you." He kept her company for a while as she waited for her husband's return, but as the sun came up, Phil was still a no show. Elias had been so kind, the kind of man she might have taken as a lover—if she'd been a heroine in a romance novel, or if she hadn't been married.

And then she heard Elias on the phone. "All systems go…we'll wait until we're out in open water…too dangerous on the dock…didn't want to risk any civilian casualties…collateral damage… wife's onboard. She's not a part of this."

He went back up to join the other men.

Hands tied behind her back, she felt for her deck knife and then finally sliced the duct tape before ripping it off from her mouth. *Who carries around duct tape?* She unzipped her backpack and pulled out the Glock.

The yacht was already out into the ocean, smooth as glass, just past the point when she snuck up on them, brandishing the gun and then pointing it at a surprised-looking Elias.

"What the fuck!" Phil yelled.

"Put the gun down," Elias said.

"Do as he says, Penelope," Phil yelled. She stood there frozen as an iceberg. Phil's eyes widened. "Bitch, you ratted me out!"

"I don't know what you're talking about," she said.

She heard someone from behind her yell, "Ma'am, drop the weapon and put your hands up!"

Before she could look, Phil had grabbed her, twisting her around and using her as a human shield.

"Phil, let her go," Elias said.

Confusion, like jetsam and flotsam, swirled in her brain as she stared into the faces of a bunch of Coast Guard officers in orange life vests standing in the salon, guns drawn, Denny, facedown on the ground, hands cuffed behind him as more Coasties and DEA agents swarmed the entire yacht. In the distance, the sound of sirens and helos getting louder.

Mind muddled, she did as she was told and dropped the gun. Phil quickly reached down to get it and then seized her by the ponytail, wrenching her into him, gun pointed now at her temple as he scooted out onto the deck. She grabbed her deck knife and stabbed him in the side.

A shot fired and Phil fell back, releasing her—the last time he'd ever yank her hair again—as he staggered toward the edge. She watched him fall overboard and remembered falling overboard as a little girl—*the shock of the frigid water as sobering as the thought of dying.* Out of the corner of her eye, she saw Elias holding a gun with a clear shot from where he stood. A Coastie immediately dove in to try and rescue Phil. Tasting bile, she licked her dry lips before emanating a scream. And just like the hero in one of those romance novels, Elias was there to catch her as her knees buckled. Gently, he set her down.

Her husband's dead body was recovered just before sunset.

Unfathomably dead calm, she watched the red and blue lights flashing all around as more law enforcement agents boarded to extract the bales of weed and bundles of cocaine and fentanyl stored to the gills in every nook and cranny of the yacht. How the vessel had cleared customs when it entered the marina was a mystery. And then she wondered about that bag of cash.

Helicopters hovered outside, their noisy blades whipping up an ocean meringue as Penelope stared out across the horizon in utter disbelief. She turned to see the lighthouse lighting the way—*a beacon of despair?*

Elias came up next to her. *I knew it.* "You're not a yacht broker, after all, Elias, or is that even your name?"

"It is. Your husband's been running drugs for some time, had a distribution going with Denny out of Del Rey. Even had a little job lined up on the way down to pick up the new boat, but with you on board, they had to abort the plan, especially after the stuff he'd slipped into your coffee wore off."

"What? Are you fucking kidding me?" *Who did I even marry?* "And during the light of day, really?"

"It's a twenty-four seven operation."

"You might have told me you were DEA before duct-taping me." *And then maybe I might have pretended this was all just another silly game. I could have stayed out of the way. My husband might still be alive.*

"Sorry." His lips smiled a small apology, and then he took her elbow to help her off the vessel back onto the land.

He was the kind of man she wouldn't mind taking as a lover if she'd been a heroine in a romance novel or—or, if she hadn't been married.

"Till death do us part," she whispered as the sun set, blazing as spectacular as her future plans, buoyed now by a fresh outlook back on land.

THE ART OF OBLIVION

by Leanne Phillips

Lydia opened her eyes. It was painful, this wrenching of herself out of heavy, dreamless sleep. She was confused, wasn't sure what woke her up, but when her surroundings came into focus, she saw the child standing in the corner of the room. A young girl—pale, skinny, staring. Always staring. Lydia closed her eyes and turned over, put her back between them. She buried her face in her pillow and had just dozed off again when the girl touched her shoulder. Lydia startled, then reached up and over and brushed the girl's hand away.

"Mom," the girl said. "Mom, it's time to get up. Dinner's ready."

"I'm not hungry," Lydia said.

The girl shook her then, softly at first, then with more urgency. "Mom. Wake up, Mom. Are you okay?"

Lydia willed herself awake and turned to look at her daughter. Rae. A barefoot, twelve-year-old girl in faded, thrift-store blue jeans and a baggy Foo Fighters sweatshirt. Rae had been born her daughter, but she was nothing like her. The girl had long, tangled, red hair that needed to be combed and James's gray-blue eyes. Rae's eyes reminded Lydia of things she didn't want to remember. Every time Lydia looked into her daughter's eyes, she felt a slight storm beginning to brew in the pit of her stomach.

There was concern in Rae's eyes now, but rather than comforting her, it made Lydia feel uneasy. "Stop trying to mother me," Lydia said. "Don't you have homework to do?"

"It's Saturday."

"Well, go play, then. Why don't you ever go outside and play?"

"I'm in junior high, Mom. I don't play outside anymore." Rae didn't budge. Didn't she have any girlfriends? Any place to be on a Saturday?

Rae was nothing like Lydia, but Lydia recognized James in her. After five years, Lydia still missed James. Her heart was still broken. Life had been perfect once, but it never would be again. Sometimes Lydia tried to force herself to look directly into Rae's eyes to see if she could feel something besides pain, but she always chickened out and looked away. She would do anything to avoid the pain. She did everything to avoid the pain.

The tinny sounds of the cheap clock radio on her nightstand drifted into her awareness. Classic rock from the sixties, a song about time and seasons and loving. *You promised me things, James.* Lydia sat up. "Will you please turn that off?" she asked. "I have a headache." She'd fallen asleep in her clothes. She pulled the sleeves of her sweater down to cover her arms, out of habit, then began rocking slowly—forward, backward, forward—and rubbing her arms to battle the constant sensation of being cold. Rae turned the radio off.

"Come on, Mom," she said. "You need to eat something."

"I'm not hungry," Lydia said again. She let out a heavy breath. "I'll be out in a minute. Just give me a minute." Rae turned to leave the room. "Shut the door," Lydia called after her. She felt the sickness creeping up on her. She rummaged in the nightstand drawer for her kit and went into the adjoining bathroom.

In the bathroom, Lydia tied off her left arm with a thin belt she kept under the sink. She opened a piece of foil and shook out the tiny bit of powder she had left onto a spoon, added a few drops of warm water from the tap, then heated the spoon over the flame of a blue plastic lighter until the liquid turned amber in color and bubbled. *This won't be enough.* It would keep her well for a couple of hours, maybe three, just long enough to make some tips at the bar and score. She placed a tiny piece of cotton onto the spoon, positioned the needle on top of it, and drew the liquid up into the syringe. When the spoon was empty, she laid the needle flat against her skin and carefully pierced a vein, then injected the liquid into it. She sat down on the bathroom floor, sank her back against the bathtub, drew her knees up against her chest. She let the warmth flood her body. The medicine pushed out the nausea and the aches that reached all the way through her muscles and into her bones. The effect was immediate. It pushed out the pain, too. All the pain.

Lydia sat on the floor, dozing in and out of consciousness for what felt like both minutes and an eternity. She never knew how long she spent in that state; she had stopped keeping track of time in any ordinary sense. When she was lucid enough, Lydia got up and changed clothes. She put on a clean T-shirt, pulled on a pair of jeans, tennis shoes, then a sweater to cover the track marks on her arms. Standing in front of the bathroom mirror, she ran her fingers through her hair and applied dark lipstick—a shade so purple it was almost black. Lydia barely recognized the woman staring back at her from the glass. The girl James had fallen in love with was in there somewhere, but she couldn't see her anymore.

* * *

When Lydia walked into the living room, Rae was watching a rerun of *Little House on the Prairie*, a half-eaten plate of spaghetti on the coffee table in front of her. She jumped up when she saw Lydia.

"Here you go, Mom," Rae said. She led Lydia into the kitchen. "I made spaghetti." Rae pointed Lydia to a place at the kitchen table and frowned. "It's probably cold now."

"It's fine," Lydia said. "Thank you." She sat down at the kitchen table. Rae brought her plate in from the living room and sat down across from Lydia. "Thank you," Lydia said again. "You didn't have to do this." Saying this was a formality. Of course Rae had to do this. Rae had been doing most of the cooking and cleaning for at least three or four years.

Rae was studying Lydia's face. Rae was always looking at her. Lydia felt like Rae was trying to figure her out. It was a creepy feeling, and it had only intensified since Lydia overdosed the month before and ended up in the hospital for a few days, her lungs filled with fluid. A neighbor and fellow junkie had checked in on Rae for her. The neighbor told Rae that Lydia had a bad flu and didn't want visitors, because she was contagious. Sometimes, like now, Lydia was almost certain Rae knew the truth.

"I'm okay." Lydia tried to reassure Rae, to answer her unspoken question. Moments like this, Lydia wanted to be better, to be stronger, to know this girl and to love her, but she'd let too much distance build up between them for too long. She barely remembered how it had started. She'd loved Rae fiercely when she was born, when she was a baby, when she was a little girl. As a child, Rae had a brave and vibrant spirit that Lydia both admired and envied. But after James died, Lydia had been too wrapped up in grief, or something, to feel much of anything except deprived of air. She began to feel…not animosity, but indifference. When she noticed how much Rae's eyes had taken on the same gray-blue shade as James's, her indifference changed to annoyance. When she noticed how James's mannerisms and his half smile seemed reincarnated in Rae, her annoyance evolved into something more adversarial. The child was a constant reminder of James, of better and happier times. That was it, wasn't it? Some days Lydia couldn't stand the sight of Rae. She continued to provide her with the bare essentials and a modicum of affection, but other than that, she felt numb inside.

The more self-sufficient the girl had become, the more the distance had grown between them. Rae would be an adult in a few more years. She would leave home, go out into the world, and make her own mistakes. *I left home when I was seventeen, and I have never looked back. You will do the same.* Soon, there would be nothing tying them together. Lydia was ashamed of how urgently she looked forward to being alone.

"I'm okay, I promise," she said again. She didn't know what else to say. Lydia ate a few bites of spaghetti, then carried her plate to the kitchen sink and began rinsing it into the garbage disposal.

"Hey, Mom? Who is Ruth?" Rae asked.

Lydia turned off the kitchen faucet and picked up a bar towel from the counter—she'd swiped a few from work. She dried her hands, her back still to Rae.

"What?" she asked, partly because she thought she couldn't possibly have heard Rae right and partly to buy time. When she was ready, she turned around.

"You got a letter from a lady named Ruth. Ruth Evans. It came this morning." Rae walked over to the kitchen counter and picked up an envelope, then handed it to Lydia.

"Who is she?" Rae asked.

Rae hadn't opened the letter. It was still sealed. And she didn't remember. Thank God.

"Her address is in Coronado. Isn't that where we used to live?"

"Yes," Lydia said. "She's an old friend. I'll tell you about her later, okay? I've got to get to work now." Lydia went into her bedroom and closed the door behind her. She sat down on the edge of the bed and stared at the envelope. She ran a finger over the lettering and the postmark. It felt strange to think this object in her hand, the ink she was touching, had been in San Diego a few days before and had traveled all the way up the coast of California to get to her here in Santa Cruz. *How did you find me?* Lydia was afraid to open the letter. She'd lied to Ruth about where they were going. She'd promised Ruth she would contact her when they were settled. She never had. Instead, she'd changed their last name and tried to pretend her life in San Diego was a sad dream. It was a horrible thing to have done. She had let James down in so many ways. But then, James had let her down, too, hadn't he?

Lydia put the letter in her nightstand drawer, unopened, tucked it in under her kit. She picked up her purse from the dresser and went back out into the living room.

"I'm going to work," she said. "I won't be too late." Lydia closed the front door behind her and began the walk downtown. As always, her ghosts followed her.

* * *

The bar was nearly empty when Lydia got there. Just a local barfly and what looked to be a new boyfriend shooting pool in the far back corner and a couple of guys playing darts in the front of the house. She'd lied to Rae— her shift didn't start for an hour. She sat on a stool at the end of the bar. Without speaking, the bartender splashed several fingers of cheap well vodka into a rocks glass and slid it toward her. "Thanks, Jack," Lydia said. She'd have preferred a bottled beer, but the owner inventoried the bottles, and clear alcohol was less noticeable on her breath. This would have to keep the edge off until her dealer got here.

A local rock cover band was loading in behind the bar's small stage. Lydia gave the drummer a slight nod. Luke. She'd slept with him a few times. She turned her back to him and fixated on her drink and the wall behind the bar. Tonight, she found Luke's loud banter with his bandmates annoying.

Lydia took a long pull from her glass and looked around the dive bar she'd worked at for five years now. Santa Cruz suited Lydia—that's why she'd come back. The funky beach town of Santa Cruz proper abutted a steel-gray ocean, but the county of Santa Cruz stretched itself up into the mountains and through thick redwood forests, like fingers weaving their way through tangled hair. The towns became more untamed and more anonymous the higher they reached—Pasatiempo, Zayante, Bonny Doon, Ben Lomond. Old logging camps, mining towns, sawmill operations. Janis Joplin and her band used to jam up in Lompico, and Jerry Garcia once lost a finger chopping wood there. San Francisco's backyard neighbor. Home.

Lydia had run away from Flagstaff to Santa Cruz when she was a teenager. It was a place where her family would never think to look—they'd lived in a dozen different places and several different states in between here and there. She'd come here with her brothers sometimes, when she was eleven or twelve. Her brothers hawked the fruits and vegetables her father stole from a ranch in Salinas while she played on the beach and ran around the boardwalk. It was the only place she'd ever felt free—an hour and a county away from her abusive father and her dishrag of a mother. Here, she'd been allowed to run wild but was still close enough to her big brothers to feel safe. They had their own problems, though, and as they got older, they didn't have time for her. Now, she didn't have time for them. Not anymore.

Increasing noise made its way into Lydia's consciousness, voices growing louder. It was the couple at the pool table, arguing.

"I swear to God, Dottie, if you don't give me my shit, I'm going to kill you."

"I don't have your shit. I don't have anything that belongs to you."

"Hand it over, bitch, before I get mad." He moved in closer to Dottie.

"You better back off, Freddie." She talked as if she was in control of the situation. Confident. Arrogant, even. Dottie didn't seem to be as afraid as Lydia thought she should be.

"Hey," Jack called across the bar. "You two, knock it off."

"You've got five seconds," Freddie said. He was right up in Dottie's face now. "One Mississippi. Two Mississippi—"

"Oh, get over yourself," Dottie said. "You ain't nobody."

Jack started coming around the bar. Lydia felt the familiar storm churning in her gut.

"Three Mississippi. Four Mississippi."

"It ain't my fault you can't keep track of your own shit."

"Five."

"Fuck you."

Freddie spat at Dottie, then pushed her up against the wall and punched her in the face—right, left, right. Lydia heard a voice raging across the bar, "Stop it! Stop it, you son of a bitch!" She left her barstool and ran toward the couple—she beat Jack there. When she stopped in front of them, she realized the screams had been her own. The rage had been her own—the storm had finally blown free. Lydia stood before the couple, shaking and breathless, fists clenched. "You're eighty-sixed," she told the man. "Get the fuck out of here and don't come back."

Lydia felt tears in her eyes, angry tears. By now, the bouncer was at her side. He pushed the man toward the door, but no one was watching that. They were all staring at Lydia—Luke, Jack, the guys who'd been throwing darts. Jack came to first and went over to Dottie, who was crumpled on the floor next to the pool table. "Fuck that son of a bitch," she said. "I don't give a fuck." Her eyes were already swelling, and blood was gushing from her nose. Jack pulled a bar towel from his back pocket and began mopping her face. "Fuck you!" Dottie yelled at Freddie's retreating back.

Lydia turned away then, still awash with so much rage she felt sick. She went into the bathroom and threw up, then rinsed her face in the sink and tried to calm down enough to start work. She felt an old discomfort all night while she worked her shift, familiar, but she couldn't quite place it. She was hyperaware, on edge, cold. Her dealer showed up around ten o'clock, and the dose helped, but not as much as it usually did.

* * *

At the end of the night, when the band was breaking down, Lydia took a pitcher of beer and a stack of pint glasses over to them. "On the house," she said. She brushed up against Luke, intentionally. He turned and looked at her, then at the pitcher in her hand.

"Thanks," he said. He took the pitcher and the glasses and set them on a table next to the stage. He poured himself a beer, tilting the glass to control the foam.

"You're welcome," she said. Then, before he had time to look up from his beer: "Want some company tonight?"

Luke looked up, and she tried to meet his eyes. He didn't answer right away. He thought she was a weird one. He'd told her so. Tonight was a prime example—she'd ignored him all night, and now here she was. But Lydia suspected the fact she wasn't all over him like some of the other women at the bar was one of the things he liked about her. He shrugged. "Sure, why not," he said. "Let me finish packing up."

"Okay," she said. She hadn't been sure he'd say yes. But then, the fact Luke could take her or leave her was one of the things she liked about him. She was glad to go home with him tonight. Sex had become another sedative.

* * *

The sun was up by the time Lydia got back to the apartment. Rae was in the kitchen making pancakes. Rae had learned to take care of herself early on. When she was about nine years old, Rae began trying to take care of Lydia, too. Looking at her daughter now, Lydia felt the pain of her own selfishness, perhaps the biggest source of the pain she fought so hard to avoid. She tried not to imagine what James would think of her now. He had been sweet to her in the beginning. She'd held on to that sweetness to get her through the days and the hours, to allow herself to miss him and to grieve. *If*

200

you were still alive, would you still love me? How could he, knowing what she had become, knowing how she'd abandoned their child? Lydia twisted and picked at her shame until it became anger. He had abandoned her. He had abandoned them both. When she allowed herself these thoughts, she couldn't help wondering what kind of father James would have been. Would he have continued to dote on Rae, liked he'd once doted on Lydia? Would he have hurt Rae, too?

"Do you want some pancakes?" Rae asked Lydia now. "Or some toast?"

"No, thanks," Lydia said.

"I can make you some eggs if you want. Or oatmeal."

"That's okay."

"You didn't come home last night," Rae said. It was matter-of-fact. Rae didn't sound accusatory or critical or angry. She never did.

Lydia ignored the statement. "I'm going to bed."

"Are you okay, Mom?" Rae asked. "Have you had anything to eat?"

"Jesus, Rae!" Lydia said. The girl stood there, silent and stunned by the rare invocation of her name. Lydia was shaking—she felt as if something she'd kept under lock and key for five years—no, longer—was trying to fight its way out. Had already emerged and was demanding to be freed. Was refusing to be pushed back down. She took a deep breath and forced herself to soften then, tried to be the thing she was supposed to be. "I'm sorry, Rae," she said. "I'm just really tired. It was a long night. I'm fine. I ate breakfast downtown." Then, "Have a good day at school." That's what mothers said.

"It's Sunday," Rae said.

* * *

When Lydia woke up, it was late afternoon. The kitchen was dark. The living room was dark, too, except for the dim light emanating from a lamp on the end table and a strip of fading sunlight coming through a crack in the heavy drapes. *She must still be at school.* Then she saw Rae's math book and a worn paperback copy of *The Witch of Blackbird Pond* on the coffee table and remembered it was Sunday. Lydia's day off. She was about to go into the kitchen when she heard a sound coming from Rae's bedroom. She walked toward the sound, fighting through a light fog in her brain. *Maybe I'll take her out for a hamburger and fries. And a milkshake. She'd like that.* She tried to remember the last time she'd taken her daughter out for dinner, but she couldn't remember anything since she'd taken Rae out for her twelfth birthday eight months before.

When she got closer to Rae's bedroom door, Lydia could hear Rae sobbing. Rae, who never cried, not even when she'd fallen off a skateboard last summer and taken the skin off an elbow and both knees. Lydia hesitated, then opened the door. Rae startled when she saw her mother standing in the doorway. She was sitting cross-legged on the floor at the foot of her bed, a sharp pocketknife in her right hand—*Where did she get a pocketknife?* Tears were running down Rae's face, and blood was running from a deep gash in her left arm. The blood was soaking into a bar towel on Rae's lap.

"Jesus!" Lydia bridged the distance to Rae in three quick steps and took the knife from her hand. The towel was almost saturated, and there was nothing else nearby to stop the blood. At a loss, Lydia tugged at the corner of Rae's thin, pink bedspread and wound it around Rae's arm. "Hold this tight on your arm and stay here," she said. She looked directly into Rae's eyes, gray-blue pools of tears and pleading.

"I'm okay, Mom," Rae said. "I'm sorry. It's okay."

"Don't move," Lydia said. "Don't move. I'm going to get help."

* * *

Rae was sleeping when the nurse led Lydia into her room. Her left arm was crisscrossed with medical tape and gauze. Lydia pulled a chair up close to Rae's hospital bed.

"She's been cutting herself," the emergency room doctor had told Lydia. He'd paused as if waiting for Lydia to answer a question he hadn't asked, his gaze firm and searching, but not unkind.

Lydia wondered if he had been the doctor on call when she was brought into the emergency room the month before. She didn't remember much about that night. She wondered if he recognized her, if he knew she was an addict. *It doesn't matter. Either way, it doesn't matter. He knows me. He knows who and what I am, whether he's ever met me before or not.*

"She wasn't trying to kill herself," the doctor had reassured Lydia. "And the cuts aren't as bad as they look. Mostly superficial. A few stitches. No nerve damage. Physically, she's going to be fine."

Physically.

Rae's arms were usually hidden under the long sleeves of a too-big sweatshirt. *When had that started?* Lydia tried to remember. Now, lying in the hospital bed in a blue cotton gown, her daughter's forearms were exposed. They were covered with angry red cuts, mostly healed, and scars, no longer red. The doctor estimated Rae had been cutting herself for about a year.

"Cutting is a sign of psychic crisis," he'd explained. "It's a way of coping with emotional pain, like drug or alcohol abuse."

At first, this made no sense to Lydia, that Rae would be harming herself on purpose. But then she understood her daughter might be something like her after all. Rae had been in pain for a long time, more pain than Lydia had allowed herself to believe or to admit. Only she'd been dealing with it in a different way. Instead of numbing the pain like Lydia did, her daughter shouted it down with even more intense, physical pain.

Rae opened her eyes and looked up at Lydia. Lydia looked back this time, searching Rae's gray-blue eyes and seeing nothing there but resignation. "Why, Rae?" Lydia said it out loud. "Why did you do this to yourself? Why have you been doing this to yourself?" This time, Rae turned away from Lydia's eyes first. Lydia was relieved Rae didn't answer the question. She didn't think she could bear to hear the truth coming from her daughter's mouth. "They want to put you in a hospital, Rae. They want to put you into a mental hospital, for Chrissake." Rae said nothing, but Lydia saw a tear slip from her eye and roll down her cheek, and then Lydia was crying, too. Lydia took one of Rae's hands in both of her own and laid her head across them as if in supplication.

"I'm sorry," Lydia said. "I'm sorry. I haven't been a good mother to you." She could avoid this if she wanted to. Rae would never say a word to hurt her. But she couldn't do that to her child. Not anymore.

"It's okay," Rae said. "You're a good mom."

"No, it's not okay, Rae. I don't want you to do that anymore. I don't want you to try to protect me. I'm supposed to protect you."

"Okay," Rae said. "But it's not that, Mom. I don't want you to think it's that."

Lydia's first instinct was to grab at those words, to hold on to them and take them as a way out. That would have been easy. But she fought against the urge to accept an unearned forgiveness.

"It *is* that, Rae. It's at the very least mostly that. I haven't been a good mother to you for a long time now. And that's not a question. It's a statement of fact. But I need you to know something. Me, the way I've been, the kind of mother I've been or haven't been, it has nothing to do with you. Nothing."

"Are you sure, Mom?" Rae asked. "You can tell me. Please tell me. Because it feels like…like I've done something wrong, like you don't like me anymore."

"No, Rae, no. You haven't done anything wrong. And of course I like you. I love you. Very much. I've just been sad. It has nothing to do with you. I promise."

"What are you sad about?" Rae asked. "Dad?"

"Yes, your dad." *But I'm not sad. I'm angry. I don't miss him. I hate him.* "Dad and some other things. Things that happened a long time ago. Things you don't know about and don't need to know about. But that doesn't matter. This isn't about me and what makes me sad. I've been selfish. I've been wrapped up in my own shit when I should have been taking care of you."

"Okay," Rae said. "I'm glad it's not me." She sounded relieved, like a burden had been lifted from her. Lydia hoped it would be enough. A start anyway. "Mom?"

"Yes?" Lydia was afraid she'd opened the floodgates.

"I miss Dad. We don't ever talk about him, and I miss him."

"I know," Lydia said.

* * *

When Rae was sound asleep, long after visiting hours were over, Lydia went home. It was dark now, the living room still dimly lit by the single lamp. It would be dawn soon. Lydia turned on the overhead light and looked around the apartment she and Rae had lived in together for the past five years. She felt like she was seeing it for the first time—the sparse, worn furniture and the bare walls where art and family photographs should have hung. She walked into Rae's bedroom and picked up the bloody bedspread and towel. She considered soaking them in cold water to try to get the blood out, but it was too much. She took them outside and threw them in the dumpster. When she came back inside, she looked around her daughter's room. Rae had nothing. None of the things a young girl should have. No CD player. No desk to sit at and do her homework. No shelves for her books. No posters on her wall.

Lydia turned on the wall heater in the living room and went into the kitchen to make coffee, taking a near-empty carton of milk out of the near-empty refrigerator. *Rae tried so hard to make this place a home. I gave her nothing to work with.* Lydia felt sick and her body ached, but she wanted to stay awake and alert a little longer. She couldn't stop thinking about the hospital the doctor wanted to send Rae to. *I don't want her to go there. I want her to get the help she needs, but I don't want her to be all alone in a place like that. She's been alone long enough.*

Lydia didn't know what she was going to do. She wanted to promise her daughter she'd go to rehab and quit using. She wanted to tell Rae she'd get a real job, a daytime job, and she'd be the mother Rae deserved, but she was afraid she'd fail. That was something she couldn't risk anymore. It was something Rae couldn't risk anymore. She owed something to this girl, this girl who was too much like her and who was so terrified of being alone and of watching her mother slowly kill herself that she'd chosen, at least in some small way, to die. *No hospital is going to be enough if we stay here.* Lydia went into her bedroom and opened the nightstand drawer. She touched her kit, spread her hand across it, almost a caress, then moved it aside and pulled out Ruth's letter.

* * *

After James died, Lydia had given up some of her memories of him. Mostly the bad ones. Remembering only the good—that seemed the right thing to do. He lost control of his car late one night and slammed into a tree, and after that, it didn't feel fair to remember some things. They were living with his mother, Ruth, in San Diego then. James had lost his job and started drinking heavily. They couldn't afford the rent on their own place anymore. Rae was only five or six. Lydia remembered the night James died and so many nights that came before that one. James yelling at her and calling her names. James punching her in the face—right, left, right—shoving her against the sharp corner of the dresser in his childhood bedroom in San Diego, standing over her, his face contorted with rage and unrecognizable. His gray-blue eyes turning dark and stormy. *I don't miss him. I hate him.*

Ruth must have heard the commotion coming from their bedroom. Maybe Rae heard, too—she was sleeping in another room. Maybe she heard, and maybe she remembered. But Lydia was certain that, time and again, Ruth *must* have heard, and Ruth did nothing. Although she was only now admitting it to herself, that's why she'd hidden Rae's whereabouts from Ruth—it was out of anger, a form of revenge. *I'm not sad. I'm angry. I'm angry at all of you. Most of all, myself.*

Ruth had been kind enough, but her grief suffocated Lydia. After James died, she talked about him incessantly, stories of a boy who bore little resemblance to the man Lydia remembered and was trying to forget. Lydia's grief for James felt all mixed-up. When she thought of him, which she tried not to do, she always redirected her thoughts to the early days. She remembered the night they'd met, their first date, the night he'd proposed. She remembered how much he had loved her. She remembered the life they'd planned together. How happy they were when Rae was born. She refused to remember anything else. She avoided Rae's gray-blue eyes because they reminded her of something she didn't have the courage to remember—*the good old days, they weren't all that good.*

* * *

Late that night, after visiting hours, when it was dark and quiet and deserted, Lydia snuck her daughter out of the hospital. She called Luke, and he came after closing time and parked in the lot just outside the hospital, near an exit at the end of the hallway, and waited for them. Lydia helped Rae out of the hospital bed. "Shh," Lydia whispered. "We have to be quiet, Rae. I'm taking you home." She helped Rae down the dark hall and out the exit, then into Luke's car. Luke drove them to the bus station in Salinas, and before they got out of his car, he leaned over and kissed Lydia on her forehead.

"Safe travels," Luke said.

Rae slept a lot on the buses and trains that took them south. Lydia did, too, but she stayed in the world, although it meant she was in pain and uncomfortable. She walked the thin line between being sick and being high, just enough so she could function. She was fueled by a determination to do what she had to do—she had to take care of her daughter first this time, and then she had to take care of herself, one way or another.

When they both were awake, Lydia did another hard thing. She told Rae the truth, at least most of it.

"I'm sick, Rae. It's not just depression. It's worse than that. I'm sick, and I need help."

"I know, Mom."

Of course you do. I've been fooling myself to think you don't.

"I'll be okay," Lydia said. "It's not cancer or anything like that. It's not anything that can kill me." Except that it almost had the month before.

Rae nodded and looked out the window at the coastline. The waves were breaking high and crashing into the shore. They were somewhere around Santa Barbara, Lydia guessed, and the sun was up.

"Did I ever tell you how I met your dad?"

"No," Rae said. She turned from the window, and her face brightened.

I'm not sure if I'll ever get clean, but this is something I can do for you. I took your father away from you. I can give him back.

"Well, I was at a party. A New Year's Eve party. I was nineteen. It was at the Portuguese Hall in Salinas. I remember my friend and I had gone shopping for new dresses and got our hair and nails done. The other girls were wearing blue jeans, but we wanted to dress up. I was wearing this pretty red dress. There were some local bands playing, and your dad was in one of the bands."

"Dad was in a band?"

Lydia laughed. "Yes, he played guitar when I met him. He was the lead guitarist in a band. I don't remember the name—Final Force? Force...Force something or other. Anyway, I thought he was cute, but he was really shy. The band took a break just before midnight, and the drummer in his band came up to me and asked me my name, and I told him, and then he said, 'Hey, Lydia, our guitar player, James. He thinks you're cute.'"

"Dad thought you were cute, too?"

"Yes, I guess he did. But he was too shy to tell me so himself. He was standing across the room with some guys, drinking a beer out of one of those red plastic cups. And when I looked over at him, he smiled at me, and I smiled back. And then his friend said, 'It's his birthday tonight.'"

"Dad's birthday was on New Year's Eve?"

"Yep. December thirty-first. He was a Capricorn. So his friend said to me, 'It's his birthday tonight. Would you make his night and give him a kiss at midnight? For his birthday and all?'"

"Wow, what did you say?"

"I said yes."

"You did?"

"Of course I did. Why not? Your dad was really cute. And it was almost midnight, and your dad's friend went over to him, and I saw him whispering to your dad. And then he brought him over to me and introduced us, and we were talking, and I told him happy birthday, and then everybody started counting down, you know, to midnight, 'Ten, nine, eight,' and when they got to midnight, everybody yelled, 'Happy New Year!' and your dad kissed me."

"Wow," Rae said. "That's pretty romantic."

"It was," Lydia said. "And then, you know what? Your dad gave me a ride home that night, on the back of his motorcycle. All the way to Santa Cruz. It was *very* romantic. It was raining, but only a little. Like a mist. And the streets were all shiny from the rain and the streetlights. It was late, and it was so quiet. And when we got to my apartment, he walked me up to my door, and he asked me for my phone number, and I gave it to him, and then he kissed me good night."

"So romantic."

"Yes." Lydia smiled at Rae. "So romantic. And the next afternoon, he called me and asked me out on a proper date, and I said yes."

"Where did he take you? On your date?"

"He borrowed his roommate's car and came and picked me up, then we drove into Salinas and he took me to A&W. We got burgers and fries and root beer floats. And then he took me driving around in the country—there are a lot of back roads in Monterey County. We drove around and listened to music on the radio. And then he drove me home to Santa Cruz, and he never left."

"What do you mean, he never left?"

"He never left. He stayed with me in Santa Cruz, and we were together after that. That was it. We fell in love, and we knew right away we were meant for each other. So we got our own place together, and then we got married, and then we had you."

Rae was soaking it all in, her gray-blue eyes bright and clear. She looked happy. It had taken so little to make her happy. Lydia was amazed to discover that Rae's delight in hearing stories about James eased her own pain, too. For Rae's sake, Lydia tried to remember the good stuff now. The sweet stuff. The ways James had made her laugh, but not the ways he'd made her cry. There was no reason to tell Rae about what James had gradually become. A monster so much like the father Lydia had left home to get away from when she was seventeen. *Is that why I was drawn to you, James? Did I recognize something in you that was familiar? Did you recognize something in me?*

* * *

Just before they reached the station in Old Town San Diego, while Rae was sleeping, Lydia pulled Ruth's letter out of her bag and read it for the dozenth time. *Please come home*, Ruth had written. *Please let me see my granddaughter.* Ruth was a mother who'd lost her son twice—once when he died, but once even before that, when Ruth must have realized he was no longer the sweet, young boy she'd raised. Ruth was a mother, a mother who loved her child without condition. Who could fault her for that? Lydia had already forgiven Ruth. She would work on forgiving James, for her own sake and for Rae's. Someday, if she made it that far, she would try to forgive herself, too.

* * *

It was early afternoon by the time Lydia and Rae got into downtown San Diego. They took the ferry across the bay, landing at Coronado, then took a cab. Lydia had the driver let them out on Ocean Boulevard. She walked with Rae down to the beach and sat with her there, in a spot where she and James had once sat together watching their little girl chase sea gulls and search the rocks for hermit crabs. Lydia was tired, and every part of her ached. It hadn't been easy to get there. There was the matter of coming up with enough money for the train and bus and food and enough medicine to get her through the daylong trip. But she'd done it. She'd brought Rae back to the place where she should have stayed with her, or left her, five years before. She felt too much shame to take any pride in this relatively small and long overdue act, especially when she thought about all the things it was too late to take back. But she couldn't live in the shame—it would take her down. And she was beginning to feel a glimmer of something she'd left behind, maybe something a little like hope.

Lydia and Rae sat together looking at the Pacific Ocean in silence. The waves were the only sound—they were crashing hard into the beach. The waves and the call of an occasional gull. Early afternoon sunlight bounced off the water. Lydia closed her eyes and breathed in, felt the sun on her skin. The salt air, the damp sand, the kelp washed up on the beach…they all combined to create the same rich, dense odor from all those years ago. How could the sounds and the smells have stayed the same despite all that had changed? Lydia felt transported. If only she really could be. If only she could do it over again.

"I have some pictures of your dad. Would you like to have them?"

"Yes."

Lydia handed Rae four worn pictures she'd kept tucked away in her nightstand drawer for the past five years. A formal posed photograph of James in his Marine Corps uniform. A fuzzy shot of Lydia and James sitting on a blanket on the beach in Santa Cruz, a can of beer in James's right hand and his left arm dangling loosely over Lydia's shoulder. A picture of James walking on the beach with Rae when she was a toddler, holding her hand. A picture taken of James and Lydia the day they'd been married in a friend's backyard. In the wedding picture, Lydia was barefoot and had a soft smile on her face, like she knew the secret to life. She wore flowers in her hair and rested her head on James's shoulder. In the picture, James looked like he wasn't going anywhere, ever. *So many broken promises.*

"I'm taking you home, Rae," Lydia finally said. "I'm taking you home, to your grandmother's house. Ruth Evans, the lady who sent me the letter, is your grandmother. Do you remember her?"

"Yes, I think so. A little," Rae said. She didn't sound surprised.

"She's your dad's mother. I'm taking you to stay with her. She loves you, and you loved her, too, when you were little, and she will take care of you while I get well." Lydia paused then, to see if Rae understood what she meant. When she felt sure she did, she went on. "She will make sure you get the help you need. She'll take care of you. You won't have to take care of yourself anymore. A girl your age shouldn't have to take care of herself." *Let alone her mother.* Lydia stopped and looked hard into Rae's eyes. She didn't see James in those eyes anymore—she only saw her daughter looking back at her. It was still painful to stare into those eyes because of all she had done to hurt her child. But Lydia refused to look away anymore. She looked straight into Rae's eyes, feeling the hurt and the fear and the anger and all of it, and knowing that feeling all those things meant she was still alive. "This is where you should have grown up, Rae. I can't change that now. What's done is done, and I can't change the past. I wish I could. But I can try to make it right. Do you understand?"

Rae nodded.

If this were a movie, this would fix everything. But it isn't a movie. Who knows how it will end?

"I can't stay. You know that, right? I can't stay here." Rae began to cry then, and Lydia felt a tempest made up of all the things she'd been avoiding begin to beat against the inside walls of her chest. She pulled Rae close to her and held her until she stopped crying. "I'll be back for you," she said. "I'm going to get some help, and I'll be back for you. I promise." Lydia meant it when she said it, and at least for now, for this moment, she refused to allow herself any doubts about whether it was a promise she would be able to keep.

* * *

It was late afternoon when Lydia knocked on Ruth's front door. Ruth answered, looking puzzled. But understanding came over Ruth's face as she must have realized the woman standing on her doorstep was Lydia, a girl she hadn't seen in five years, a girl whose picture once hung in her living room and who stood before her now with hollow eyes. When Ruth looked at Rae, Lydia could see she recognized her granddaughter immediately—Rae looked so much like Ruth's son, James, which would make what came next for Ruth both so easy and so hard. Lydia knew all about that.

Ruth's eyes began to fill with tears, but she smiled at Rae, then at Lydia. She looked straight into Lydia's eyes, unblinking. "Come in," she said. "Both of you. Please, come in."

PULP HEMINGWAY

by Nik Xandir Wolf

"But man is not made for defeat. A man can be destroyed but not defeated." -Ernest Hemingway, *The Old Man and the Sea*

"Does that one over there look like it is moving to you?" Hemingway said, sitting between my son and me, our surfboards beaded with water and our feet still numb from the cold.

Hemingway held a .30-06 deer rifle and sighted down the corpses of the tech bros still washing up on the shore a few at a time. Every once in a while, they weren't quite dead and would try and take a bite out of you when you surfed or walked past. Like a large fish after it's been gaffed in the brain, a flash of life still in its nervous system.

"The one on the right?" I said.

"The one on the right that just washed in, yes. I think I can see his fingers clawing at the sand there. You know, these remind me of the war when the Krauts would come up over the stone walls, and we would pot the bastards when they did, and each time they had the same absent look of surprise, and that is what stuck with me all these years. That look of surprise, then falling dead into the mud below." Hemingway half smiled like this was a fond memory; then the rifle bucked. I looked out at the shoreline, and a plume of red spray caught the sun just right so it glowed pink in the dusk sun.

"Good shot," I said, and pulled my surf parka up over my shoulders as the chill set in from the waning sun.

* * *

Half the drive here to Ketchum I had daydreamed of ways to murder Edward J. Hawks. Not just because he conned my father-in-law, Jack Harper, into selling him our family-owned company a year ago—right before my father-in-law passed away rapidly from stage 4 pancreatic cancer—but also because now the sinister prick was living with my goddamn wife. Well, soon-to-be ex-wife. And I'm pretty sure my son liked him better than me. His own flesh-and-blood father. The kid wouldn't even return my calls or texts. However, I can't blame him too much. Edward epitomized the airbrushed hypermasculine cliché that dominated the views and clicks on the social sites. I was middle-aged, overweight, balding and cried a lot.

I ran my fingers over the smooth, wooden stock of the hunting rifle that I'd brought with me on the trip, my father-in-law's old deer rifle, a .30-06 that had been fired probably once—in a range. There was supposed to be a hunting contest on this corporate bonus trip to Ketchum that Edward had put together, so I had dusted the thing off, oiled it, and here it was. I'd still never fired it, though I let the daydream of running Edward Hawks down in an empty forest and slowly filling him with bullets replay in my head all the way out here from San Jose. His blood leaving splatter marks through the woods for miles. I would never do it, of course. I was no murderer, but goddamn I hated him. My daydreams were the innocuous *The Secret Life of Walter Mitty* type. The truth was even worse. I'd never stood up to anyone in my life. Not as a child and certainly not as an adult. Growing up, I was the only white kid in an all-Latino school in a poor California ag town and got jumped every day from K through twelve. And that wasn't even the worst of it.

Two blocks into town and to the right, neon lights lit up a group of young people smoking on the sidewalk. I turned, and when I got closer to the bar, Whiskey Jacques, I noticed that the crowd was a line to get inside. Across the salt-glazed street, however, was a sign for Casino Club, with no line. I parked a few blocks up and shifted off the hemorrhoid donut cushion I had been sitting on; sharp pains exploded from my asshole. As some sort of sick parting salvo, right before my wife, Melinda, informed me she was moving in with Ed, she convinced me to let her fuck me. Or peg me. Whatever it's called. Apparently, I'd menaced her with my ungainly phallus for years, and she wanted me to feel what it was like. How could I say no? And now I knew. It felt like getting split open by a goddamn jackhammer. And the equipment, I shit you not, the equipment she strapped on and tore me apart with—I checked the label in the trash—was made by Petro Industries, a subsidiary of BMA Financial. This was the same private equity firm that owned WorldCom—and Edward J. Hawks was a massive shareholder. I literally got fucked in the ass by my own company. Or, parent company. Sort of a sick Oedipus-incest situation that now haunted me. And my ass.

The Casino Club had a Hans Christian Andersen vibe with storybook Nordic lines, wood siding, and the scent of decay. A placard out front said it opened in 1936 and had continuously operated. Inside, it was dim and smelled of stale beer and vomit. A dozen older locals limped around the place, playing pool, darts, standing over the jukebox, and a few sat at a very long, wooden bar top. I bellied up with a stool between myself and an old man with a long, gray-and-white beard and a black beanie clinging to his thinning scalp. The stool between us didn't serve as the buffer I'd hoped for, because he immediately turned my way and glared. I could tell his eyes were clouded with drink without even looking. At a glance, he was the town drunk.

"You don't look like the ski bunny type." His raspy voice was too loud. He leaned in, and I could smell his breath several feet away. Raw fish, tobacco, and peated malt.

"Probably because I'm not." I looked straight ahead, hoping to avoid encouraging him. "I'm here for work." The old man waited. I sighed. "A sales conference. For an insure tech."

He rolled his leathery lips. "I could tell by your hands. You have the most precious little hands I've ever seen on a man." He hacked out a laugh. Finally, the bartender saw me and came over.

"What can I get you, handsome?" She was muscular with thick, black hair pulled into a bun, a black tank top, and rockabilly tattoos sleeved down both arms. She had a hard, local-mountain-town look to her, and even though calling me handsome was probably how she greeted all her guests for tips, it had been a long time since I'd been flirted with. It felt good.

"Just…" I looked at my new old-man friend, who looked away now, watching an infomercial for Lexapro, a drug I'd tried to help me out of my depression and had nearly killed me by causing my heart to arrhythmia for three days, landing me in the hospital—pharmaceuticals kill. "Two shots of Jack."

"Beer back for another dollar," she said.

"You drive a hard bargain," I said, and she half smiled like she'd heard it all, and that it was tiresome. I hated that, being a cliché.

"Somebody's got to. Name's Darlene. Holler if you need another." She poured two shots and cracked a bottle of MGD.

When Darlene was clear, the old man leaned over again. "She don't like me talking to the yuppies that come in here. She says I scur them off." His teeth were pointed, black at the gumline. His eyes had half circles of lined flesh under them. "But you're different, aren't you? You look like you've seen your share of real life. Hard life. Are you doing okay?"

I wanted to ignore the guy, but I am a sucker for pity from strangers, though I try very hard not to spend too much time feeling sorry for myself. But fucking hell, my world had gotten ripped upside down over the past year. Lost my father-in-law, Jack Harper, whom I loved dearly. Who had coached me into insurance, helped me succeed and win business by using a personal touch and love, and made me believe in this dumb old machine of late-stage capitalism. That a nobody, an adopted kid from a poor farm town could make a damn good living with some effort and the right mentorship. But then he'd died. But not before selling his business to WorldCom, getting every penny he could for Tanisha, his newest wife who was half his age. A contract that he promised me would take care of me as well. But it was a dog-shit contract, and the truth was, Jack hadn't cared. And how WorldCom handled it from there, that disgusted me to the point of night terrors, panic attacks, and a bout of A-fib that put me in the hospital, the first time. That piece of shit Edward moved immediately, fired everyone that had built Jack's business over the years, stole all of my accounts, remanded me to an entry-level sales role, and persistently threatened my job security for not reaching wildly impossible sales goals, and then savagely beat me in front of the whole company. Yes, the contract that I had to sign or lose everything required I participate in physical altercations in the ring as a form of "sports-oriented therapy." Then, off the books, Ed stole my wife and son. I took to drinking to rid myself of the pity, and it worked. Until it didn't.

"I can't remember the last time anyone asked me that. And, for the record, you don't scare me any," I said.

"Nobody cares how a guy like you is doing, so long as you keep your head down and get your work done and provide, am I right? Treat you like livestock, don't they?"

"Goddamn right," I said.

"If I guess who you work for, how about you buy me a drink?"

I chuckled and said, "Sure."

"Ed Hawks, he your boss?"

I almost choked on my shitty beer. "How the hell?"

"I'll take a Johnnie Walker and soda." He smiled, his eyes glistening in the dim bar light, and it hit me like a jab from Edward: There was something else to this old man. He clearly wasn't what he appeared.

"I'll add it to my tab."

"And how is that? Working for WorldCom? As bad as they say?"

"I don't think I fit in there," I said. "They are trying to put microchip implants in our brains so we can use office software with our minds, and we have to fistfight our bosses. It's like a Philip K. Dick universe gone awry."

"You're not wrong, kid. And I'm sorry for it. Sorry for it all. But I'll fix it. I have the cure. You think you can beat him? Ed, I mean?"

"I'm not even supposed to be on this sales trip, I didn't make the cut," I said, and fought an urge to weep in front of this old fool.

"And yet here you are."

"Here I am—I don't know what the hell I am doing here," I said, but the comment burned in my stomach like a shot of 151. I had never stood up to anyone in my life, and yet I did come here; I did bring the rifle. And I did plan to compete, didn't I? Maybe a man, even a sad sack like me can only take so much?

"Aren't you a little curious to know how I guessed your boss?"

I sipped my beer and really looked at this man. He wasn't as old as I'd guessed initially, seventies maybe. And he was certainly a lot more mentally acute than I'd summed him up for.

"I guess a big conference coming into town from Silicon Valley is big news out here," I said.

The old man reached over and grabbed my wrist. "The reason I know is because Edward J. Hawks Jr. grew up in this town. That's why he's come back. He wants to show me, all of us, what a big shot he's become. How he's going to take over the town, buy the whole place, then the world."

"He's the second-richest man in the world at thirty. What does he need to prove to you people?" I said, peeling at the condensation-wrinkled label on my bottle of beer, then taking a sip. "No offense."

"Christ. He's a fraud. I know, I raised the little twerp."

This time I spit beer across the bar. Darlene gave me devil eyes. I waved an apology and motioned for another shot. "That's utterly impossible. The statistical odds that I run into Edward's parents at the first bar I stop at in town are nil."

Darlene came over, and I ordered two more shots, a beer, and a Johnnie Black and soda. Once she was clear, the old man stood, moved closer, and sat at the stool immediately beside mine.

"The odds are better than nil. I came here tonight because I knew one of you conference guys would need a drink. I knew I'd find my man tonight."

"You *wanted* to run into one of his employees?" I said, confused.

The old man smiled with a wicked glint in his eyes. "That is correct. Name's Melvin Hawks. Edward Sr. was my son. Passed away in Iraq twenty-five years ago. Army Special Forces."

"I'm sorry," I said, and sipped a shot of Jack, feeling my equilibrium shift slightly, like the alcohol was building beyond a buzz and toward inebriated.

"Sorry for losing my son, or raising a megalomaniac?" Melvin hacked a laugh.

"Both, I suppose. You know, I daydreamed about killing him today. I know I shouldn't tell a soul that, but somehow I feel like you get it," I said. The shots were loosening my lips more than I preferred. I hated waking up in a panic in the early morning hours, when everything that happened the night before came rushing back to me in cringey, fragmented clips.

Melvin sipped and peered at me carefully like he was considering something of grave importance. Setting his drink down, he said, "Listen, you hate the guy, right? Don't be ashamed. From where I sit, it means you've got a good grasp on reality. His kind, what they do to guys like you. The meek. It's not right." He paused and looked around. "I have a proposition for you, Jared. And I think you're perfect for it."

"Oh god. I am not your man, whatever it is. I promise I'm pretty useless," I said, feeling icy terror trickle through my heart at the thought of any form of confrontation. "Wait, I didn't tell you my name."

"Jared Pleasant, I know who you are. Former vice president of Harper Insurance Services, one of the few companies left in the country not owned by the private equity firms. Got fucked over hard in the acquisition. Lost your wife, your dignity, your everything. I know a thousand like you that he's done this to. But they're not here, are they? You are. You made this journey for a reason, and that reason is me."

I nodded, stunned into silence. The old man knew everything. I mean, I supposed most of it was public information, but how the fuck did he know I'd come here?

"Did you take the chip in the head?" Melvin asked, his face inches from mine.

"God no. Never."

"Then congrats," Melvin said. "You're hired."

Melive raised his glass to cheers me; I obliged and then slammed my shot and sipped my beer to guide the bile back down my throat.

"Congrats for what—" I started to say, but my head rocked hard like I was on a cruise ship in a storm. I held on to the bar to steady myself.

"Easy there, son. I am going to give you a gift. It started with that shot Darlene just poured you," Melvin said.

I looked over the bar, and it slid back and forth, pixelated and swimming. Darlene stood there watching me. "You okay, handsome? Need a lift to your room?" she said, her smile wide and friendly.

Melvin put his arm over my shoulder and spoke into my ear. "I entrusted my inventions to that savage beast of a man who went on to become Edward J. Hawks. I am an inventor. Well, *the* inventor. The AI software that Ed is using came from me. So did a lot of things my grandson has peddled as his own. The savage brat took what I gave him, and went legion on the world."

I rubbed my eyes to clear my blurred vision, my heart sprinting in my chest like a trapped bird. "Why did you do this?" I stammered. "What did you give me?"

"The drugs I gave you, which haven't fully taken hold yet, will open your mind fully so that I can train you the way I trained Edward when he was young. To be a fighter. To be bully proof. With a little training, you'll be able to beat Ed Hawks."

"Are you telling me that *you* created that monster? And now, *me*?"

"The training is virtual but works deep, altering your subconscious mind and improving your perception of yourself, confidence, and you come out a real man. A warrior. It won't change who you are, you just become better at everything you do. Edward was always Edward, I just gave him a significant competitive edge."

"What if I don't want to run around ravaging people like some sort of caveman?"

"Maybe you should be. Let me ask you this, is your family safe? There is always war, and for us civilians, business is war. Here the lions are billionaires and corporations in trench coats, and as they grow more powerful, they grow eviler and more corrupt. They must be stopped. And when you need a fighter, the kind that go bump in the night and put the fear of God into the hearts of evil men, you need that masculinity. Don't you? And you will be that. A pure heart with savage capability. You just have to stay incorruptible. Unlike Ed."

My heart pumped hard in my chest, a cloudy sensation filling me up, spiking my adrenaline. "How are an old man and a middle-aged insurance salesman going to stop the corporate Eds, and worse yet, BMA Financial, regardless of some mind tricks?"

"You're going to give him this." Melvin held up a syringe with blue liquid and tiny gold specks in suspension. "I call it iCeNyNe. It will stop Ed."

"You want me to stick Ed with another crazy invention of yours?" I said, trying to control my breathing so I didn't go full-blown panic attack.

"Look, Ed's going to unveil his latest tech tomorrow. A chip that he wants to have in every employee as soon as possible. Hell, probably the world if he could make that happen. It's a technology I invented, and this is the antidote."

"What the hell does that mean?" I said.

"Ed's going to paint the most beautiful picture. Like all technological innovations have done for the past two decades. A gorgeous woman on a sandy shore, or a goddamn slicked-up muscleman, whatever you're into for objectification purposes—that's what they sell. Dopamine bumps for free. Meanwhile, the backside of those beach mannequins is a leprosy-ridden corpse of rot and decay. Festering sickness. That's what they do—sell the dream, then steal your life. Every detail of it, everything they can get their greedy goddamn hands on. The porn you watch, the shits you take, your heart rhythm, your medical records, DNA, sexual predilections, how you make your money, what shows you watch. All of it. And they want it now to sell advertising, sure. But what is the endgame of that kind of power, that grasp on humanity?"

"You still haven't told me how subjecting me to this experiment of yours is going to change any of this." The veins in my neck and forehead felt full and searingly hot, like lava had taken the place of my blood. I closed my eyes and rubbed my temples.

"The drugs I gave you plus the virtual training you'll undergo will reprogram you. You're going to stay at my hunting lodge tonight—it's set up for you already. It's where Edward transformed, too. I made it fun. I mean, it's going to hurt, but I have chosen the perfect specimen as your guide. The grandfather of masculine energy and a Ketchum legend, Ernest Hemingway."

"I'm staying at the Sun Valley Lodge," I said, wondering how Hemingway was going to fit into this with his Nobel prizes and adventure swagger.

"I'll get you to the lodge tomorrow, but we need to go to my cabin now. The drugs are going to really take hold soon."

"Christ. I just want to go home." I wanted to scream, run, call the police, but my legs felt cemented to the floor.

"Sorry, but I chose you when you walked in that door with a hunting rifle in the car. You are ready, whether you know it or not. After tonight you'll never be bullied again. Not ever. Just remember this when you're scared, right now included—even if you lose the fight, you win in the end because whatever is on the other side is going to be better for you, even if you don't know what that thing is. Just trust that the only way out is through, and you have to nut up and do it. Do the thing you are afraid of, goddamnit."

I wanted to protest, but now my mouth felt painfully dry, like cement had spread across my tongue. I was being lifted from my seat. I was vaguely aware of Melvin telling Darlene that I had one too many—there was another set of hands on me. Bouncer? Accomplice? Then something was slipped over my head, and things went dark.

* * *

I wasn't unconscious; I could tell I was in the back of a car, or van, and we were moving. There was a seat belt across my waist and a cloth bag over my head.

"It's not too late to take me to the hotel. I won't tell anyone you drugged me." Even as I said this, I knew it wouldn't work. There was no way I could even walk into the lobby, let alone get to my room.

"Just rest, the drugs will kind of tickle your mind before they really get started. It's the perfect time to tell you a little story. The event that got me started on this project to make real men out of the weak. Because I was like you once. Afraid of people, afraid of my boss, afraid of girls, afraid to even open my mouth in public. But then, one day when I was a teenager, it all changed thanks to one man. When I was working at the Saw Tooth Club, a lot of celebrities came in there, and it was such a buzz, like the whole restaurant would get charged with electric energy.

"But one Sunday afternoon in the summer, the place was slow—this must have been in '59 or '60—*he* sat in my section. Ernest Hemingway. I rushed to the coatroom and grabbed my book. When I went over to clear his plate, I pushed the book in front of him and asked him to sign it. A first edition of *The Sun Also Rises*. My all-time favorite. He snatched the book from me and stood. Told me if I could knock him down, he would sign it. I was certain the old man was messing with me, but decided to play along anyway.

"He was older then, almost sixty, but looked eighty. So I said sure, I'd box him. Soon as I stepped outside though, he put me down on my ass. Twice. I clipped him good in the chin, and the old bastard just *smiled*. I could have landed a real haymaker on him but didn't have the heart. He helped me up and signed my book anyway. His knuckles bled, and I gave him my apron to wrap it up. My manager came out and fired me on the spot. I went home with a black eye and a signed book."

"You fought Ernest Hemingway?" I said. The car bounced hard on a pothole; then we turned off the main road, and I could hear gravel crackling under the tires.

"Bet your ass I did. And I worked tirelessly for decades to recreate that experience. And I have, to a large extent, succeeded. Though it does require a bit of a drug mixture to make the simulation feel truly real and immersive."

"What the hell does that mean?' I said, color beginning to bloom in cascading patterns against my closed eyelids.

"It means you're going to fight him too," he said. We pulled to a stop, and he killed the engine. "And he'll get you ready for tomorrow."

The car door cracked open, letting a rush of frozen air slice through my clothes and into my bones. Rough hands pulled me from the back of the car, then shoved me forward; something pushed sharp and hard against my back. Then a swift kick knocked me onto my knees. The damp, hard pack of snow made my shins ache through my jeans. I heard a car door slam, then start and peel away. Tearing the bag from my head, which appeared to be a thick pillowcase now that I could see it, I looked around to get my bearings, the red taillights fading into the distance.

I wasn't at a cabin; I was in the woods, in a cemetery. A long, fat tombstone lay in front of me. An ocean of color throbbed all around my line of sight, and it all felt like a dream. A levity, a distance, a feathery patina existed here. A fissure in reality. An *alternate* reality. I dragged my fingers through the snow, and I could feel the icy chill, the granular texture. I didn't need to pinch myself; I knew it would hurt.

In front of me lay the final resting place of Ernest Miller Hemingway. And somehow, impossibly, my right hand clutched a book. I turned it so I could read the title in the dim moonlight. *The Sun Also Rises.* Cracking it open, I read the inscription. *That was a hell of a punch, kid. Just like Cohen, you're going to do okay.* It became clear to me that I was, for some reason, holding Melvin's signed book.

I stood to get a better look at the grave. It had a flat, ground-level slab of marble at least seven feet tall and four feet wide. The inscription was plain, *Ernest Miller Hemingway. July 21, 1899 – July 2, 1961.* Hemingway had survived until just shy of his sixty-second birthday. A shotgun to the face. Suicide, just like his father. Even though I hadn't read much Hemingway, I had watched his Ken Burns documentary, so I knew that much.

There wasn't a lot around the grave. Some dead flowers and a collection of corroded coins. It might have been the drug elixir or all the alcohol, but standing over the gravestone, I started to feel impossibly heavy. The cement returning to my body. It was below freezing; my breath unfurling in thick clouds, and I wasn't sure what the hell I was supposed to do here. It dawned on me that this might be some sort of hazing ritual my boss was subjecting me to. Drive me out here as some sort of fucked-up learning experience. My body tingled all over, my vision bursting with peripheral color, and so I turned and walked toward the street. There would have to be a car soon; I could hitchhike back.

I was turning toward the road when something snagged my shoe. I tripped, fell forward, and slammed hard, face-first in the dense snow. Looking back, I found an exposed root caught in the laces of my New Balance. Scooting on my ass, I pushed myself until my back rested against the trunk of a large pine to recover. I rubbed my knees, cracked the book, and put my nose in the spine to smell deeply the aged pages. A scent that brings profound joy to my heart even in the darkest times.

Snow began to fall, creating a beautiful, muted silence. Silken layers piled over me that worked to slowly encapsulate me in a cocoon with Hemingway's corpse.

"How the hell did you do it, Hem?" I said. Down below, a car zipped past. "I can't do a single thing I want to, and you? Well, you did everything your way." I chuckled. "Not sure either is the exact answer."

Someone had left a bottle of Jim Beam. I picked it up, and though the label was frayed from exposure, its seal was intact. I cracked it, took a long, hot pull, and then poured the rest onto Hemingway's headstone. The liquid splashed against the marble. A small rivulet traveled over the side and down into a crack between the headstone and the earth. I leaned back, my head against the tree, and the world swirled around me in streaks of glowing snow.

I looked at Melvin's book and ran my finger over the inscription. "I guess I need a boxing lesson, old man," I said, feeling completely foolish for still being out here, knowing I'd be hypothermic soon.

I tossed the book onto the grave, and it slid on the snow, clearing a little trail on the marble. I held my breath as if some miracle would occur. After a moment, I began to laugh. I laughed hard until tears formed and felt cold in the corners of my eyes.

"I'm sorry, Hem. I'll let you rest. I don't know what the fuck I was thinking."

I stood and reached for the book but tripped again. The damn root was still caught in my shoelace. I sat back and tried to tug it out, but it kept getting more tangled. I looked closer and could swear it was actually growing. I blinked hard and focused. But instead of clearing an insane vision away, it made it more vivid. The root was growing, getting longer, fibers extending from it like netting enclosing my shoe. I ripped at it, tried to pull free, but it grew faster.

I pushed with my feet hard against the tombstone, trying to crawl backward, but the root made quick progress. It wound itself tightly around my ankles. Then it had my wrists, face, and chest. My heart skipped and fluttered like I might have a heart attack. I tried to scream but couldn't. Paralyzed from the roots working through my body. Then, as if in answer to my most primal fears, the side of Hemingway's grave hinged open. A wide mouth gaping at me, roots dangling inside the darkness like gnarled teeth. The roots began to pull, dragging me toward the opening. In utter terror, I dug my fingers into the earth, fingernails splintering against rocks while my body slid into the cold opening in the earth. Finally, I let go and began to fall into a soundless pit. Down the rabbit hole. Above, the tombstone slammed shut, choking off the pale moonlight. Plunging me into darkness.

* * *

I never landed. Instead, I slowly became aware of my surroundings again. I was sitting at a bar in a huge cabin, and it felt like I'd been sitting there awhile. There was nobody else around, and the bar and cabin seemed to stretch on forever in all directions.

I called out, "Hello?"

Nothing. Not even an echo.

My hands probed my body. I wasn't cold anymore, but my fingers hurt, blood and scratches on my fingertips. I gingerly sucked at a bloody cuticle when a heavy hand landed on my shoulder. I jumped an inch off the stool, and my heart somersaulted. I turned and found a bearded man in his fifties staring at me. Stunned into a state of shock, I could say nothing at all. The man with his hand on me was Ernest Hemingway, which meant the psychotic, kidnapping, mad scientist wasn't mad. Not completely, anyway.

"That was a good, strong liquor you poured down for me, and I should thank you for that. I can't remember the last good man who had a sound enough mind to give it to me instead of leave it up top for that grave robber to make off with. People the world over bring me good whiskey and absinthe and fine French Chablis, and every week that bastard rounds it up. And I am sure you can see for yourself, there isn't a drop of anything down here."

I tried blinking hard again; I even pinched my leg. It hurt; this was real. Or, as real as reality could get. My drug-addled mind was fully inside this thing. Hemingway stepped around the bar and picked up a few bottles. He smashed them, tossed them into the void all around us, but they just reappeared on the shelf. Dusty and completely empty.

"I don't know who runs this terrible place, but this bar is worse than the night after a Fiesta in Pamplona. Nothing left there but sore jaws and empty leather wine bags. You have anything else on you? A good rye? I didn't catch your name, boy."

"Jared Pleasant," I said, and I realized I was still holding the bottle of Jim. "It's gone." Hemingway's eyes widened, and he snatched the bottle, tilted his head back, and lapped at the drops of whiskey from the rim. Licking his lips, he tossed the bottle into the white void outside the bar. Then it was back in my hand. I set it on the bar.

"That all you have?" he said. His beard was fully gray, and he looked like his most famous photos with his broad chest and long, heavy forearms.

"It's all I had with me," I said.

"Christ. I finally get a drink, and it's just enough to give me the thirst."

"Can I ask you, sir—"

"Call me Papa, for Christ's sake. Everyone knows that."

"Papa. Where the hell am I?"

"Some form of it. Hell, I mean. Best I can figure, you're in a kind of purgatory, old sport. I knew a guy who loved that line. Old sport."

"Scott Fitzgerald?" I said.

"You know of him? I guess his overcomplicated drivel must have survived him. Yes, that is the fellow. Good fellow, sensitive one, he and Zelda. Couldn't handle their liquor, but she took a liking to me anyway." Hemingway winked.

"Did you say 'purgatory'?"

"Some great joke, right, boy? I don't know how I ended up here, either, but you've apparently been granted a goddamn wish." Hemingway tossed the book onto the bar top. "Somebody thinks you deserve a second chance out there. Hell, all I got was goddamn dementia after getting every hand in government shoved up my ass. All I wanted to do was write my stories and die like a real man, in battle. Instead, they pull me out of Cuba like a war criminal, and then they start drilling me about Castro, like he's my longtime pal. Then the Russkies. I can't help it if Castro and the Russkies like my books. You write books about war; you get fans of all different kinds. Then the FBI follows me all the way to Ketchum with all this rot about counterintelligence."

"Counterintelligence?"

"Let's not get caught in the wrong current. Just do me a favor, if anyone ever says I worked for the Russkies, you goddamn well pot him for me, you got that? I was a double agent. Not a goddamn sellout. Now, come here, boy. I'm going to show you something."

Hemingway came back around the bar and stepped close. He reached for my face with rough, massive hands, and he squeezed. He pushed his forehead against mine so hard, it felt like my head might crack and all of my life would pass into Hemingway's spirit. Then I was off my stool, my body suspended by my head in Hemingway's thick hands. He held me there for a moment longer, then, getting what he needed from my brain, dropped me.

"Huh. You're not the type I normally see. Question, you shoot well, boy?" Hemingway asked.

"Shoot, like, a gun? I shot clay pigeons as a kid in the Scouts."

"That thing with your boss, you need to do something about that. I won't tell you what to do about your wife, God knows it took me three or so tries to get that one right. Love, power, then friendship, that's the order for marriage—for wives. You'll find that one out, boy, but you need to pot that son-of-a-bitch boss. Maybe pepper him with a light bird shot. Men have been killed for much less than what he's done to you. I've seen it all over the world. Capitalism is murder on the human soul. It's a mechanism that puts profit above all else, above human life. It strips men and women of their beauty, their sensuality, their pride. You end up with fucked-out husks of men. Better to die in battle. At least then they use those hollow but lovely words like valor and bravery when you're gone."

"I'm not going to shoot my boss. I'll go to prison," I said. "And while capitalism has fucked me, hard, it's better than communism or any other bullshit system."

"Yes, well. That is a fair point about prison, and communism—fucking Russkies—and I'm no one to talk about the other thing, but you are a good and honest man, Jared Pleasant. Your boss, he might be the Antichrist. He lives and breathes destruction in the name of progress. He knows your fear because he exploits it. Ruins you for it. You have to charge into the thing you fear most, like a goddamn bull. Same thing runs true for about everything in life. Women, hunting lions, game fishing, war. Stare through your challenges, find the soul of it, and show it you don't give a damn if it kills you because you will keep coming. That's the key to everything. Feeling like a thing will kill you, but going on anyway. Not because you are resigned to die, but because death is what you came for. And you're ready for it. That will put the fear into anyone. And you know what I mean, you've met someone like that, I am sure."

"I would rather take the bullet," I said.

"Don't talk such rot! If you're not going to pot the bastard, what you need to do is fight the man. You land one good, square punch and knock him down, then you'll feel better and like yourself again. Or maybe like yourself for the very first time, and you can go on making plans with your son. Good plans that make you both very happy."

"I can't," I said, my stomach lurching at the thought of losing my son. "He dominated me like a child when we fought at the WorldCom office."

"Well, you're here for a reason, aren't you? To stand up for yourself. So stand up." Hemingway came close again and pulled my hands up in an old-school boxing stance with the wrists facing upward, as if in supplication to the gods—one of whom, in this particular setting, was Melvin. I was slightly taller, but Hemingway was stockier. Hem turned hip to hip with me and demonstrated how to shift your weight into the punches for knockdown power. "You step into the whole thing and punch through the man's face, into that soul you're staring into. You understand that, and you will have the power you need. Now face me and throw a punch."

I turned and faced the old man; his eyes shined and his presence flickered. A halo of energy seemed to glow around him. Hem's eyes were focused, his jaw was set, brow furrowed, and he looked murderous. I turned my hips and weakly tried to hit him, but my right shoe slipped, and the blow glanced off Hemingway's shoulder. He rubbed the spot on his arm and laughed.

"You have to want it, boy. It has to feel good and true. Like this." Hemingway turned with his whole body, a fist attached to a massive forearm collided with my chest and sent me smashing against the glass bottles lined up on the bar. I lay there for a moment, broken glass around me, gulping for air. Hemingway walked over to me and jerked me to my feet. "Try again," he said.

After I caught my breath, I planted my feet, squarely this time. I wound back, turned my hips the way Hemingway had, and swung with everything I could gather. My fist smashed Hemingway solid in the jaw. The big man staggered and blinked. His whole presence flashed like changing the channel on an old television set. He was old, then young, twenties, then forty and out in Key West, then a child dressed like a little girl. He spun in a pirouette. The little boy in the dress approached me, reached back with a balled fist, then swung. He flashed through the figures, landing back on gray-bearded sixties Hemingway who connected with my stomach like a kick from a horse. I doubled over, the air rushing out of me.

"Now that's how you land a punch. You put a good hard turn on that one, boy. Sorry if I put you down with that body shot. Take some slow breaths," Hemingway said.

I puked and tried to brush off an ache forming deep in my bones. "That was a cheap shot," I said through panting breaths.

"Boy, do you think that boss of yours, Edward, will give you an easier time when you challenge him? No, he will put you down like he wants a kill. Embarrass you with blow after blow and make you wish you had never lived at all. Is that what you want with your life? To end up a punchline?"

"No." I started to cry. "I just want my wife and my son back."

"Make certain you know exactly what you wish for, boy. What do you want true and most in the world?"

"I want my son back."

"Not your wife?" Hemingway said.

I felt a sense of strength gathering. And with that strength, that confidence, I realized I didn't want her back. I wanted to be with someone who respected me, loved me, cherished me. Deserved me. Someone who didn't take advantage of my childhood abandonment trauma manifesting as a people pleaser. "No. I don't. I want my son, and I want this all to be over. All of it. I don't want to fight. I don't want to scratch and claw for existence. I don't want to feel daily terror over losing a job I hate because I need the money to survive."

"What would you do if you didn't work at that shit place?"

"I want to learn to surf. I want to write bad poetry. Raise my son. And I want to be in love again. I want to love living again."

"Then you have your answer. Melvin gave you the iCeNyNe, and I will help you with the hardest part. Standing up to the biggest bully you've ever had. Hell, possibly one of the worst in the world save for Mussolini. Melvin has you plugged into one hell of a machine. What you go through tonight will bring you closer to the path you are looking for. The machine will feed basic martial arts into your subconscious mind: boxing, Brazilian jujitsu, Tae Kwon Do. It will also interrogate your life and challenge your soul."

"Do you think I will live through this?"

"Boy, you haven't even lived a day in your life. Not yet."

With that, Hemingway reached back and swung at me with every ounce of his strength, and the last thing I remember was a bright flash of color with a black spot blooming like blood at its center, spreading until it lifted me off my feet. I floated there and never came back down.

Then I was a child again. My father cracking his worn leather belt like a whip. Landing it sharply across my bare ass, a bottle of Old Tennis Shoes whiskey in his left hand. The pain spilling hot down my legs. Then I was in my first foster home, my foster mom catching me pulling an extra Twinkie from the box, a wire coat hanger wracked hard across my knuckles, then my face, neck, ears. Pain splitting me apart. Then I was in junior high, in the locker room. All the recently pubescent kids surrounding me, beating me with soap in socks. One cracked my nose, and I choked on blood rushing into my mouth. My whole body now bursting bright with pain so great, I hoped my heart would give out. Then my wife wearing that fat, black dildo out of the bathroom. Walking toward me with it dragging like the cock on a stallion. But this time, I felt a welling, a surge of something primal. An emotion I'd never allowed myself to express. Anger. Rage. I stood and unclipped the massive phallus and threw it out the back window. I told her it was over. I took my son and walked out. Then a tide of emotion stirred in me, a cyclone of emotion, a battle. A sense of confidence overpowering my fears and anxieties. A sensation I never knew was possible.

Then I was back in my father's bedroom. I grabbed my father's belt and ripped it from his hands, slapping the whiskey to the floor and rushing out the front door to safety. In the locker room I tore the sock from one of the boy's hands and helicoptered like a savage until every guy in the locker room bled from split lips and busted eyes. I ripped the coat hanger from my foster moms hands and took every Twinkie in the house and sprinted down the road, shoveling them into my mouth to quench my starvation. I stood. Tall. Hands at my hips like a goddamn superhero, head toward the sky. Triumphant.

Then I was sitting on a couch, facing a full-wall projection television. A rapid feed of mixed martial arts instruction displayed in front of me, and a wave of relief washed over me. I touched myself. My legs, arms, neck, and my body felt strong and hard. My emotions were steady, subdued. The cement hardening inside of me. A certainty crystalized in my mind that I was done being bullied. I would never be a people pleaser again, no matter how hard the conversations were. I would never be walked over, beaten, or picked on again. Not ever. I was goddamn Jared Pleasant. And that was finally going to mean something.

* * *

I woke the next day and sat up, rubbing my crusted eyes. Every muscle and fiber in my body felt tight, sore, and firm. I wasn't sure how the drugs worked, but I felt pretty damn good and clearheaded. As I glanced around the space I was in, it dawned on me that everything I'd witnessed the night before had been some sort of illusion, hallucination. A fever dream.

I was indeed in a cabin. It was old, dilapidated, mice running through the corners, insects, mold, filth everywhere. Branches and vegetation inside the home. At the far end was a bar with empty bottles lined up along its surface. A virtual reality headset lay on the couch next to me. My phone was dead. I had no idea where I was, or how to get back, but it didn't matter. I would figure it out. Nothing could stop me now. Nothing would stop me ever again.

* * *

For a boutique hotel, the Sun Valley Lodge had a massive convention center—there must have been over three thousand associates there. Edward J. Hawks Jr. spoke effortlessly, animatedly, controlling his audience with calculated precision, so nobody noticed when I slipped in through one of the back double doors. The way his intensity was building, I could tell his big reveal was coming, and I had to get to him first.

The sea of people grew denser toward the front; the bigger more athletic of the group usually stood there. A pecking order by muscle mass. I would normally be squeezed out, pushed to the side, stuck in the margins. But today, thanks to Melvin, I felt good and strong, my brain racing with ways to win a fight.

"So are you ready for our company—*your* company to lead the world in global innovation? To completely dominate our competitors? Because the answer is right here in the palm of my hand. And every single one of you are holding one as well," Edward said, his voice echoing through the crowded auditorium.

Edward held up a vial of some sort of glowing green liquid that looked like a shot of absinthe with black, swirling flecks inside. "This is the key to our future. The future of everything. This little beverage contains over a thousand microprocessors that will revolutionize your abilities. With this invention you will be able to control all the devices that we make, you will be able to speak to each other with no words. You will virtually have the powers of telekinesis and ESP. You will be gods among men. Us, our team. Gods! Drink this with me and join the hive!"

Everyone in the room took their shot, and the room fell to an eerie silence. Some coughing, throat clearing, and then as if he couldn't be any more of a cliché, Edward began to thump his chest and hum. *The Wolf of Wall Street* style. Then they all started humming, the whole room becoming a vibration. A cause. It felt infectious, like joining them would make me a part of something bigger than myself. A real part of it. Not an expendable by-product. I wasn't sure I could go through with injecting Edward with the iCeNyNe. Who was I to stop global commerce? The inexorable forward march of technology and improvement?

Then I got a text: *When are you coming home? I miss you, Dad.* It was my son, Avery. I didn't cry, not this time. I clutched the phone in my palm until the screen cracked; then I breathed deeply, clarity revealing itself again. I was coming home very soon, Son.

I shoved my way to the front, knocking a few company alphas to the floor. Then I approached at stage right, where a burly, bearded guard stood with his arms crossed. I approached the stairs; he blocked access with his bulk, a sleepy-eyed scowl daring me to try. I felt electric with energy, like this could be fun. A sensation I had never experienced.

I stepped to him, feinted to the right, and he flinched, his body thrown sideways. I shoved him hard the same direction. His body dropped and slammed hard into the stage supports. I heard a groan as I ascended the stairs, the stage-right curtains blocking me from the audience. Finding a backup microphone, I switched it on. A loud, magnetic howl screeched over the speakers, and everyone went to cover their ears.

"We seem to be having a technical issue—" Edward Hawks said, his big speech interrupted.

"It's not a technical issue. I am here to challenge you to a rematch," I said, still behind the curtains.

Ed laughed in a manner meant to placate the audience. "I would normally respond with 'anytime,' but right now is not great." Ed tried to go back into his speech.

"Right now. Spiff Off. In the Octagon." The Spiff Off was the contractual language that Edward had forced me to sign, that forced any employee challenged to fight in the ring or lose their monthly Spiff bonus, which accounted for the majority of our commissions.

"It's going to be hard to fight a man I can't even see. Are you going to stay hidden in the shadows?"

I stepped from the curtains and moved in fast, sure strides until I was six inches from Edward. I glared into him, to his soul. My hatred for him vibrated in my chest. I could rip him apart right here. And then I saw it, that glimmer in his eye, that reversion to childhood. That fear. He recognized me, and for the first time in my life, my bully was frightened by *me*.

"Christ, Peasant? Didn't you get canned—"

"My name is Pleasant, with an *L*. Let's go. Now. That's the rule. *Your* rule."

"Look, Peasant, what happened to you…it's just business," Edward said, then looked toward the stage exits. "Security, little help?"

Three large men moved from behind the curtains toward me, and Edward turned his back to me to address and assuage the audience. I stepped quickly behind Edward, and *300*-style kicked him in the back, sending him scorpion flying off the stage, where he landed with a bounce inside the Octagon cage below. The Octogen that Ed had installed to host employee fights at this conference. A place he'd had never been defeated by a colleague, or anyone, for that matter.

Casually I stepped to the edge of the stage, and just before the men got to me, I dropped, trying to make my landing as much of a statement as possible. But Ed saw me coming. Ed was pissed. He swept my legs before I touched the mat, and sent me sprawling against the chain link. Then he was on me, his grotesque weight on my chest, his fists hammering down on my face, forehead, nose, ears. I covered up, tasted blood, Ernest Hemingway's shimmering likeness raging in my thoughts. *Pot the bastard.*

* * *

Edward hit me hard in the forehead, jaw, chest, ribs. He was coming at me from every angle, and with all of the UFC footage I'd watched, I knew I had to cover up and minimize damage. The truth was, before, when Edward did this to me in front of my wife and son, all I wanted to do was disappear into the mat. I was so humiliated, I wanted him to kill me. And now, with this meat wad hammering on me with everything he had, I started to smile. It didn't hurt all that badly. For the first time in my life, I realized I wasn't made of glass. I wasn't anything but water in a stream. Reaching low, I turned my body sharply left, taking Edward's ankle into a vise grip and twisting hard.

He knew it would break, so he rolled with it, and I let go, then leapt to my feet, feinting right, then delivering a hard roundhouse to Edward's chin, snapping his head back. He stumbled, fell. Sat for a second to shake off the blow. Then he stood, smiling.

We faced each other. Blood coming out hot from my nose and feeling cool as it trickled down my chest, blood leaking from his right ear. I pulled my shirt off, wiped my face and threw it at him. I reached back quickly to grab the syringe of iCeNyNe, and I rushed him, the needle tip aimed directly at his neck with my finger already pushing firmly against the plunger.

Ed swatted my shirt away, sidestepped my attack, and landed a knee hard in my solar plexus, sending me sprawling to the canvas. I heaved, trying to get my breath back, the spent syringe on the ground near Edward's feet.

The crowd hummed louder, cheers popping up. Someone yelled, "Finish him!"

"It looks like you dropped your little shot. Let me guess, Melvin gave you some injections, and you thought you could come here and what, stop me? Kill me? Change me back? That poor, crazy bastard. Look what he did to you. He made you believe in yourself."

Edward laughed and bent down to pick up the syringe, holding it up against the dim lights to inspect it. "Looks like you wasted your little shot." Edward dropped the syringe to the canvas and crushed it with his foot, the glass shattering into small shards.

"Peasant. You know what I thought when I first met you? That you were the anonymous henchman that dies first when a hero jumps into action. A flash on the screen. Nothing but a bullet taker. A nobody. A body. A nothing. A never will be. And this. I am offering you a gift. A cheat code. It's not too late to join us. You can rule this future with us."

"You're the last thing on earth I would want to become," I said, and spit blood at Edward's feet.

Edward leaned down next to me, placing his meaty hand on my neck, squeezing so hard it felt like the vertebrae might snap. "Don't you understand, you dense, little prick? I am not the bad guy, and you're not the good guy. Or a nice guy. We're all just code." He leaned forward so close, I could feel his breath hot on my ear, and whispered, "Our entire existence is just a fucking simulation. Once you know that, it takes the sting out of getting shit done that hurts people. Fuck them. Fuck the world, they're all just code. And I am offering you a cheat that will help you evolve faster than the script. All you have to do is drink it."

Edward slipped the bottle he'd displayed onstage into my palm, just like I knew he would. I looked at it. I nodded, my head hanging in false defeat. Unscrewing the cap, I put the liquid to my lips, smelled strawberry, and chugged the drink.

For a moment I felt nothing. Then the flood hit me. The voices in the room, chaos, but also orderly in an ineffable way. Like their humming became a chant I could feel and understand. The strange elixir summoned something dormant inside of me that was built in but never expressed. I ran my fingers over the chain link, and my skin melded with the steel, ran through it, the ones and zeros flowing through my fingers like blue, translucent water. I slowly rose, the hum emitted from my chest involuntary. The room around me a refractory prism of glowing binary code. The sea of bodies around me humming louder, and Edward standing in front of me, grinning like the devil. *You're one of us now,* he said, but his lips never moved. *He's one of us. Welcome. We will take over the world together.* Voices. So many of them at once.

When my hand moved to my back pocket and I removed the small, black pen tube, the voices changed. *What is he doing? What's in his hand? Somebody should take that from him.* And it took everything I had to force the syringe from the casing; the voices were trying to slow me. Stop me. Edward willed me to stop, but the elixir he'd given me hadn't taken hold fully. Not yet. I held the syringe up for the room to see. The voices began to scream— concern, fear, hatred.

"You'll never reach me with that, Peasant. Not before you get crushed by these men," Edward said.

"It's not for you," I said. I drew my hand up, my thumb on the plunger. "It doesn't matter what your implant does. It doesn't matter if it is a cheat code for a simulation. Your design takes us into a future where we are eventually indistinguishable from the machine, from the code. Where we lose ourselves. I do not want to become the code. I want to destroy it, and I don't know what that means, but I hope it means we go back to living, truly living. Without the machines. The future is ours, not theirs."

"What the hell is in that shot?" Edward said, a panic rising in his voice. The voices in my head screaming louder. My willpower, my ability to even move autonomously was a window rapidly closing.

"It's iCeNyNe, and it shuts you and your whole hive down."

"No!" Edward screamed, and rushed me.

I dropped to my knees, landing a powerful punch to his groin. He doubled over. I stood. He glanced up at me, wheezing with his hands covering his destroyed cock.

"Fuck you, Peasant," he croaked.

I grabbed Edward by the back of his hair, pulling him up to face me. "Don't worry, Edward, it's just business," I said.

Hands grabbed at my clothes through the chain link; bodies descended from high above, splashing all around me. A million fingers ripped at me, my hands, my grip, and ripped the syringe from my free hand and flung it into the chasm of the auditorium.

But it was too late. The iCeNyNe was inside of me, and the pain was instant.

Edward writhed in my grip, too. A buzzing of circuitry flashed and flickered under the surface of his skin above his right ear. I let him fall to the canvas.

I fell to my knees, too. In front of me, Edward J. Hawks clutched and clawed at his face, his head, his brain. Then, as if blasted by a shotgun, the right side of his head exploded. Circuitry and gray matter splattering the canvas floor, popping and hissing, then crystallizing solid. The virus worked quickly, spreading through the room, through the software Edward had stolen. Bodies dropped to the floor, convulsing, puking, dying. My own brain felt like a vise was crushing it, and if I had let the implant take hold a minute longer, I would be dead too. The virus continued on, through every infected human unlucky enough to come into contact with Edward over the past year. Which numbered in the hundreds of thousands as the virus spread from Ketchum, all the way to the Silicon Valley and beyond.

I stood at the center of that octagon, the corpses piled around me like a mass burial site, and looked out toward the entrance of the auditorium. Two uniformed janitors stood at the doorway, mouths agape, mops in hand. They had a lot of cleaning to do.

* * *

A small, shoulder-high wave began to form out on the horizon, that beautiful bell-shaped curve that gave you options on which direction you wanted to surf. Clean, offshore, partially sunny. It was a perfect morning.

"I'll go left," I said, knowing my son, Avery, preferred rights. We both paddled, popped up, and charted our lines down the face of the wave, and it felt so pure, being connected to the ocean, my son, and this new reality of ours without WorldCom and a dozen smaller tech companies that it had owned. I maneuvered around several probably dead bodies floating in the surf.

When the circuitry that millions of the tech bros had either intentionally implanted or Edward Hawks had surreptitiously implanted froze from the iCeNyNe, they'd died—whomever they had been before had died when the circuitry took over—they had been more AI robot than human. The trouble was, sometimes the circuitry freezing up killed the computer, but the body went on ticking with no human presence. Shell humans. And they would, out of some primitive instinct, track toward the ocean. Mostly they would drown, but once in a while they would come climbing out of the sea, biting and thrashing.

I sold my house in San Jose and bought a boat and docked it at the Monterey harbor. I wrote bad poetry that was slowly getting better, mostly about nature. I paddled out with Avery every morning, and the three of us surfed whatever waves we could cobble together—Hemingway was there, and old man Hemingway could rip some waves. Melvin, who had made it out for a few weeks before going back to Ketchum, apologized for that. The procedure he'd put me through had created a permanent imprint on my occipital lobe, like an image burned into an LCD screen. Sometimes I would box the old man, and when I tagged him up, he'd flip through the channels again. Sometimes I would leave him as a kid in a dress playing in the sand.

Avery and old Hemingway and I all sat in the sand, watching the sun set. A sailboat drifted by, a dark silhouette against a liquid-peach sky. I moved to sit next to Avery in the sand, smiled, and put my arm around him. He leaned into me, put his head on my shoulder. Tears of pure joy spilled from my eyes. We got to beat on, to love living again, and it felt so right.

Then Hemingway fired another round into the ocean, red spray geysered crimson into the sun strata. *Potted the bastard*, he said. *One of those zombie fish. God, have I seen it all now.*

HAPPY CHRISTMAS

by Joyce Carol Oates

S he flew home at Christmas, her mother and her mother's new husband met her at the airport dazzling-bright with Christmas neon in the long mall of shops and restaurants. Her mother hugged her hard and told her she looked pretty, her skin had cleared up hadn't it?--and her mother's new husband shook hands with her and looked her eye-to-eye like no bullshit between them telling her Jesus yes, she sure did look pretty, prettier than her pictures where she never seemed to be smiling but frowning and welcome home. He was younger than the girl's mother by maybe six, seven years. His sideburns grew razor-sharp into his cheeks and were jet-black, not a graying hair visible, not the sideburns and not the thick-tufted hair springing back from his forehead as if shellacked. His cologne or after-shave or hair gel cloying-sweet made her nostrils pinch. On his right hand he wore an onyx signet ring. In his lapel, a sprig of mistletoe. In his handshake her hand felt small and moist, the bones close to cracking. Her mother hugged her again, half-sobbing God, I'm so happy to see you, almost thought I'd lost you. Blue veins in the backs of her hands startling, the skin looking thin, papery, but her mother was happy, that was a relief. You could feel that all about her like a thrumming of the soul. The pancake makeup on her mother's face was a fragrant peach shade that had been blended skillfully into her raddled throat. On her left hand she wore her new rings: a small glittering diamond set high in spiky white-gold prongs, a white-gold wedding band. The girl tried and failed to recall the old rings like you might try and fail to remember a dream that must not have been important since it faded so quickly upon waking.

The girl was surprised, they stopped so soon for a drink at Easy Sal's at a Marriott off the Turnpike, she'd gathered that her mother and the new husband had had a drink or two at the airport. In Easy Sal's there were more dazzling-neon Christmas lights, a ten-foot silver-tinsel tree with glittering ornaments in the shapes of bottles: whiskey, wine. The girl ordered just Perrier with a twist of lime (*That's* fancy, her mother said with a kissy purse of her lips), her mother and her mother's new husband had martinis on the rocks, which were their "celebration" drinks.

For a while amid the festive buzz of the cocktail lounge they talked about what the girl was studying and what her plans were for the summer though the mother and the mother's new husband didn't appear to be listening to what the girl said and the girl had the impression that they were clasping hands beneath the wobbly chrome table or possibly the mother's new husband was clasping the mother's chubby knee exposed below her tight-fitting gold-lamé skirt, and when that subject trailed off they talked about their own plans, putting the house on the market, that was the first of the chores after the massive clean-up *top to bottom* as the cleaning service boasted which wasn't cheap, not an ideal time to sell a luxury property (as it was called) but now that the grand jury was behind them, that was the next step. A year and a half of fucking hell but no indictments which was what their lawyers assured them of course, not a shred of evidence that could constitute *beyond a reasonable doubt* if there was a trial and why'd there be a trial?—no crime had been committed, that was the bottom line. The insurance company had finally paid, *that* was the bottom line. There's a fantastic new condominium village on the river, the girl's mother said, we'll show you when we drive past, there'll be a room for you whenever you want it, reserved for *you.* Radiant happiness in the mother's face, the girl could not help but see. The mother smiling so hard you'd think her lower face would crack. Giggling, shivery. It's like I died and was reborn. Just makes me so happy, the two people I love most in the world right here with me. Right here right now. So if I died, you would both hold me tight. Wouldn't you? Wouldn't you both hold me tight if I died right now? The mother's new husband laughed startled and kissed her saying, Hell nobody's going to die tonight or any other night. That's a promise. A waitress in a tight-fitting satin-Santa costume with a Santa hat tilted on her head brought two more martinis and a Perrier though the girl hadn't finished her first Perrier. And a tiny glass bowl of beer nuts. Thanks, sweetheart! her mother's new husband said happily squinting up at the waitress the tip of a pert pink tongue between his lips.

* * *

The girl had spoken with her mother no more than three times since her father's funeral in December of the previous year, they'd tried Skype but something went wrong or (maybe) the girl had sabotaged the call, she'd been high, but a bad kind of high, a toxic high, started laughing and then crying and had to shut down the computer and her roommate had to clasp her hands tight to keep them from fluttering like crazed birds saying in a calm voice *You're OK. You're going to be OK. We've decided, you are going to be OK. You're beautiful, you don't need them, maybe they are not murderers you can transcend them. You have got to rise above them, you will destroy yourself if you keep on like this* and eventually it was OK really, actually she'd been able to speak with her mother in a normal voice a few days later about her mother's plans to be remarried. Not that this was a surprise, it was not. Not asking is this the one from online. From, what's it for older people, *match.com.* Not asking how can you. Just, how can you. Her mother was maybe a little drunk. Or high too. A different kind of high. Saying, trying not to sound accusing, Oh I understand it's sudden in your eyes but you know, your father is not going to come back, we have to accept that. He is gone, we loved him so much and our hearts are broken but he *is gone,* it was a totally random tragedy, it always seems soon to the children, you are not a *child* any longer you know. You have to understand, Jay was there for me during all that ugliness. He was there for me, he was the *only one.* You were not, I am not blaming you but the fact is, you were not. And all your father's family—monsters... But that is water under the bridge, that is over with now, we are here now. All the back tuition has been paid, that's all cleared up now. Your degree—that's the bottom line. Jay said, we aren't going to turn our backs on that little girl, she needs us. This is a time of need. Mutual need. But it's over now, except for selling the house. We love you. Wait and see. *Both of us*—we are here for you. The girl had fallen silent feeling something nudge her knee, possibly it was the knee of the mother's new husband beneath the wobbly chrome table. As if unconsciously the girl moved her leg away causing the chrome table to tilt, fortunately they were clutching their drinks which did not topple over. The girl laughed nervously saying Yes, or maybe she was saying no. Or, I guess. Her mother said in a husky voice, He makes me feel like living again, I feel, you know, like a woman again, after twenty-three years, and the girl felt her throat shut up tight too stricken to reply. As long as you're happy, her mouth tried to say.

Now it was 8:30 PM and had been pitch-black outside for a long time. The girl was light-headed with hunger, she'd had just Diet Cokes and pretzels on the plane but her mother and her mother's new husband were on their third round of drinks. Easy Sal's had entertainment, first a piano player with a sad gargoyle face and a red Santa hat drunk-tilted on his head playing background music, old-timey pop songs the girl did not recognize, then a singer, female, ebony-black, V-necked red spangled dress, Santa cap drunk-tilted on her head, then a stand-up, anorexic-looking, of no sex or gender or ethnic identity you could determine, small bony angular face like a wizened monkey-face glittering with piercings, no makeup, punk hairdo, waxed-looking purple-pink, black faux-leather jumpsuit, pelvis thrust forward in *mock-Vogue-model* stance, delivery fast brash deadpan like rap lyrics: great thing about havin' your abortion early in the day is uh like y'know the rest of the day's uh gonna be fuckin' uphill, right? There's these half-dozen people in a uh Jacuzzi, hot new game called musical holes, uh maybe it just ain't caught on yet in New Jersey's why nobody's laughin', huh? words too machine-gun quick for the girl to catch but her mother and her mother's new husband seemed to hear, and were laughing though afterward her mother's new husband confided in disgust he did not approve of dirty language issuing from women's lips, whether they were dykes or not.

* * *

They stopped for dinner off the Turnpike at a brightly lit Polynesian restaurant surrounded by faux palm trees adorned with winking Christmas lights, on the faux-thatched roof a neon-red Santa with sleigh and reindeers at an alarming tilt. The girl's mother was explaining that there wasn't anything to eat at home, also it was getting late, tomorrow she'd be preparing a terrific dinner from Whole Foods, was that OK? She'd wanted to have a welcome-home dinner but ran out of time, then the plane was delayed anyhow, so was it OK? The mother's new husband interrupted sharply to say it's OK, no need to repeat yourself like a parrot, then made a joke of it winking at the girl like they were in it together whatever it was.

In Mauri's Polynesian Paradise they perused menus so large, the girl could barely see her mother and her mother's husband over her menu, the two seemed to be quarreling or maybe not, maybe it was a kind of foreplay, or after-play, sipping drinks from halved coconuts, laughing together. In high spirits, this was still their honeymoon as the mother's father said. Holding hands between courses, sipping from each other's tropical-hued drink. When the girl's mother excused herself to use the restroom moving unsteadily on her feet in high-heeled sandals the new husband leaned close to the girl to confide, Jesus I'm crazy about that woman. Your mother is a high-class lady. She was very hurt, he said, very devastated by things said about her. Erroneous charges. Outright lies. Slander. You know, we never met until—until after. It was all news to me. Shifting his cane chair closer, leaned moist and warm, meaty, against her, an arm across her shoulders too heavy for the girl to shake off.

Saying in a lowered confidential voice, there's nobody in the world precious to me as that lady, I want you to know that. I cannot and will not allow slander to be uttered about that woman, d'you understand? No matter who it is and I think you know who it is—was. But never again, OK? Is that an understanding? You and me, an understanding? The girl who had been sleepy-eyed was wide awake now and tasting cold and very frightened hearing herself say stammering Yes, yes I know it, and her mother's new husband said in a fierce voice close in her ear, gripping her shoulders with his arm heavy as a hose, Damn right, sweetheart: you better know it.

Francesca Lia Block, MFA, is the author of more than thirty books of fiction, non-fiction, short stories and poetry, and has written screenplay adaptations of her work. She received the Spectrum Award, the Phoenix Award, the ALA Rainbow Award and the 2005 Margaret A. Edwards Lifetime Achievement Award, as well as other citations from the American Library Association, and from the *New York Times Book Review*, and *Publisher's Weekly*. Currently she teaches creative writing at UCLA Extension, Antioch University, Pocket MFA, and numerous workshops across the country. Francesca also edits *Lit Angels*, an online literary journal available on Substack. Her most recent novel is *House of Hearts*.

Bev Vincent is the author of several books, including *The Road to the Dark Tower* and *Stephen King: A Complete Exploration of His Work, Life, and Influences*. In 2018, he co-edited the anthology *Flight or Fright* with King and has published over 140 stories, with appearances in *Ellery Queen's*, *Alfred Hitchcock's* and *Black Cat Mystery Magazines*. His work has been published in twenty languages and nominated for the Stoker (twice), Edgar, Locus, Ignotus, Rondo Hatton Classic Horror and ITW Thriller Awards. Other recent works include "The Ogilvy Affair" and "The Dead of Winter," the latter in *Dissonant Harmonies* with Brian Keene. To learn more, visit bevvincent.com

Mike Newirth grew up on Long Island and now lives in Chicago. His fiction received a Henfield-*Transatlantic Review* award and a Pushcart Prize, and his stories, essays, and reviews appear in many publications and anthologies, including *The Baffler*, *The Louisville Review*, *Another Chicago Magazine (ACM)*, *VOLT*, and *They're at It Again: Stories from Twenty Years of Open City*. He's a faculty member of the Department of English at the University of Illinois--Chicago.

Lawrence Block is an American crime writer best known for two long-running New York-set series about the recovering alcoholic P.I. Matthew Scudder and the gentleman burglar Bernie Rhodenbarr. Block has won every award imaginable for his works, had numerous film adaptations and was named a Grand Master by the Mystery Writers of America in 1994.

Curtis Ippolito is a two-time Anthony Award Finalist, a Derringer Award Finalist, and the author of the crime novel *Burying the Newspaper Man*. His short stories have appeared in numerous publications, including *Ellery Queen Mystery Magazine*, *Vautrin*, *Tough*, *Mystery Tribune*, and *Shotgun Honey*, as well as being included in several anthologies including the Anthony Award-nominated *Trouble No More*, and *The One Percent: Tales of the Super Wealthy and Depraved*. He lives in San Diego, California, with his wife. Learn more about him at curtisippolito.com.

Kathryn E. McGee's horror stories have appeared in *Kelp Journal*, *Lit Angels*, *Ladies of the Fright*, *Gamut Magazine*, and the Bram Stoker Award nominated *Chromophobia* anthology. She writes about horror books and film for *The Lineup* and is an active member of the Horror Writers Association. She manages the MFA Program in Creative Writing at UC Riverside Palm Desert. Learn more at www.kathrynemcgee.com.

Megan Jauregui Eccles lives in the foothills of San Diego and is a writer, poet, and professor. When she's not rehoming rattlesnakes, she plays Dungeons and Dragons with her five sons and hatches a variety of poultry. She holds an MFA in Fiction from UCR—Palm Desert. Her novel, SING THE NIGHT, debuts with 8th Note Press in 2025.

Jeff Kronenfeld is the capitol reports coordinator for the Arizona Capitol Times. He's also an author, comic writer and screenwriter based out of Tempe, Arizona. His articles have been published in Discover Magazine, Vice, and many others. His scripts have been produced by WatchMojo and placed in the Austin Film Fest, Big Break Screenwriting Contest, and Screencraft Film Fund. His fiction is featured in So It Goes: The Journal of the Kurt Vonnegut Memorial Library, Four Chambers Press, Ripples in Space: A Sci-Fi Journal and others. His graphic novella Dog Years was funded by the Arizona Commission on the Arts and has been featured in events at colleges, libraries, comic conventions and correctional institutions. The Phoenix Office of Arts and Culture is supporting an expansion, which is due out in 2025.

Hoda Mallone is a journalist and writer based in Los Angeles. She has been a managing editor, book editor, and has worked for then Senator, Presidential Candidate, and now Vice President Kamala Harris. Her writing has appeared in *The Los Angeles Times, Electric Literature, Premium Magazine, Press Telegram, OC Register, Los Angeles Daily News*, and more. She holds an MFA from the University of California Riverside Palm Desert.

Craig Clevenger is an American author of contemporary fiction. He was born in Dallas, Texas and raised in Southern California, where he studied English at California State University, Long Beach. He currently lives in California, where he divides his time between the Mojave desert and the central coast, where he works at a local library and runs a community writing workshop. He is the author of The *Contortionist's Handbook, Dermaphoria,* and *Mother Howl.* His works have been translated into 30+ languages.

Sara Marchant received her MFA from the University of California, Riverside/Palm Desert. She is the author of THE DRIVEWAY HAS TWO SIDES (Fairlight Books), a memoir, PROOF OF LOSS (Otis Books), and her latest novel BECOMING DELILAH (Fairlight Books). Her essay Haunted was a Notable Mention in Best American Essays and Nonfiction 2021. Sara is a founding editor of the literary magazine Writers Resist.

David Zimmerle lives with his wife and two young children in the rural Southern California town of Fallbrook and grew up in South Orange County. In 2023 he published a short story, "The Rolex," with Kelp Books in The Dark Waves of Winter anthology. He continues to publish creative non-fiction and feature stories / profiles in *The Surfer's Journal.* He's also published poetry in the *99 Poems for the 99 Percent* anthology. In early 2023, Zimmerle also completed his first novel, *MULEBOY*, a fast-paced coming-of-age upmarket story set in the bleached-out, glowing allure of late 90s South Orange County that tracks an underprivileged prep school athlete who can no longer accept his bad hand in life. He then rationalizes that becoming a drug mule for his dad's best friend — using the team bus as his cover for transport — is his slim chance to transcend it all, while setting in motion a sequence of serious events that will change his life forever. Zimmerle is currently working on a second novel.

Ioannis Argiris is an award-winning filmmaker, writer, and zinester. He's driven to tell stories about working class immigrants, crime, and mental health. He illustrates these themes through surrealism with offbeat visuals--blending his love of Rothko and the weirdness of Cronenberg. ioannis adapted and directed his short film *Blends,* which has won multiple awards and has been selected in over a dozen film festivals around the world. He's working on new short stories for his collection *Encinal Nights.* His work has been featured in the Kelp Journal, Coachella Review, and his zines are available in many bookstores along the West Coast (Powells, Silver Sprocket, Spectators). He holds a MFA in Creative Writing from UCR Palm Desert. You can find him urban cycling through Oakland while he thinks of new tattoos to add to his sleeves. Check out more of his work at ioannisargiris.com and blendsfilm.com.

Ruthie Marlenée is a Mexican-American novelist, poet and award-winning screenwriter born in Orange County, living now in the California desert of the Coachella Valley and too far from the ocean. Marlenée earned a Writers' Certificate in Fiction from UCLA and is the author of *Isabela's Island, Curse of the Ninth,* nominated for a *James Kirkwood Literary Prize* and *Agave Blues,* which received an Honorable Mention by the *International Latino Book Awards* for the *Isabel Allende Most Inspirational Fiction Book Award* and is currently in pre-movie production. Marlenée is a two-time Pushcart Prize nominee in fiction. She is a member of Macondo Writers Workshop, Inlandia Institute, Palm Springs Writers Guild, and is a WriteGirl Mentor. Her poetry and short stories can be found in various publications.

Leanne Phillips lives, reads, and writes on California's Central Coast. Her work has appeared in publications including The Rumpus, the Los Angeles Review of Books, Kelp Journal, The Coachella Review, and the New American Studies Journal. She earned an MFA from the University of California at Riverside's Palm Desert program in Creative Writing and Writing for the Performing Arts.

Nik Xandir Wolf is a Monterey, California based writer and surfer. He attended Stanford's OWC program in novel writing and holds an MFA from UC Riverside-Palm Desert. His debut chapbook was published in February 2022, and his bestselling novel, *Shadow Valley*, is out in paperback. His essays, fiction, and poetry have appeared in various publications.

Joyce Carol Oates (born June 16, 1938) is an American writer. Oates published her first book in 1963, and has since published 58 novels, a number of plays and novellas, and many volumes of short stories, poetry, and non-fiction. Her novels *Black Water* (1992), *What I Lived For* (1994), and *Blonde* (2000), and her short story collections *The Wheel of Love* (1970) and *Lovely, Dark, Deep: Stories* (2014) were each finalists for the Pulitzer Prize. She has won many awards for her writing, including the National Book Award,[1] for her novel *Them* (1969), two O. Henry Awards, the National Humanities Medal, and the Jerusalem Prize (2019).

www.ingramcontent.com/pod-product-compliance
Lightning Source LLC
Chambersburg PA
CBHW010742310726
48971CB00010B/2909